THE SOUTHWICK INCIDENT

A NOVEL
BY

Jeb Ladouceur

America Star Books
Frederick, Maryland

© 2017 by Jeb Ladouceur.
All rights reserved. No part of this book may be reproduced, stored in a retrieval system or transmitted in any form or by any means without the prior written permission of the publishers, except by a reviewer who may quote brief passages in a review to be printed in a newspaper, magazine or journal.

First printing

All characters in this book are fictitious, and any resemblance to real persons, living or dead, is coincidental.

America Star Books has allowed this work to remain exactly as the author intended, verbatim, without editorial input.

Softcover 9781683946175
PUBLISHED BY AMERICA STAR BOOKS, LLLP
www.americastarbooks.pub
Frederick, Maryland

Books by Jeb Ladouceur

The Palindrome Plot
Calamity Hook
Frisco
The Banana Belt
Sparrowbush
The Oba Project
Mark of the Zodiac
The Dealer
Harvest
The Quantum Syndrome
The Ghostwriters
The Southwick Incident

Dedication

To Louis Greenblatt:
Skilled physician,
Superior wit,
Stalwart reader,
Steadfast friend.

Chapter One

ELIZABETH BANNING HAD SPENT the entire week decorating her house for Christmas. She'd affixed small electric candles inside every window of the white clapboard colonial, and their dim glow provided a perfect, understated holiday touch when the two-story home was viewed from the street. Even the Banning Christmas tree, decorated with small white lights and festive red balls, and positioned on the far side of the living room fireplace, could be seen through one of two large front windows. A second identical casement in the dining room flanked the Bannings' red front door and its large wreath.

Since the leaves had all fallen from surrounding oaks and dogwoods, passersby on Stony Path sixty yards distant had a clear view of the handsome Banning residence with its black shutters and bright door. From mid-spring until late fall, the house and its pair of north and south extensions, was almost invisible from the quiet roadway. The same was true of the other widely spaced neighboring homes in this wooded section of Southwick that sloped toward Caleb's Creek. Now one could even make out the chimneys of the Thomas and Fifer residences a quarter mile away. The area was known as 'The Landing.'

The traditionally festive season notwithstanding, it was the time of year when days were depressingly short…little more than eight hours long…and the privacy-conscious residents of 'The Landing' had, weeks ago, battened down the hatches in preparation for whatever the next two months held in store. The previous winter had been an oppressive one, with snowfall in Massachusetts breaking all records. Power outages had been commonplace in Southwick, Springfield, and even Boston, and observers of the worldwide 'climate change' phenomenon were predicting more of the same for 2016.

But so far, Mother Nature, notorious in these parts for her unpredictable whimsy, had more than lived up to that capricious reputation. This Christmas was easily going to be the warmest ever!

Elizabeth hadn't had time to read the weekly Southwick Messenger…she'd barely had a chance to make a quick cup of tea after packing Carter off for his regular checkup at the VA Hospital. As usual, he'd skipped breakfast despite his wife's insistent plea that he *at least have coffee and a slice of toast… perhaps some shredded wheat.* But there was no persuading the man. Whenever he had an appointment that called for even the slightest amount of travel (and the Southwick VA Medical Center was a mere fifteen-minute drive from Stony Path) Carter Banning could find a thousand-and-one reasons to leave the house unduly early. Elizabeth assumed he'd experienced some traumatic incident involving tardiness, probably as a child, something that had left an indelible imprint on his psyche. Well, if obsession with punctuality was to be counted his worst fault, Elizabeth Banning figured she should consider herself a fortunate wife indeed.

She turned on the radio in the kitchen and prepared to polish her good silverware. The main topic of discussion on WBZ Radio was, of course, the weather. Cardinal O'Malley, Archbishop of Boston, had observed that in all his years as a priest he could not recall ever preparing for Midnight Mass...and wondering if the church's air conditioning should be turned on!

In another weather-related vignette, an official of the National Park Service in Washington had noted that a number of Cherry trees near the National Mall were currently in partial bloom. A horticulturist of the first order, Elizabeth Banning scoffed at the implication that high temperatures had fooled the flowering trees into thinking it was spring. She knew that autumn-flowering Cherries were sparsely interspersed with the spring-flowering variety in D.C. It was the former, Elizabeth was certain, that were now blooming near the Tidal Basin...seemingly against all odds.

Before leaving the house Carter had at least taken the few minutes his wife asked for, to help her add two large leafs to the dining room table, and now she floated her best, tablecloth over the resulting ten-foot-long surface. When the patterned linen had billowed and settled, and as Elizabeth smoothed its white surface, the WBZ newscaster announced that there'd been an apparent hit-and-run accident on Route 25-A...west of Southwick...and all traffic in the area was being diverted to College Road.

Oh dear, Elizabeth thought, *that's going to add a good ten minutes to Carter's trip. I hope he doesn't rush.* She pulled aside the curtain on the kitchen window and scanned the length of the driveway. As usual, her husband had backed swiftly to the street and the westbound car was already well out of sight.

The announcer stated that authorities were looking for a blue Chevrolet Impala, described by a jogger at the scene as "...an older model 2-door..." last seen headed in the direction of Southwick proper. *Area residents with information regarding the suspect vehicle are asked to call LAW-BREAKER at 529-273-2537.*

Five-foot-one Elizabeth Banning jotted the phone number on a 3 by 5 card from her recipe box, then, standing on tiptoes, she reached for the silver polish on a cabinet shelf over the sink.

Chapter Two

JUST AS THE WEATHERMAN HAD PREDICTED, it was starting to rain—a light mist that vaguely dampened one's car windshield. *What a lousy Christmas Eve this is turning out to be,* Carter Banning said under his breath. He turned the wiper control two clicks clockwise, and the blades smeared the grime that had built up overnight. Carter was rendered momentarily blind by the blurry film that coated the glass in front of his face. Impatiently, he jammed his foot on the brake, and the Volvo skidded, then fishtailed to a stop a few feet from a pair of barricades erected at Middleville Road.

A tall policeman in a yellow raincoat sauntered toward the silver sedan. He raised one hand, palm forward, and twirled the forefinger of his other hand in a gesture that said, *Turn down your window*…which a sheepish Carter Banning promptly proceeded to do.

The policeman peered into the front of the Volvo…then the back…then he walked slowly around to the rear of the car…noted the license plate…and methodically examined the vehicle's entire exterior, paying special attention to the front fenders and grille.

Carter poked his head out of the window, and called, "Is there a problem, Officer?"

The policeman nodded toward the barricades that shut down traffic on both lanes of Route 25-A. "Another two feet and there would have been. What's the big hurry?"

"No hurry," said Carter. He shrugged with both hands on the wheel. "Appointment for a physical at the VA, is all."

The brusque patrolman in the raincoat nodded and re-examined the empty right front seat. "Have you been taking any sort of medication today, Sir?"

"No. I haven't even eaten anything today."

"Don't suppose you've been drinking this morning."

Banning looked askance at the obviously annoyed patrolman. "Hardly...it's nine o'clock in the morning!"

The policeman glared at Carter through half-lowered eyelids, then stepped away from the driver's door. "I'm aware of the time, Sir. And for your information, you're very close to invading a crime scene." He motioned toward the dash. "Turn off the ignition, please."

Carter's wipers had been passing over the windshield on the next-to-lowest setting...intermittently...once every three seconds or so...and through the streaked glass, he could make out three middle-aged men in civilian clothes maneuvering methodically inside the barricades. One man was taking flash pictures, and the other two were systematically making calculations with a long tape measure and writing in small notebooks. Another officer in a yellow coat, this one to the rear of the Volvo, was turning traffic around and sending it back in the direction of Slater's Lake. Carter also noted with dismay that the policeman confronting him had removed a ten-inch, leather-covered pad from a side pocket of his raincoat.

"Don't tell me you're going to give me a ticket," Carter Banning said...and immediately he realized the ill-advisability if his objection.

"If you don't turn off your ignition, I'm going to give you more than a ticket," the patrolman said, his voice rising enough to draw the attention of the other officer fifteen yards away. Carter hastily switched off the key.

"Now get out of the car, Sir...and let me see your license and registration."

This was unreal.

Recognizing that at the very least he was going to be late for his physical exam, Carter pushed his door open with uncharacteristic abruptness, and simultaneously reached for his wallet. The policeman's raincoat was not fastened down the front and he pushed it aside revealing the handcuffs and gun holster on his wide, black belt.

"Slowly," the officer cautioned. "Now exit the car, Sir...that's it...slowly...face away from me, please...and hold your license and registration out to one side." Banning did exactly as he was told.

As the patrolman took the documents and examined them, Carter scanned the shining asphalt roadway...the wooden barricades...the yellow tape that defined the crime scene he'd very nearly penetrated with his skidding car. "Is this really necessary?" he said over his shoulder. "I didn't hit anything, did I?"

The policeman reached inside the Volvo and removed the keys from the ignition. "That's what we want to establish," he said, "...isn't it?" He unbuttoned one of his shirt pockets, dropped Carter's keys into it, and buttoned-up again.

"You'll be more comfortable over there in my car," the officer said, gesturing toward a white late model sedan with large blue letters that said *'Southwick Police.'* He escorted Carter to the idling vehicle and, as the light bar's six blue strobes flashed in hypnotic sequence, Carter Banning reluctantly took a seat behind the vehicle's wire mesh divider.

The patrolman slammed the door and it locked automatically.

* * * * *

ON THE FAR SIDE OF THE INTERSECTION where Middleville Road met Route 25-A, a lean man in his early twenties sat answering questions in the passenger seat of a squad car identical to the one where Carter was now confined. Obviously, he was a jogger; he wore a loose-fitting sweatsuit, as far as Carter could tell, and a white headband. Will Beamish, the officer who had detained Carter, approached the vehicle and a plainclothes detective seated behind the steering wheel lowered the driver's window. The detective accepted Banning's Massachusetts license and registration card from the patrolman, and raised the window again. In the rearview mirror he visually checked the Volvo against the information on the registration form...*2014... 4-door sedan...silver*...then he called headquarters to determine if there were any outstanding warrants for 70-year-old Carter A. Banning.

While the detective's request was being processed, he held the driver's license before the fellow in the jogging clothes and asked if he'd ever seen the man pictured there. The photo on the license was five years old, but Peter Wilkinson recognized his Southwick Landing neighbor immediately.

"Yeah. That's Mr. Banning. He lives in my area. I *thought* that looked like the Bannings' car."

"Then it's not the vehicle you saw leaving the accident scene earlier?"

"No. Like I said: it was an old Impala, maybe fifteen years...a two-door. And it was light blue."

The sector car's radio squawked with: *Southwick unit 231... Carter Alton Banning...6/1/45...ID-798503486-21...negative warrants...negative history...HCPD out.*

The detective plucked a hand mic from a bracket on the dash and mumbled, "SC...231 out." He switched on the squad car's roof-mounted loudspeaker and summoned Sergeant Beamish. "Volvo man's clean...come pick up his stuff, Sarge."

The uniformed officer retrieved Carter's documents from the plainclothesman and brought them, along with his keys, to where Banning was waiting impatiently in the squad car. He opened the door of the cruiser and said, "You're free to go, Sir. Please drive carefully. The roads are a bit slippery."

Carter Banning elected not to say anything. He got into his Volvo, made a careful three-point turn, and doubled slowly back to College Road. Better to keep Doctor Song waiting than to spend part of Christmas Eve in the goddam Southwick jail.

Chapter Three

IT HAD BEEN an unseasonably warm fall throughout most of Massachusetts, and even now, three days into winter, midday temperatures were in the high fifties. For December 24th in Hamden County, that translated into a very pleasant fourteen degrees above normal. Consequently a sort of mellow lethargy had overtaken the staff of the Southwick VA Medical Center. Everyone was moving at a slower pace, it seemed; even the normally intense doctors, nurse practitioners, and clerks, most of them usually overburdened and on edge, appeared enervated by the summerlike weather that, except for this morning's brief shower, had produced sunny, dry conditions as far north as Bangor.

Carter Banning stood clad only in a disposable surgical gown. He was clearly self-conscious and uncomfortable as petite Dermatologist, Dr. Meili Song, untied and parted the front of the green paper garment he wore. 'Millie' (as she was referred to by everyone at the hospital) shifted a pair of stylish eyeglasses from the bridge of her nose to the top of her head, and examined Carter's genitals by leaning and peering through a hand-held dermatoscope.

"Nothing here," she proclaimed after what seemed to Banning an interminably drawn-out inspection. Doctor Song then switched off her blue polarizing light, gathered a fistful of the flimsy gown at the hem, and lifted the bunched garment to chest level. "Hold this," she instructed, "...and turn around, if you don't mind." The Dermatologist re-activated the scope's intense light and played it over her patient's buttocks. Detecting nothing of note, she extended her visual examination, unaided by the device, to the back of the elderly man's thighs. There, Doctor Song noted a few slightly raised, eighth-inch-diameter spots that she deemed deserving of more incisive scrutiny.

Kneeling on the examination room floor, Song levelled the dermatoscope the way one might hold a small pistol, and she winked one eye, as with her other she looked below Carter's summer tan line for the telltale pattern that would reveal the presence of basal cell carcinoma, the type of cancer that typically grows on parts of the skin that are subjected to excessive exposure to the sun.

The 32-year-old woman regained her feet effortlessly, whereupon Carter Banning quickly dropped the lower half of the now-wrinkled surgical gown. He tied it securely at the waist utilizing the garment's two attached plastic belts.

"What's the verdict?" he asked, and he sat in the chair toward which the specialist motioned with a flick of her hand.

Dr. Meili Song had swiftly cleaned the business end of her black scope with an antiseptic wipe. She'd then removed her Latex gloves, and was now typing away rapidly, entering notes that became inscribed in the Medical Center's sophisticated computer system.

'Visual scan...lesion: BCC...mid-right forearm...12 mm...recomm: incis, remov...surg. 12/24/15.'

"You virtually get a free pass for the time being," the Dermatologist said as she typed, "...but that growth on your arm—I want to take it off."

"When?"

"This afternoon."

"But it's Christmas Eve, Doc."

"Your basal cell carcinoma doesn't know that," said Millie Song. "This is the least serious type of skin cancer we find," she said with a shrug, handing her patient his underwear…"*if* we catch it early. Happily, in this case we did. So let's continue to do this my way, shall we?"

The Korean War veteran looked out of the window longingly. "I was hoping to play golf this afternoon." He said it more than a bit wistfully.

"Carter, basal cell is unlikely to spread on one's skin to other surface parts of the body, but it can move into nearby bone or other tissue *under* your skin." Doctor Song cocked her head, "You really don't need that. It could play absolute havoc with your backswing someday."

Carter Banning glanced at the large analog clock on the examining room wall. Eleven-fifteen. He turned his back and climbed reluctantly into his boxer shorts. "There's a sign posted in the waiting room that says this place is closing for Christmas at twelve noon."

"And?"

"So, who's going to be around to do the surgery?"

"You're in luck, young man…I'm on call for ER back-up 'til 12:00. I'll do it myself."

"You're the doctor, I guess." Carter looked with disdain at the small, round growth on his arm, then, with a sigh, he clambered into his trousers.

"I wouldn't try an appendectomy without assistance," she said, "…but all that this 'basal' thing entails is a local anesthetic, an inch-long incision, and five or six sutures. I've done similar procedures a hundred times…at least!"

Banning had donned his shirt and buttoned it. He slipped into his light, unlined New England Patriots windbreaker, and turned toward the door.

"Get a bite to eat," said Doctor Song, "...and be back here at twelve-thirty. No alcohol, okay?"

"I'll be back in an hour," he said, "...right here...sober as a judge. You do the same."

Meili Song smiled coyly. "I had my first and last drink when I was sixteen, Carter. It almost got me in trouble, and...let's just say...I never went back for more." She smiled and held the door open for the tall man.

"Twelve-thirty...sharp," said Carter Banning...and he left the examining room. He would be Meili Song's last patient before Christmas...barring some afternoon crisis in the main floor Emergency Room.

* * * * *

FREDDIE YOUNG, a Korean-born US Army veteran and naturalized American citizen, was one of four assistant greens keepers who tended the golf course that semi-circled the Southwick VAMC. He was also a recovering Stress Disorder patient at the Center.

At 1145 hours on this balmy Thursday, Young was steering an electric golf cart stenciled 'USVA' toward the north guardhouse. There, two busy VA policemen paid the approaching worker little mind as they hurriedly waved him and his bundle of rattling garden tools through their checkpoint and onto the hospital grounds proper. They were intent only on closing the installation's high iron gate to incoming traffic. It would soon be time to lock up the mostly vacated medical facility for a rare three-and-a-half-day Christmas weekend...and the eager uniformed men had some last minute shopping to do in town.

Chapter Four

IT WOULD HAVE BEEN A SIMPLE MATTER for him to decline, Carter Banning thought…to negate Doctor Song's suggestion that she perform the surgical procedure on his arm that afternoon. Christmas Eve was, after all, one of perhaps half a dozen days in the year when a person needed to be available at a moment's notice to respond to family matters…to be ready at the drop of a hat, if called upon, to fill any number of holiday obligations. Hell, in less than twelve hours he was due to drive to Saint Stephen's in Sawyer Bluff for Midnight Mass.

But what if Millie Song said he wouldn't be able to? Carter's wife, Elizabeth, though a few years younger than he, was showing signs of incipient macular degeneration and already she feared driving at night. Why hadn't he considered that?

Nonsense! he told himself.

The procedure Doctor Song was going to perform an hour from now was as simple as having a tooth extracted. Carter would be locally anesthetized over only a small portion of his forearm, and he was assured the small, bandaged wound wouldn't interfere with his driving home. What's more, the doctor had advised him he'd even be permitted his traditional six-ounce cup of brandy-laced egg nog while decorating the tree. There was nothing to be concerned about. Why complicate matters with dreamed-up problems for God's sake?

Confident that the accident scene on Middleville Road would be open to normal traffic by now, Carter pulled the car out of the VA's usually jammed parking lot, noting that the three-acre paved area was as empty as he'd ever seen it in all the years he'd been treated at the Southwick Center. Nor would the lot be any less accessible when he returned from lunch…because the incoming lanes that led from Route 25-A would be blocked by the barrier gate at the guardhouse. And surely the East entrance checkpoint near College Road would be closed as well. That would leave only the ambulance gate accessible…the portal with the automatic barrier controlled from the Emergency Room itself.

Carter frowned. *But with the access roads cordoned off for the holiday, how the hell am I supposed to get back in here?*

He cursed aloud, wishing now he'd eaten breakfast, and he stopped the Volvo just short of the vacant Lexan guardhouse. *Maybe the hospital cafeteria's still open*, he said inwardly. He knew for a fact the janitorial staff sometimes ate midnight chow there on holidays…he'd seen them last July 3rd. The flustered septuagenarian checked his mirrors, made a three point turn in reverse, and drove back toward the near-deserted parking lot by way of the North exit lane.

As Carter Banning turned into the area marked-off with hundreds of empty yellow rectangles, the only other person in the vicinity of the VAMC's Main Building 200 was a thin landscaper who scratched idly at the ground beneath a nearby elm, his long-handled rake producing only thin brown ruts in the rain dampened ground under a naked tree.

* * * * *

CARTER PARKED THE VOLVO, entered Building 200 through the revolving Main Door, and walked through the now empty lobby toward a corridor that led to the cafeteria. It was 12:00 noon when he reached the end of the hundred-yard hallway. To the left was Cardiology...the Lab entrance was straight ahead... and the arrow next to it pointing right said 'Countryman's Café.' Carter turned and walked quickly to his right along the quiet corridor whose overhead lighting had been reduced to half its normal radiance.

The café door was closed but it opened easily, and once inside, Banning saw that only two medical personnel, a man and a woman, both of them in green scrubs, sat at a round table in the center of the room. Left of the entrance, against the wall, a middle aged woman occupied a tall stool by the cash register, where she sat with her legs crossed, absorbed in a paperback.

The steam table and salad bar had been shut down, but assortments of Saran-wrapped sandwiches...mostly salami...a few egg salad...were arrayed on a glass shelf at eye level. Beneath the sandwiches, a dozen or so containers of white and chocolate milk sat partially covered in slowly dissolving cracked ice. The coffee urn at the end of the counter still steamed.

Carter selected an egg salad and opted for white milk, which he carried, along with three paper napkins, to the register. He paid his five dollars to the grim-faced cashier. She seemed to resent being here on the near-vacant premises, and he strode to a seat far from the unpleasant looking woman and her dog-eared book.

Carter could take his time.

Meili Song's examination room, where the tall man assumed the procedure on his arm would take place, was virtually overhead from where he sat. Getting to the second floor would take no more than two minutes. If the elevators were running. *They must be*, he said to himself. *Then again, the lights have been dimmed, haven't they? It might be best to take the stairs.* What the hell, even given the delay he'd encountered at Middleville Road earlier, Carter Banning had plenty of time.

He pried open the paper spout on his half-pint milk carton, bit into the sandwich, and washed down a bland mouthful of egg salad. Ten minutes ago he'd been starving, but now he seemed to have lost much of his appetite.

The man and woman in the green scrubs gathered up their lunch wrappers and paper cups. As they left the cafeteria, Carter noted that she was fanning herself with an open hand. *The air conditioning's been turned down too*, he realized. Except for the cashier idly flipping the pages of her 'dime novel,' the normally bustling Medical Center had become as still and quiet as an empty tomb.

Chapter Five

ELIZABETH BANNING FINISHED POLISHING her sterling silver service for eight, and now ran warm water in the sink as she prepared to wash and hand-dry the 5-piece Gorham sets. She'd been collecting the graceful Melon Bud design since long before her wedding and she gently handled the knives, forks, and spoons as if holding each of the gleaming utensils for the first time.

Her husband should be returning soon, Elizabeth estimated. WBZ reported that the Old North Highway (as the Boston stations called 25-A between Southwick and Turner's Falls) had been re-opened at Middleville Road. Unless his physical had revealed some problem other than his troublesome lower back…or something had come up regarding the 20/20 vision that inexplicably seemed to be failing…Carter would be turning into the driveway any minute.

Should she make some lunch? Not yet. He always called when leaving the VA. Maybe he'd surprise her with a nice salad from Mannino's. *It's only 12:25,* she said to herself, looking at the clock on the stove. *If he doesn't call by a quarter 'til, I'll go ahead and make myself a cup of soup.*

She hummed a familiar melody as she tenderly rinsed the silverware…then dried it…always in the same sequence…first forks (dinner then dessert)…spoons next (tea and soup)…and finally knives, the heaviest, but easiest to clean of all five pieces in each setting.

The WBZ newscaster repeated the description of the blue Impala…followed by the LAW-BREAKER phone number… and Elizabeth checked the card on her kitchen counter to be sure she'd copied it right. *I wonder if Carter's got his radio on,* she mused. Then she stopped drying the last of the dinner knives and frowned. *Roseanne Turbish…the woman who lived next door to the Wilkinsons…didn't her husband have an old blue Chevy when he was alive? Or was that a ford?* She shrugged. *Carter would know.*

Elizabeth Banning dried her hands on her apron. "Now, where's my good cheese knife?" The tiny woman scanned the kitchen counter, then looked toward the dining room table. "You might know…right in front of my nose." She shook her head and rolled her eyes. "Maybe I should have a hot cup of tea."

*****

CARTER BANNING LEFT the 'Countryman's Café' and walked to the end of the first floor hallway. There, beneath a red and white 'Exit' sign, he entered the dim-lit stairwell where wide concrete steps led down to Radiology, and up to the Vision and Dermatology clinics. Before climbing the stairs, he tried the door through which he'd just come, to reassure himself that it hadn't locked behind him. All he needed to make this Christmas a total disaster was to be locked in an empty, stifling stairwell for the next four days! As far as he could tell, there wasn't another patient in this building that on any given day probably accommodated a thousand. If he got stuck here, he'd stay here… probably 'til Monday. Jesus!

On its interior, the heavy metal door was labeled 'Lab' and 'Cardio' and its brushed steel knob yielded to his twist as he checked it. Okay, the door was accessible. He proceeded up two steeply inclined groups of ten steps each, and at the second-floor landing, he opened an identical green door that bore the inscriptions 'Vision' and 'Derm.'

This door, too, opened freely and Carter stepped into the soundless second floor corridor...but immediately he was taken aback. Never before had the tall man seen the line of various specialty clinics arrayed in full 'security' mode. The place looked for all the world like a sanitized prison. Not only were the wide clinic entrances stretching along the hallway for a hundred yards, now enclosed by bronze, roll-down grates...but each of their empty interior spaces was vaguely illuminated by only one, faint, corner light that blinked every five seconds and cast along the floor, distorted shadows from the countertop Christmas trees and pointed Menorahs...newly darkened symbols that once had given the place at least some semblance of life and optimism. Now this place...that usually was vibrant with confidence and the promise of healing...seemed hopeless and despairing...a facility designed more to house the dead than accommodate the living.

But not all the second floor clinics were cordoned off by their impermeable bronze enclosures. The motorized cage suspended over the entrance to Doctor Song's empty waiting area had not been lowered, and the suite itself, though cloaked in darkness like the others all along the corridor, was unblocked and easily accessible.

Slowly, Carter approached the uninviting atrium he'd left some fifty minutes earlier. He peered into the now gloomy foyer, reluctant to cross its threshold—defined as it was by a recessed metal track in the floor. The half-inch-wide trough was the slot into which the stout overhead grate would be secured when dropped electronically.

He shifted his gaze upward.

Eight or nine inches of the barrier protruded from the arch that delineated the upper proscenium of the Dermatology vestibule. There had to be some logical reason why the roll-down grille had not been lowered when all the rest of them on this floor apparently had. *Doctor Song must have access to the mechanism that controls this thing,* he concluded. *She's obviously left the place open for me.*

Carter checked his watch. He was still ten minutes early for the scheduled 12:30 surgery. Though hesitant to enter the waiting room, lest the cage somehow suddenly descend and thus entrap him there, he was equally unwilling to stray from the immediate area of the vestibule. If Meili Song were to come looking for him and find him gone, she might assume that her skittish patient had balked at the last minute. In that event she'd simply leave for her slated duty in the Emergency Room. Of course she would!

Branning chastised himself inwardly.

What the hell was this sudden obsession with imaginary confinement all about? He'd never been claustrophobic, for God's sake! Why the perplexing fear of being restricted? He'd even felt it in the back of the squad car. And if he were to be honest with himself, it was this new, mysterious sensation that concerned him most of all…more than the incipient minor surgery…more than the incident with the Southwick Police… more than his screwed-up Christmas Eve.

Shit, be reasonable! he told himself. *If one were to select the safest location in the world to be isolated, what better place to choose than a hospital…or a police car…or a goddam military installation. Get a grip, old man!*

He tentatively entered the dismal foyer, took a seat nearest the hallway with its diminished lighting, and warily eyed the long bronze trellis that, his attempts at self-assurance notwithstanding, seemed ready to slam down and imprison him at any moment.

Chapter Six

DETECTIVE LIEUTENANT FRANK BROGAN sat in Southwick police headquarters reading witness Peter Wilkinson's signed statement for the third time. He was in his shirtsleeves, a wrinkled suit jacket draped over his chair. From a straight-backed seat on the opposite side of the desk, lanky Yale grad-student Wilkinson examined a dozen simply framed documents that adorned the wall above Brogan's head. Most of the citations were municipal commendations from various organizations ranging from the Greater Southwick Chamber of Commerce…to Miss Farrington's third-grade class at Southwick Elementary. The children's letter of appreciation, young Wilkinson noted, occupied the place of honor, centered as it was, in the exact middle of the array. It was also the only hand-written award…and it bore a small gold 'Teacher's Star' in the upper right hand corner.

Lieutenant Brogan rose from his wooden swivel chair and walked to a dusty laser copier to the right of the desk. "Seems specific enough," he said. "You certainly got a good look, m'boy."

Peter shrugged without comment, and Brogan ran off three copies of the deposition.

He returned to the desk, one of whose six-inch legs had broken off and been replaced by two thick, unused volumes on 'Prosecutorial Misconduct,' and he placed the duplicates in front of Wilkinson. "Initial these next to your name, if you don't mind." He pointed a nicotine-stained finger toward the signature. "Anyplace down there will do."

Peter scribbled PLW beside his name on each copy.

Brogan scooped up the facsimiles of the declaration that bore the stated place, time, and circumstances surrounding the accident that had critically injured 19-year-old pedestrian, Renaldo Vega, as he attempted to cross Middleville Road in Southwick. The detective returned to his seat. "Can we give you a ride home, son? It's Christmas Eve, after all."

"Sure," said Wilkinson. "Our house is down by The Landing... just on the other side of Preston's tobacco farm."

"I know the place," said Brogan. "Nice area. Quiet."

Again, Peter Wilkinson merely hiked and lowered his shoulders indifferently. The detective wriggled into his jacket and both men strode to the SPD parking lot where Brogan's unmarked sedan sat, dotted by droplets from the rain shower that had now stopped altogether.

Once inside the car, the heavyset plainclothes officer buckled his seatbelt, waited for his passenger to do the same, then slowly departed the parking area. He wheeled the dark sedan onto Point Grove Road and followed it around the perimeter of Edgewood Links Golf Course. The neatly-trimmed facility that separated The Landing from the Southwick VA hospital appeared lush, even in early winter, and as the chimes from the nearby Veterans' Chapel carillon wafted over its manicured expanse, Frank Brogan said, "That's a French Christmas song playin'... 'Bring a Torch, Jeannette Isabella.'"

"Yeah," said Peter with another shrug, "...I know."

"I'm impressed," the Detective murmured, as he turned onto Stony Path. "Nine out of ten people in this country couldn't tell you the name of that carol."

"Nine out of ten people in this country are assholes," young Wilkinson said. "That's my place at the bottom of the hill...after the mailbox marked 'Turbish'...the house closest to the lake."

Brogan eyed Peter in the mirror, and he pulled into the tree-lined driveway of number 22. "Here ya' go. We may need you to confirm the ID when our blue Impala turns up."

"Sure," said Peter. "Tell the Vega dude I hope he's okay." He exited the unmarked car and loped toward the shingled ranch house. It was all but invisible amid a profusion of mountain laurels and boxwoods that sheltered the property from chilly Slater's Lake.

Lieutenant Brogan backed out of the narrow drive. He turned toward Point Grove and the west side of Edgewood Links. Once he had Stony Path in his mirrors, the Detective Sergeant lifted the mic from its bracket on the car's dash. He depressed the 'talk' switch, squawking it twice. When the dispatcher answered, Brogan identified himself and said, "Retrieve Volker's Dash Cam video of the Wilkinson statement. I'll be there in ten minutes."

* * * * *

WHEN FRANK BROGAN PULLED BACK into the eight-car lot on the west side of police headquarters, everything was as it had been when he'd left with eyewitness Peter Wilkinson as his passenger...with one exception. The dispatcher had summoned Officer Steven Volker, advising him that the Lieutenant wanted to check the Dash Cam footage of Wilkinson making his deposition, and Volker's car, in which the statement had been taken, was now waiting, locked and empty, in the precinct yard. The camera had been removed from its swivel mounting on the dash, and the fist-sized, black device was sitting on Brogan's desk.

Detective Brogan strode into headquarters and the Duty Officer nodded toward the far side of the cluttered room...in the direction of the wall full of framed certificates.

The Bluetooth camera was positioned in the middle of the Lieutenant's desk blotter. Its late morning video had not yet been replayed, and Detective Volker was as eager as anyone to see the recording of Peter Wilkinson's statement that he himself had taken. He had, of course, filmed the interview by turning the Forzen device 180 degrees to the rear of the windshield, and activating its fisheye lens.

All of the policemen under Brogan's command studiously actuated their Dash Cams in this manner when interviewing witnesses or suspects…inside the sector cars and out. There was no department-wide edict requiring the procedure, but failing to do so would earn the Lieutenant's subordinates a severe reprimand, and everyone knew it. There were far too many nuisance claims of brutality and other forms of police malfeasance being leveled at cops everywhere to suit Frank Brogan.

"Okay, Stevie," said the Lieutenant, "…let's go to the movies." He picked up the Bluetooth device and passed his folded handkerchief gently over the display screen on its back.

"What are we lookin' for, Chief…anything in particular?"

"I'll tell you when we see it," Frank Brogan said. "Or more properly put…when we *don't* see it." He activated two small switches on the state-of-the-art camera, and replaced it on the desk…where both men could clearly see Officer Steve Volker writing…and hear Peter Wilkinson talking.

Chapter Seven

EVEN IF HE'D BEEN SO INCLINED, Carter Banning wouldn't have been able to read one of the dozen or more magazines arrayed on the end tables in Doctor Song's waiting room…there simply wasn't enough light. Although the rain shower that had sprinkled Southwick and vicinity had stopped, the typically gray early winter overcast remained, and the resulting dim daylight barely illuminating the skylight-like windows jutting out from Building 200's second-floor, was insufficient to relieve the dreary atmosphere in the shadowy atrium.

Carter wished he'd thought better of leaving his Galaxy Core at home to charge. Its cheery screen would have been especially welcome right about now, he mused…not to mention the reassurance that access to the device's phone feature would have provided. He doubted he'd have experienced the claustrophobia episode that began in the stairwell if he'd had his smartphone with him. *I just hope it doesn't ring while it's charging in the kitchen,* he thought. *Beth will think I'm calling, and she won't have the foggiest idea how to answer the damn thing.*

He reconsidered the scenario he'd just envisioned, and shook his head in disbelief. What the hell was going on with him? Did he really think a woman of Elizabeth Banning's intellect would conclude Carter would be calling *himself*...on his *own* cell phone? And if he were trying to reach *her*, wouldn't he be calling on the house landline? "I don't need a Dermatologist, he muttered, "...I need a fucking psychiatrist!"

Precisely at that point in his displeasing reverie, Carter Banning's spine stiffened and his breath caught in his constricting throat. A long, low scream originated down the hall and grew in intensity until its high-frequency wail filled the gloomy corridor to his left.

The former Army codebreaker lurched to his feet and stumbled into the hallway. Someone obviously was in severe distress... either that, or a disturbed patient had managed to gain access to Building 200 from the Psychiatric Ward. That must be it. The poor souls there were known to screech from the iron-barred windows of Building 150—the Psych Center—particularly during holidays, when they felt more abandoned and alone than ever.

With his eyes trained on the passageway's east end, Carter could detect only the glowing red and white sign above the corridor's emergency exit. Without question, the hallway was empty...still, the screaming persisted...an uninterrupted howl that echoed along the full length of the second floor in eerie resonance.

What should I do? the tall man wondered. There'd been no announcement on the hospital's loudspeaker. If a dangerous inmate had broken away from the confinement of Building 150, it was standard procedure to sound the two-tone horn over the public address system. And a general advisory stating the emergency always followed...he'd heard both alerts issued on a few occasions in the past.

But today, there had been nothing to forewarn the occupants of Building 200 that something was amiss. Could it be that hospital authorities concluded the Southwick Medical Center was unoccupied? Was he alone in this huge, bleak facility with a psychopath...possibly a physically fit soldier one-third his age…some former combat warrior trained to kill quickly and stealthily?

He moved his eyes furtively from left to right.

Carter Banning backed up slowly, retreating into the security of the waiting room. If he had to confront an unstable individual, better that he give himself the benefit of a darkened area in which to fend him off. At least he was familiar with the layout of the Dermatology Clinic. If need be, he could slither beneath one of the two long settees positioned against the facing walls of the vestibule.

Then, as Carter backpedaled with slow, deliberate steps…he felt a firm hand grip his shoulder.

* * * * *

LIEUTENANT BROGAN AND DETECTIVE VOLKER hunched toward the Dash Cam in the middle of Brogan's desk. "Pull down that blind," the Lieutenant instructed, pointing to the window behind the illuminated camera. The Duty Officer complied.

The grainy video playing on the device's viewing screen showed Middleville Road wobbling out of view as the camera lens was obviously being swiveled in order to photograph the interior of the police car in which Volker sat with the sweatsuit-clad Peter Wilkinson. The date and time of the filming were superimposed on the lower right corner of the screen.

The Dash Cam's fisheye lens suddenly became engaged, and as Volker's hand was withdrawn from the mounted piece of equipment, the picture stopped shaking and the images of both the detective and the young jogger became stationary and clearly visible. In another second, the sound was activated and the squeak-thud…squeak-thud…of the sector car's windshield wiper could be heard.

Lieutenant Brogan frowned at his Sergeant.

"Establishing precipitation conditions," Volker said.

"Good thinking," said Brogan. "Any conversation to this point?"

"None," said the sergeant. "You can see me holding my hand up to keep him from starting…now I'm showing my shield… there's the kid holding up his license…here's where the interview begins."

For ten minutes the two men watched the Dash Cam screen intently. Both seemed satisfied that standard on-site interview procedure was being followed to the letter. Even Sergeant Volker's handwritten notes were discernible in the recorded document. At the conclusion of the video…when Wilkinson exits the police car and Volker rotates the camera back to its normal forward-facing position…the Dash Cam clicks off, and the image of Middleville Road dies.

"See what you wanted, Lieutenant?"

"Sure did," Frank Brogan responded, getting to his feet.

"Which was?…" Volker asked, "…if it's any of my business."

"You never told him the name of the victim, did you?"

"'Course not."

"I didn't think so," said Lieutenant Brogan. "I wonder how he knew."

* * * * *

CARTER BANNING WHEELED AROUND swatting wildly at the hand that had surreptitiously grabbed him. Envisioning an assailant even taller than he, Carter then swung a clenched fist blindly into the dim void where his accoster's face was most likely to be. But the lunging effort found no target, and Carter stumbled in his futile attempt at self-defense. Immediately, he felt the attacker's arms encircle his waist from behind, and he seized the hands that were clasped at his sternum. If he could get sufficient leverage, perhaps he could use the man's hold on him to advantage. Grabbing the clenched hands with his own, Banning secured their grip even tighter and thrust his torso swiftly downward...lifting the five-foot-two-inch body of Doctor Meili Song from the floor...and flinging her onto one of the waiting room's two leather-covered divans.

The startled woman weighed little more than one hundred pounds, and as she scrambled to secure her rumpled gabardine skirt, the slippery leather of the couch provided little purchase for the smooth soles and heels of her glossy, black shoes.

"Carter!" she yelled, "...for Christ's sake!"

Stunned and disbelieving, Banning held his arms outstretched and frozen as if crucified. Doctor Song swept her black hair from her face with one hand and fumbled with the other to adjust her white lab coat, one sleeve of which had been torn at the shoulder.

Taking the air in deep, hungry gulps, Carter Banning stared down at the squirming woman before him. He backed up slowly. "Jesus, Millie...I'm sorry. I had no idea..."

"Just help me up...hand me my glasses," she said. "And come inside. That damn howling vacuum cleaner's driving me crazy!"

Chapter Eight

AMONG OTHER THINGS, Peter Wilkinson had become an avowed vegetarian in his sixth and final year at Yale. First, he'd changed his curriculum from the fairly common *Master of Arts in History*, to the related, but considerably more specialized, *Master of Arts in Historic Preservation*…and now he'd announced himself a confirmed lactovegetarian, of all things. "That boy's a strange one," people would say.

Of course, adopting a diet that excluded the ingestion of slaughtered animals was a modest lifestyle adjustment that affected no one, especially Peter's frail mother who was herself, indifferent at best when it came to consuming red meat. But switching his course of study to the considerably more expensive, architecture-focused discipline he'd curiously opted for…well, that was something that could hardly have been expected to go unnoticed.

By nature however, Mary Wilkinson wasn't one to quibble over a thirty-thousand dollar increase in her only child's already steep Ivy League tuition. No one living in The Landing area of Southwick was what one might term 'hard pressed' economically. If you weren't financially 'comfortable,' after all, you simply didn't live there. What bothered Mary was that

Peter was becoming more and more withdrawn...to the point of being almost secretive, she thought...whenever the conversation during her son's brief visits home turned to academic issues.

In that regard, Peter's stepfather, Bradley, could not have cared less. What mattered to Mary's second husband was that "...at least we don't have to look at the fucking ingrate more than nine or ten days a year!" To which he'd added sardonically, "If it takes ninety-thousand for Yale to babysit him, so be it." After reacting bitterly at first, Mary had learned to bite her tongue... and wonder if her otherwise considerate husband hadn't, in truth, been unjustly provoked beyond all endurance by the boy he'd legally adopted...that leach of a son who now, like it or not, bore his name.

Actually, Peter Wilkinson had been nudged toward 'Historic Preservation' as a preferred discipline by his newly appointed Yale counsellor, the Iraqi scholar Mujab Baghdadi. Neither the peevish student nor his profoundly deaf mentor had shown any laudable desire to preserve buildings of historic importance; in fact, the opposite would soon prove to be true. But Baghdadi quickly perceived in his rebellious protégé the desired combination of restlessness and intelligence that he'd been trained to detect in the young. Furthermore, Peter had displayed an abiding confidence in Dr. Baghdadi...he'd even begun an online course in *'Basic American Sign Language'* the better to communicate with his favorite professor.

The gullible Mister Wilkinson will more than suffice, Mujab Baghdadi had concluded.

On the appointed December day, that of the winter solstice, he'd wired an encrypted message to his associates headquartered at a small hotel in Kirkuk:

```
    one Period in life surpasses four
eternities.
    three Will be as three kinsmen...nay...
three sons.
```

```
    two heroes out of five shall all five
serve.
    after the four, then shall three die
in allah's bosom.
    when the last two, at two mystical
moments know him...
    ...then the major seven commandments
will be fulfilled.
```

The code was so simple that the Islamic cabal considered it foolproof, thus the message was relayed without alteration to Stonehenge in England. There, thousands of druids and other pagans had gathered to chant and dance while welcoming the last spectacular sunrise of the fall.

In nearby Amesbury Abbey, Mujab Baghdadi's dispatch would be decoded once more by his fellow jihadists…this time, huddled in an ancient, inhospitable bunker now disguised as a haven for Druid pilgrims. Then the 53-word communiqué would be summarily destroyed.

At least, that had been the original intention.

Hamid al-Jamil was the youngest member of Baghdadi's terrorist group and the only other *'Husam'* collaborator (the word means *'Sharp Sword'*) who could boast a Western education. Al Jamil and Baghdadi were close friends, and indeed in college they had traded the ultimate in intimate gifts among Muslim males—a colorful taqiyah, or Islamic skull cap, inscribed with the word, *'Husam.'*

Some insisted one could hardly call the University of Istanbul, from which both Hamid and Mujab had won degrees a 'Western' school, since the city sits astride the border between Europe and Asia. But in Mujab Baghdadi's case, Yale considered the geography insignificant. Indeed, upon learning of Baghdadi's aural disability, the bastion of Liberalism in New Haven had virtually salivated over the opportunity to flaunt its own double edged exercise in brotherly love…and the Eli faculty had immediately adopted Mujab as one of its very own. Not in spite of his disability…but because of it.

Hamid al-Jamil was out of matches, so he merely pocketed the oblique letter from his friend and former classmate. There would be plenty of time to destroy it following the noon *Adhan*. After all, how was he to know he'd be dead fifteen minutes after the midday *Call to Prayer*?

Chapter Nine

AS FREQUENTLY HAPPENS during fluke Massachusetts winters, warm spells when temperatures reach into the fifties have been known to spawn erratic nor'easters and produce copious amounts of drifting snow. This was precisely the unwelcome weather pattern that was predicted for the New England coast beginning the day after Christmas and continuing right through the weekend.

Many in Connecticut, Massachusetts and Rhode Island felt that the timing of this threatened early blizzard was fortuitous. *If a storm is inevitable,* they reasoned, *what better time for it than during a two or three-day period when virtually everyone can stay safely indoors?*

Elizabeth Banning, however, could summon up no such pragmatism. Her unmarried twin daughters living in New York and Pennsylvania were planning to arrive in Southwick late Saturday, two days hence, which meant, should current forecasts hold up, they might possibly be driving right into the teeth of the nor'easter.

Elizabeth decided to make herself another cup of tea.

She would have to give some thought to calling the girls... though she was secretly terrified that whatever she might say would dissuade them from coming at all. *Mary Wilkinson doesn't know how fortunate she is,* Elizabeth mused enviously, as she filled the kettle for the third time today. *Her son can get here from New Haven in little more than an hour.*

As for poor Roseanne Turbish down on the *cul-de-sac,* she had no one now that Herman was gone. Carter would look in on her, of course...and in bad weather, Brad Wilkinson always did the same, if only briefly. Furthermore, with Peter home from school there would be no shortage of able-bodied men to lend a hand in emergencies.

Elizabeth Banning filled her good porcelain teapot and brought it to the kitchen table. *Sometimes we don't realize how fortunate we are here in quiet little Southwick,* she thought.

* * * * *

THE WIDOWED ROSEANNE TURBISH had observed young Peter Wilkinson's arrival in Lieutenant Brogan's unmarked car... just as she witnessed everything that happened on the dead-end portion of Stony Path where she lived with nothing better to fill her days than watching the infrequent comings and goings near the river.

As always, when her neighbor (whom she considered a brat spoiled beyond redemption) had come home from his Ivy League school in Connecticut five days prior, he'd immediately donned his running togs and gone out jogging...promptly at ten...daily... and he never returned before one.

Running...for three hours...every day?

For the rest of the afternoon and evening, Roseanne assumed, he'd habitually kept himself glued to the Ham Radio apparatus in Mary and Bradley's attic...that infernal contraption whose eyesore rooftop antenna had landed the Wilkinsons in so much trouble with the Zoning Department the week before Herman's accident.

She attempted to cast the three-year-old image of her husband's broken body from her mind. "What a perfectly terrible boy," she said aloud, the bitterness reverberating throughout her big, desolate house. "I'm surprised Frank Brogan would have anything to do with him."

* * * * *

BUT GIVE THE DEVIL HIS DUE…Peter Wilkinson had always been a bright boy. In fact he'd earned his Ham Radio ticket from the International Telecommunications Union at the age of 15. With an array of non-commercial radio equipment constructed entirely in the manner known as 'Homebrew' (or privately-built), young Wilkinson was broadcasting as an amateur to other Hams around the world a few months after he'd first subscribed to 'CQ Amateur Radio' magazine. In no time, Peter had been awarded the Call Sign AAA3ASD, and from his elaborate cubby hole in the Landing area of Southwick, the precocious teen was soon broadcasting to…but more importantly, *hearing from…* the part of the world he found by far the most interesting—the inscrutable Middle East. And in particular, Iraq!

It was the first giant step on his road to radicalization. And who would have dreamed it? Certainly no one in the Wilkinson family…nor anyone in this upper class neighborhood…well, maybe Rosanne Turbish might have.

Her distrust of Peter had begun when she'd observed him, while he was still a pre-teen, cultivating the trust of flocks of unwary seagulls…then abusing them in the most inhumane and Machiavellian way.

His practice was to venture into the salt marshes in Herman Turbish's duck blind armed with sacks of small round pretzels, dozens of which he would cast onto the surrounding shallow water of the estuary. Of course the always ravenous gulls competed in droves for the crisp treats, and when they'd cleaned every last one from the surface of the marsh, they persisted in their begging, battling one another in a frantic, squawking crowd above the camouflaged jon boat.

Peter would further encourage the birds' frenzied competition by occasionally tossing a single hard-baked delight high amid the flock, where the luckiest and most agile among them would snag it on the fly and make off with it, only to return seconds later for still another delicacy.

When the general complaining had reached a crescendo...so loud and insistent that Roseanne Turbish could hear it from her upstairs reading room...even in winter...it was Peter's cue to take an inch-and-a-half M-80 firecracker from his pocket, light it's two-inch fuse with a match, and hurl the gunpowder-packed explosive up into the midst of the screeching throng.

Once again, a battle for the prize would ensue...but this time the gull that proved successful would win a hollow victory indeed. Snatching the flickering device in the determined clamp of its beak, the sharp-eyed seagull would fly but a few wing flaps away...before the inevitable explosion would tear the creature's head from its body...and the decapitated animal would plunge, trailing blood from its shredded neck, and splash into the brackish waters of the estuary.

This was the ideal result, as Peter Wilkinson saw it. For if one of the huge birds were to swallow the M-80 whole, the spectacle would prove far less dramatic. To be sure, the explosion would take place, and yes, the voracious seagull would perish, but the assassination would have become a rather ordinary, strangely muted exhibition; one far quieter...more subdued...and infinitely less satisfying than the in-flight beheading.

It was hardly surprising, then, that a year earlier...almost to the day...following the winter solstice, when Hamid al-Jamil's friends at *'Husam'* mailed their prospective recruit in Southwick, Massachusetts, a graphic video wherein a masked and black-robed executioner wielding a ten-inch knife severed the head of a helpless, kneeling 'Infidel'...the wicked seed of radicalization took instant root.

The emailed letter with its stomach-turning attachment was untraceable to any individual, of course, even though it had been intercepted by the clandestine British Censor's Bureau and tracked to the Woodstock Wi-Fi Café in Salisbury.

The stark landscape where the subject beheading had occurred appeared to be someplace in the Middle East, but even if such were the case, that could be almost anywhere in a vast area that stretched from Turkey to Pakistan…Iran to Somalia.

Why, then, was Wilkinson's letter mailed from Salisbury?

Obviously to disguise both the true locale of the crime, and the intent of its transmission the BCB's Inspector Miles Plumber had concluded. "The originators of the correspondence no doubt knew it would be spotted seconds after its electronic broadcast," he proclaimed. And wasn't it commonly known, after all, that Salisbury, a mere 18 miles south of Stonehenge, was literally crawling with Druids at this particular time of year? "Many of these bloodthirsty pagans, believe in multiple rebirths, and dabble in the sort of ritualistic behavior shown in the video," he'd insisted. The fanatics behind all this might well have contributed to the victim's being ushered into another (and by their lights possibly far better) incarnation. "To put it another way," said Plumber, "…one man's massacre can be another's ticket to paradise, if I may be so blunt."

At any rate, every letter mailed from Salisbury fell within Scotland Yard's jurisdiction, not the Censor's Bureau's…and 'The Yard' was known to have little stomach for injecting itself into the mysterious practices of the world's various religions. Especially when it was not at all clear that any British national was involved.

Like it or not, the golden age of colonialism is over, was Scotland Yard's mantra. As far as the agency was concerned, they would have no legitimate reason to judge the propriety, or otherwise, of anyone's sending a ten-minute film from Salisbury to Southwick, Massachusetts, regardless of its content.

That was the end of it.

Under less 'sensitive' circumstances, perhaps when budgetary considerations were not as stringent, the US State Department might be contacted...but only if there should be recurrences.

"Flag this *'Wif.en.poof'* email address if you must," instructed Commander Shelby Whitmore of The Yard, "...but for Cripe's sake, don't let the FBI know you've done it." He shook a Benson & Hedges from its box, twisted it into a black cigarette holder, and realizing that his tea was getting cold, set it aside. "Let me know if this sort of transmission to the US becomes habitual," he said.

With that, the Commander bit into a sugared scone and sipped his tepid tea.

Chapter Ten

IN DOCTOR MEILI SONG'S small operating suite, Carter Banning had been instructed to remove all of his clothing from the waist up. With the heat having been significantly reduced throughout the entire Medical Center, he was grateful that at least he would not be required to strip down to his boxers once again. It was getting downright cold in this building!

The petite Dermatologist lowered the examining table to its horizontal flat position, pulled the long rolled sheet of disposable paper the full length of the table, and tore it off. She crumpled the section to be discarded, deposited the crushed ball in a tall trash receptacle, and motioned for Carter to lie on the table on his back. When he had done so, she stood on tiptoes to reach the broad overhead light, moved it into position, and turned it on with a wall switch…making certain the powerful beam did not shine on her patient's face.

Having donned her surgical mask, Doctor Song rolled a narrow, padded table to Carter's side and placed his arm on it with the fleshy side down. She scrubbed and dried her hands and arms for what seemed to Banning the hundredth time, but now she followed up by slipping on a pair of green Latex gloves plucked from a box.

After cleansing her patient's forearm with some sort of liquid that Banning assumed was alcohol, the doctor swabbed the cancerous section of Carter's arm with an antiseptic solution. As it dried, she lifted a thin syringe from the small table and, holding it up to the light, forced the air from its clear cylinder. With four or five shallow injections she proceeded to anesthetize the three-inch-square area where her five centimeter incision would be made. Then she dropped the spent syringe in a wall-mounted repository marked with the triangle of six rounded hooks that identified it as a hazardous material container.

As he lay submissively on the table, the palm of his free hand cradling the nape of his neck, Carter Banning was struck by the calm precision with which Meili Song performed her task. Certainly, she had every right to be perturbed by the events that had marked the past half-hour. One could hardly have blamed her if the manhandling she'd undergone in the vestibule, even though unintentional, had prompted her to call off the surgical procedure altogether. But clearly it would take more than a physical jostling to dissuade this dedicated young woman from the completion of her noble task.

Carter could hear, more than feel, the incision.

It was the purring sound of a razor slicing through velvet. This was followed by an insistent series of pressing probes...then a swift change of instruments. The exchange was followed in turn by more pressing...additional probing...and finally by the sound of something metallic being dropped into a steel kidney-shaped bowl.

"How're you doing?" the Doctor asked idly...and she reached for the first in a row of sutures that she had pre-arranged on a small table at her right elbow.

Carter had felt nothing but slight pressure in the still-tanned area of his outer forearm about six inches from his wrist. "I've had teeth-cleaning sessions that were a hell of a lot worse," he responded.

Meili Song smiled, Carter could tell. Her mouth was obscured by the surgical mask, of course, but the woman was one of those people whose smile invaded every area of her face, and her eyes fairly twinkled with amusement. *Things must have gone well*, Carter thought. And they had.

The stitching of the wound took three times as long as the incision and removal of the small, elongated tumor had. The process consisted of applying eight absorbable interior sutures that secured the dermis, and ten black non-absorbable stitches that effectively closed and held the abutting epidermis in a neat, two-inch line. By the time Doctor Song had applied the bulky gauze dressing, an inch-thick bandage that was easily four times the size of the wound beneath, it was obvious that the Dermatologist was pleased with the result.

She removed her mask and dropped it in the tall waste cylinder. "Sorry it took so long," she said winking. "We usually have three pairs of hands involved in one of these procedures…but that's just a union requirement. I can do it with one arm tied behind my back."

Meili helped Carter to a sitting position, lowered the foot portion of the table, and pointed to his t-shirt, sweater, and Patriots jacket that hung beside the door. "You can put on your things," she said, pointing, "…while I clean up here. Then you can buy us a cup of coffee in the cafeteria. Do you know where it is?"

*****

THE TRANSMISSION IN HAMID'S POCKET might not have been considered particularly significant had it not been inscribed on both sides of the cheap, all-purpose paper from the printer in al-Jamil's Istanbul flat. But configured as it was, the document clearly held the key to the original message's encryption. The deaf professor Mujab Baghdadi's dispatch was printed on one side in English with the coded message:

The Southwick Incident

    one Period in life surpasses four eternities.
    three Will be as three kinsmen...nay... three sons.
    two heroes out of five shall all five serve.
    after the four, then shall three die in allah's bosom.
    when the last two, at two mystical moments know him...
    ...then the major seven commandments will be fulfilled.

...but certain words and phrases sprinkled throughout the message were underlined in pencil. Thus the original side of the resulting communiqué now looked like this:

    <u>one Period</u> in life surpasses <u>four eternities</u>.
    <u>three Will</u> be as <u>three kinsmen</u>...nay... <u>three sons</u>.
    <u>two heroes</u> out of <u>five shall</u> all <u>five serve</u>.
    after the <u>four, then</u> shall <u>three die</u> in allah's bosom.
    when the last <u>two, at</u> <u>two mystical</u> moments know him...
    ...then the major <u>seven commandments</u> will be fulfilled.

On the reverse of the page, all the underlined phrases beginning with a spelled-out number were handwritten and listed in order as follows:
<u>one Period</u>

<u>four eternities</u>
<u>three Will</u>
<u>three kinsmen</u>
<u>three sons</u>
<u>two heroes</u>
<u>five shall</u>
<u>five serve</u>
<u>four, then</u>
<u>three die</u>
<u>two, at</u>
<u>two mystical</u>
<u>seven commandments</u>

Clearly, each underlined term began with a spelled-out number…but that fact in itself would mean nothing to the uninformed observer. In actuality the cipher depended on applying the number that began each two-word phrase ('one Period'…'two heroes'…'three Will'…etcetera…) to the letters of the following word (first letter…first and second letters… first, second, and third letters…and the like)…specifically, to the number of letters with which that follow-up word began. This explained the next grouping that the terrorist, Hamid al Jamil, had written…with the indicated letters hand-printed in large, bold form…and the undesignated ones, partially struck through.

~~one~~ **Period**
~~four~~ **eternities**
~~Three~~ **Will**
~~three~~ **kinsmen**
~~three~~ **sons**
~~two~~ **heroes**
~~five~~ **shall**
~~five~~ **serve**
~~four~~, **then**
~~three~~ **die**

> ~~two,~~ **at**
> ~~two~~ **my**~~stical~~
> ~~seven~~ **command**~~ments~~

```
Peter Wilkinson he shall serve then die at
                my command
```

The explosion that leveled the building and killed Hamid al Jamir where he'd lived since enrolling at Istanbul University, also destroyed the off-campus residence of sixteen American transfer students, killing them all as well. That latter structure, it was assumed, had been the primary target of the bomb. The twelve young men and four women housed there had been warned of the inappropriateness of playing loud music during the *Adhan*, and otherwise disrespecting the city's *Muezzin* as they summoned the Islamic faithful to prayer five times each day as prescribed in the Holy Qu'aran.

That Hamid had been slain in the process was considered collateral damage.

It was customary for passersby to search the bodies of the dead in such cases, not because Turkish authorities suspected the presence of anti-Islamic contraband, but in a failing economy, first rescuers on the scene were wise to help themselves to windfall loot when the opportunity arose. And with the strange, encrypted letter from Yale, 15-year-old Abdul Sanzir correctly concluded that he'd hit the jackpot.

Chapter Eleven

DURING THE USUALLY HARSH MONTHS of December and January, Roseanne Turbish confined her food shopping to one morning every two weeks…usually a Tuesday when fresh produce had been newly washed, trimmed, and placed on display. Living alone as she did, there was little reason to visit the Big Y supermarket on Sheep Pasture Road any more frequently than that. As for essentials other than food, everything except prescription medication and fuel for the car was available within a few blocks of the Big Y.

Most of Rosanne's medical supplies were mailed to her promptly under a special Massachusetts Senior Citizens plan, and even those were brought right to her door by Conner the mailman whenever it snowed. The only basic requirement that presented a problem so far as the 85-year-old widow was concerned…was gasoline.

Rosanne had never in her life pumped gas into an automobile, nor could she picture herself doing such a vile thing…even if she'd known how. Accordingly, the terrifying prospect of dispensing the 'liquid dynamite,' as Herman Turbish had described it to his wife of sixty years, had fallen regularly to Herman until the day he died in 2013. After that, it had become Roseanne Turbish's practice to fill up at the 'Gas 'n Go' on College Highway once a month. There, Richie Grudens still pumped gas for regulars who, for whatever reason, requested the convenience.

Police Lieutenant Frank Brogan was fairly sure that Herman Turbish's car was a Chevrolet...a two-door, he thought...though he wasn't sure of the exact model, year, or color. Brogan knew only that Roseanne kept the vehicle garaged, and that neither she nor her husband had ever been involved in a motor vehicle accident in Southwick.

Still, as he left Police Headquarters and turned toward his home on Hart's Pond Road, the Lieutenant had a nagging feeling that the automobile described by Peter Wilkinson as the one having fled the scene of a serious accident...was somehow familiar. Of course, veteran policeman Frank Brogan was not about to alarm an old woman by approaching her directly with questions about her personal automobile. The implication would be clear. The Southwick Police Department would be looking for a car resembling hers. It would be enough to terrify any octogenarian.

But Richie Grudens the mechanic would know.

The Lieutenant turned right on College Highway and drove north.

At the 'Gas 'n Go' Richie was engaged as always in repairing something. This time it was the air hose that hung on a stanchion beside the rest room door. It had inexplicably developed a slight hissing sound near the inflator air chuck, and Richie had immersed it in a pail of water. The trail of bubbles clearly showed that the source of the problem was a pinhole mere inches from the brass chuck.

Frank Brogan parked his unmarked sedan near where Grudens squatted with his sleeves rolled to his elbows. He exited the car and walked casually to the proprietor. "Looks like you're gonna lose a couple inches of hose, Richie."

"Uh-huh," Grudens responded, wiping the air hose with a greasy rag. He raised his steel-rimmed eyeglasses to his forehead and squinted at the offending pinhole. "At least the damn compressor'll stop runnin' day 'n night." He flung the bucket of water in an arc that washed down a swath of the tarmac near Brogan's car. "What's up, Frankie?"

Lieutenant Brogan helped Grudens coil the 25-foot length of hose and hang it on its semi-circular bracket. "Nothing much. I was down by one of your customers' house on The Landing a little bit ago…Herman Turbish's."

"Uh-huh. Roseanne. In here first of every month like clockwork. 'Less it's Sunday."

"What's that car of Herman's…the Chevy…a Lumina?"

Richie rubbed his arms with the oily rag. "Nope, '99 Impala."

Frank Brogan nodded. "Yeah…that's right…I think I remember when he got it. What color again?"

"Black," said Richie.

"Ah, yes," said Brogan. He smiled as if relieved. "Black. I shoulda' remembered that."

Grudens tucked the greasy rag in the back pocket of his overalls. "Herm never really liked drivin' a black car, though… claimed it's too hard t'keep clean…so he had me paint it."

Frank Brogan frowned. "You painted The Turbish's car?"

"Yep." Richie pointed to the air hose. "First job I did when I bought that hose n' compressor…painted 'er robin's egg blue." The mechanic rolled down his sleeves. "So what'll it be, Frank? You can't be outta gas…just filled you up Wednesday."

"Naw," said the Lieutenant. "Only stopped for the paper. You got any copies of The Globe left?"

* * * * *

A CONCERNED FRANK BROGAN drove south on College Highway. Now he had no choice but to take a statement from Roseanne Turbish, and at the very least examine her 1999, blue, Chevrolet Impala…maybe even have it impounded. Furthermore, he would need a substantiating statement from eyewitness Peter Wilkinson.

But all that can wait 'til morning, he told himself It was nearly dark, and the Lieutenant preferred that examination and verifying identification of the Turbish vehicle be conducted at approximately the same place, and time of day, where and when the accident occurred.

He pulled over to the side of the road, and as a precaution, turned on the flashing blue lights built into the grille and rear fenders of his unmarked cruiser.

Brogan took a cell phone from his shirt pocket and called Baystate Medical Center in Springfield. He identified himself by name, rank, and shield number…then asked for the condition of the injured patient, Renaldo Vega.

As he waited for the information, Frank Brogan lifted his folded copy of the Boston Globe from the passenger seat of his sedan. He held the phone to his ear and scanned the paper's front page idly. Of course, the spring-like weather was the Globe's lead story; record temperatures were in prospect for Christmas. A sub-headline announced that another Improvised Explosive Device had claimed a number of Americans in Turkey…this time, sixteen students in Istanbul.

An efficient sounding voice on the phone said…"Lieutenant Brogan?"

"Yes, Brogan here."

"This is Tammy Morgan…the ER Charge Nurse…at Baystate."

"Yes, Ms. Morgan."

"I'm afraid Renaldo Vega has expired. He was pronounced fifteen minutes ago. Cause has been established as irreversible cardiac arrest induced by severe trauma. The family has been notified, Lieutenant,"

Frank Brogan gritted his teeth.

The accident on Middleville road had become a case of vehicular homicide. He looked at his watch. Two minutes to four. Vega's time of death would thus be designated 3:43 PM, December 24th 2015…already Christmas Day in far off Istanbul…

where sixteen plain wooden caskets were being loaded on an Air Force C-130 aircraft bound for Dulles International Airport.

"Thank you Ms. Morgan," said Brogan. He jotted "*Vega— 3:43 PM—12/24/15*" in a small black notebook, turned off his flashing strobe lights, and drove toward The Landing where Roseanne Turbish and young Peter Wilkinson lived.

Chapter Twelve

AT A LITTLE AFTER 4:00, Doctor Meili Song and her patient sat in the middle of the 'Countryman's Café' drinking muddy coffee and comparing notes about Carter Branning's medical prospects. He poked gingerly at the fat lump on the forearm of his Patriots jacket. "What are the chances this thing's gonna grow back?" he said.

"Slim to none," said the Dermatologist, "…that's the good news."

Carter Banning sipped from his plastic cup and looked uneasily at the petite woman over the rim of the container. "Sounds like a 'but' coming."

"You're a big boy…and you've obviously been a lifelong sun bum…so you should face facts." She added another packet of sugar to the bitter black brew in front of her. "When the sun's ultra-violet rays hit your epidermis, they can damage the DNA in your skin cells over time. Research has shown that the DNA holds the code for the way these cells grow. We're also aware that damage to one's DNA can cause carcinomas to form." She nodded toward Carter's arm, and stirred her coffee. "The tumor-formation process takes years…and the growths aren't all the same type…nor do they all pop up at one time. It's likely we'll be digging basal cell tumors out of you 'til you zoom off *'into the wild blue yonder.'"*

"I've heard a lot about melanoma lately."

"Whoa! That's a whole different ballgame," said Meili. "If we detect melanoma early, the cure rate is about 98%…" she pointed to the bulge in Carter's sleeve, "…almost as high as removing your former basal cell buddy, there. But should melanoma go unnoticed and invade the lymph nodes, for instance…" she shook her head, "…then you and I would become steady pals for a long time to come."

Banning was overtaken by a gallows humor moment and wondered if, at his age, being afflicted by the universally dreaded 'Big C' might not be a bad price to pay for keeping non-stop company with a woman of Meili Song's obvious charms…but he promptly dismissed the ridiculous equation. *For Christ's sake, she's young enough to be your granddaughter*, he said to himself. *You're a living, breathing example of how silly a worn-out old goat can be!*

The morose cashier seemed to have only a few yellowed pages remaining to be read in her paperback. Carter could now see that the book was a battered copy of T.J. Clemente's *'Triangle Love,'* and he was hardly surprised. The woman was not exactly the type you'd find engrossed in a scholarly Elise Pearlman biography, he'd already concluded.

"It's the shortest day of the year," Carter said, looking at his watch. "I'd better be heading home. My wife's been having trouble driving at night, so she thinks it should be outlawed for everybody."

Doctor Song too checked the time. "I'm not due in the E.R. until 6:00," she said, standing. "I'll head back to my examining room. Have to send that chunk I took out of you over to the lab."

"You don't just dispose of it?"

"That's optional. I prefer to have the laboratory examine my tumors. They dissect them and make sure that a growth this size has at least one millimeter of non-cancerous dermis surrounding it…just to be sure we got it all."

Carter stood. "I'm all for that." He walked with her toward the door. As they passed the cashier, he took the Doctor's elbow and said with a wan smile. "I'm sorry if I got a bit rough upstairs, Millie. When you grabbed me around the waist that way, I couldn't help…"

"Let's forget it," Meili Song said hastily. "It was dark. I think we both got carried away somewhat."

Cashier Edna Brawley glanced up from her steamy romance novel, and her sidelong gaze followed the pair through the door.

Hmmpf! She arched her eyebrows and returned to the well-thumbed book. *Pretty cozy if you ask me.*

* * * * *

THERE WAS NO NEED for Roseanne Turbish to lock the garage door. Still, she made it a practice to bolt the interior entrance to the house itself. So far as anyone in The Landing knew, there had never been a break-in on Stony Path. There were a number of reasons why this would be the case, if one looked at the matter from a purely logical standpoint.

First of all, the exclusive area was bordered on the south and east by the marshland that defined Slater's Lake…on the west by dense trees and busy College Highway…and on the north primarily by the exclusive Edgewood Links Golf Course. The only way in and out of the fashionable neighborhood was via Point Grove Road, a narrow north/south thoroughfare that began at Southwick…and ended in a *cul-de-sac* by Caleb's Creek. Anyone entering The Landing from Southwick would have to leave the way they came—by regularly police-patrolled Point Grove Road.

Thus, Peter Wilkinson had easy access to Roseanne's spacious attached garage when he entered it in the early twilight of December 24th. There was little likelihood that anyone would see him in the semi-darkness…and what if they did? He was merely a protective neighbor…one who thought he'd seen a mysterious figure lurking in the wooded area between the Wilkinson and Turbish properties. As for the heavy three-foot stick he held in his gloved hand…that's what he'd use to pummel the intruder if and when he cornered him.

The dark-clad Wilkinson had completed his business quickly. First he'd yanked open the car's passenger door, placed something on the right-side floor mat, and slammed the door shut. Then, with one powerful swing, he'd driven a foot-long gouge into the grille of the blue Impala just above the built-in bumper…finally he dashed back outside, pulling the single exterior door closed behind him. All in less than a minute.

Roseanne Turbish, having heard from her second floor bathroom what she considered a suspicious, muffled noise, tiptoed downstairs and armed herself with a butcher knife. The plucky woman eased open the door leading from her mud room and raising the broad knife threateningly, she gingerly turned on the overhead light. There was no one in the garage…and nothing was amiss.

The audacious but relieved widow realized she must have been imagining things and retreated to the kitchen to prepare her Christmas Eve dinner.

Hidden by an evergreen on the west side of the Turbish's driveway, Peter Wilkinson saw the garage light go out. Smirking in the darkness, he heaved away the stout branch he'd used to pound the Impala, and casually sauntered the fifty or so yards past the canvas-covered jon boat…past the decaying wooden dock…and back to the sanctuary of his house next door.

Just as with the killing of the innocent birds…Peter Wilkinson had once again demonstrated his strange capacity for unprovoked malevolence!

* * * * *

The Southwick Incident

BY THE TIME Lieutenant Frank Brogan turned onto Stony Path from Point Grove Road, he'd rehearsed his speech three or four times:

Hello, Roseanne...Merry Christmas. We're helping Motor Vehicles to inventory some of the older automobiles in the area. Mind if I get the mileage on Herman's Chevy? Is it in the garage? Just take a minute.

Surely no one would be alarmed by such an innocuous approach. He pulled into the Turbish's driveway with his brights on to assure that Roseanne wouldn't be surprised or alarmed by the doorbell.

When she opened the door after peeking through the hall window and turning on the porch light, Roseanne invited Frank Brogan into the house, but he demurred and recited his prepared speech...and he added, "I can't stay. If I can just get a look at the car's odometer. It's a '99 Impala, right?...is the car locked?"

The Turbish woman frowned, holding a forefinger to her cheek in recollection. "Locked?" She grinned feebly. "To tell the truth, I don't remember. I haven't driven it in a week." She reached into a shallow candy dish on the hall table. "Anyway here's the key. You can go through the far side door. Are you sure you don't want a cup of coffee?"

"Thanks, no," The Lieutenant said over his shoulder, "...the family's waiting for me. Just be a minute."

Brogan put the car key in his pocket, circled the garage, and let himself inside. Roseanne had turned on the garage light and was standing in a doorway at the top of three wooden steps, watching. Immediately, Brogan noticed that two of the horizontal ribs in the Chevy's narrow grille had been smashed, and the centered blue Chevrolet logo was askew. He crouched and shone a pocket flashlight on the damage.

"If you're looking for the odometer, it's inside...on the instrument panel," Rosanne called out.

Frank Brogan had seen all he needed to, but he decided to play out the charade. He circled the car, opened the driver's door, and examined the odometer. It read 69480 miles…he also took note of a nearly empty pint bottle on the floor…the label read *'Paul Masson—Grande Amber Brandy.'*

He pressed the button that would lock both the Chevy's doors and exited the car.

Before Roseanne Turbish could say another word, the veteran policeman left the garage the way he'd entered…and with the key to the blue Impala still in his pocket, he drove his unmarked vehicle back to headquarters. It would be seven-thirty before he would finish his detailed report and head home.

Though his heart wasn't in it, Frank Brogan had promised to go Christmas caroling with the kids.

Chapter Thirteen

ABDUL SANZIR was a veteran practitioner of such things… all 15-year-old street hooligans in Istanbul were. By that age, every enterprising orphan adrift in the city formerly known as Byzantium, then Constantinople, had learned to search through the still-smoking rubble of bombed-out buildings with all the skill of a cadaver-sniffing dog.

Moreover, when one lived penniless in the world's sixth largest city…specifically on the shoddier Asian side of the uniquely transcontinental metropolis…one quickly became adept at rummaging for, and more importantly, fencing at the optimum rate of exchange, whatever plunder one might be able to retrieve in a day's work.

With the growth of Radical Islam and the expanding of Sunni-Shia hostilities, the production of Improvised Explosive Devices had become a major source of income for those who could afford to buy and assemble the required components. But for the city's impoverished…like Abdul…acquiring of such deadly (and expensive) constituent parts such as Semtex, timers, and detonator caps, was out of the question. Thus, for Abdul Sanzir and his fellow urchins, the searching and stripping of dead and injured bodies had become the new cottage industry of choice.

In Turkey, and throughout the Middle East, a generation of hard-bitten ruffians was growing more expert by the day at removing rings, bracelets, body piercing adornments...and even dentures and contact lenses...from IED victims.

Some, unable to function in the field because lost limbs made it impossible, had adopted a career of teaching new recruits the macabre techniques that the most successful casualty vandalizers practiced.

Such a one had been young Sanzir's mentor, the one-armed teacher Evrim Yildiz. Indeed, thanks to Yildiz's patient tutelage, keen insight, and thorough attention to detail, Abdul now found himself possibly in a position to graduate from the ranks of Turkey's common Street Thieves. Because Abdul Sanzir had recognized his find on the mangled body of Hamid al Jamir to be not only a coded message...but one whose annotations obviously provided the *key* to the code itself...the enterprising lad envisioned a once unimaginable prospect...namely, his ascending the slovenly pecking order all the way to the infinitely more respectable level of 'Islamist Informant.'

But the dream was to be short-lived.

Flushed with the exuberance that so often betrays youths the world over, Abdul had stuffed al Jamir's decrypted cipher into his shoe (also stripped from a bomb victim two days earlier) and rushed to the hovel where Yildiz lived with only his dog in the shadow of the massive Bosphorus Bridge.

There, Evrim Yildiz eagerly reviewed and analyzed Abdul's treasure, as the boy slept, and Evrim's muscular Corso guard dog growled...all the while warily eyeing the lad whom the restrained animal regarded only as a snoring intruder.

Without question, Abdul had evaluated the situation well.

His discovery was a find the likes of which Istanbul's plunderers only dreamed about. Clearly, the mysterious note's correspondents were men of power and prominence in the Radical Islamist ranks, otherwise how could the originator of the cipher state that this *'Wilkinson'* person should *'...die at my command'*?

And such vast power translated into great wealth in the narrow avaricious world of Evrim Yildiz. For wasn't this coded message transmitted from the same esteemed American university known to have produced the endlessly wealthy George Bushes?...not to mention the philandering billionaire, Bill Clinton?

There was but one problem, as Evrim saw it—this treasure ironically contained the seed of its discoverer's destruction. It would be impossible to ransom the communiqué, because the very recognition of the cryptogram's significance...and its profound value...would mean that its bearer was himself also privy to the clever code. Evrim Yildiz was too familiar with the bloodthirsty methods of his radical associates to estimate that anything short of excruciating torture and ultimate death awaited the possessor of the message Abdul Sanzir had come upon.

He looked at the sleeping boy...and the watchful Corso whose twitching muzzle was crawling with flies as it lay in the grime that was the dirt floor of Evrim's lean-to. There was no way to know whether the boy had committed the code to memory, but even if there were, what the one-armed Yildiz must now do, was apparent. With the speed of a cobra, Evrim snatched one of the half-dozen chickens that he kept, snapped it's neck with a whip-like thrust of his wrist, and severed the hen's head with a knife. He sprayed the bird's warm blood on the face and shoulders of his stunned former student, and as Abdul wiped the crimson from his eyes in disbelief...Evrim Yildiz released the frantic hundred-pound dog.

Amid the Sanzir boy's screams, and the roar of overhead traffic on the Bosphorus Bridge, Evrim burned the coded message from professor Baghdadi to the careless Hamid al Jamil. Then he re-chained the dog...and threw Abdul's mauled and mangled body into the rushing Bosphorus Strait that ultimately fed the Black Sea.

* * * * *

THE CLOSEST AMERICAN AGENCY to the bridge was the U.S. Public Affairs Section of the American Embassy. The five-story structure was a modern edifice on the Boulevard of Peace, incongruously surrounded by a spiked fence, with machine gun emplacements at all four corners of the block-square building. All visitors who lacked up-to-date identity credentials were required to submit to a retinal scan at either the north or south checkpoint before admission to the next examination post could be granted. Once approved, the applicant for temporary admission would undergo a full body scan that included a cavity check, and only then would the caller be issued a one-hour visitor's pass.

Evrim Yildiz, having lost his left arm in the defense of an American soldier in the Aegean town of Yalikoy, was one of those Turkish nationals who quickly passed the retinal examination, as well as the subsequent checks designed primarily to detect the presence of internally planted explosive devices. His history was well known to U.S. authorities at Public Affairs, and had it not been for some minor red flags sent up because his person smelled heavily of his seldom-washed Corso watch dog, Evrim might have promptly gained admission to the office of the Consul General himself; such was the esteem in which the partially disabled 30-year-old Turk was held.

Like Evrim, the Deputy Consul General was fluent in Turkish, Kurdish, and Arabic, and the two men sat in a well-lit anteroom drinking tea and making small talk. They conversed in Arabic; it was Nicholai Douniat's custom when given his choice of spoken languages. After an appropriate few minutes of introductory banter, Douniat looked at his watch ostentatiously and said, "What brings you today, Evrim."

"I have something for sale," said Yildiz. "A very valuable product."

Nicholai merely smiled and rested his chin on his folded hands, waiting.

"It is a coded message from an Iraqi...in your country...an enemy of the U.S."

The deputy continued to smile...and he nodded.

"No doubt you have intercepted the communiqué," said Evrim. "It arrived here in Istanbul yesterday. You know the sender as *'Wif.en.poof'*...a professor at Yale University...his name is Mujab Baghdadi."

The smile left Douniat's face. "Perhaps you would like another cup of tea," he said.

Evrim Yildiz looked at the recently pilfered watch on his wrist. "My one hour will be over in fifteen minutes. Perhaps we do not have time for more tea."

"Leave that to me," said the Deputy. "Tell me more of this... this *Coded Message*..." he said. "Do you have a copy?"

The one-armed man tapped the side of his head with his finger. "I have it...here," he said. "If you can bring the sequestered dispatch...and the sum of ten thousand Turkish Lira...I think I will like to decrypt it, and tell you precisely what your adversary *'Wif.en.poof'* has to say."

Douniat picked up the secure phone on his desk and his thin smile returned. "I am confident that such a thing can be arranged." The Deputy Consul General cleared his throat and uttered a few terse commands in Greek...a language he was confident Evrim neither spoke nor understood...then he hung up the phone. "For such a vast sum, you will, of course, provide me with the key to this *'Wif.en.poof's'* code." It was not a question.

"Vast sum?" said Evrim. "What vast sum?"

He looked offended. "I have intentionally been moderate in my request so that you may determine the purity of my heart. Ten thousand new Turkish Lira translates into only $3,500. American. It can barely buy the nine millimeter Beretta of my dreams...and a year's worth of horsemeat for my dog 'Benito.'"

Evrim Yildiz tugged at the left sleeve of his threadbare sweater...the one that contained no arm and thus hung loose and lifeless at his side. "You must understand, Deputy, one in my untenable position must insure that his services will continue to be required…is it not so? I believe the American term is 'a steady job.'"

Nicholai Douniat offered the informant a cigarette from the box on his desk and took one himself. "Have I ever given you reason to question the good will of this office?"

Evrim studied Douniat's face through lazy eyes whose lids were half-lowered. "And have I ever given you reason to think me more valuable dead than alive?"

"I don't understand," said Nicholai.

Yildiz drew deeply on his cigarette and blew the aromatic Turkish smoke toward the high, vaulted ceiling. '*Wif.en.poof's'* coded communiqués are of value to you only insofar as the good professor feels that they remain encrypted, is it not so?"

"Of course."

"Accordingly, my services are required by the Consul General only as long as these messages require decoding…correct?"

"Indelicately termed, perhaps…but if you must…alright, correct."

"Then why would I knowingly put my livelihood in jeopardy, Deputy?"

Douniat's face grew cold and still. Only the slow blinking of his dark eyes revealed any life whatever in his features. "Suppose my superiors were to increase the sum you request by a factor of ten? Our Department of State has been known to extend a generous hand to those whose fidelity they value."

Evrim Yildiz extinguished his cigarette in the Deputy's large ash tray. "True," said the one-armed man, "…but the activities of your Central Intelligence Agency are equally legendary regarding moles who have outlived their usefulness."

There was a knock at the door, and Douniat pressed a concealed button that unlocked it. An orderly entered, placed an attaché case on the Deputy's desk, and left the room without a word.

Nicholai Douniat opened the case, counted out ten thousand Turkish Lira in 20 and 50-TL banknotes, and set them to one side. He then withdrew a computer-printed sheet from a Manilla envelope. It began:

```
one  Period  in  life  surpasses  four
eternities...
```

The man from the American Embassy handed Evrim the encoded cipher, a pen, and a plain, white pad…and he sat back to watch. Slowly, the informant wrote:

P ETER WIL KIN SON...

Chapter Fourteen

IT WAS DARK BY THE TIME Carter Banning turned onto the long driveway that led from Stony Path to his house. Doctor Song had been right about his arm…he'd experienced no sustained discomfort whatever from the procedure. In fact, the only inconvenience so far as he could tell came from the substantial inch-thick dressing that covered and padded his new wound. There, the adhesive tape holding the bandage in place stung his shaved skin whenever he made a ninety-degree turn of the Volvo's steering wheel, thus stretching the epidermis of his forearm.

Not even worth mentioning, he told himself as he pulled into the open garage, exited his car, and pressed the remote control that lowered the overhead door.

Elizabeth stood waiting for him in the middle of the kitchen. "I expected you earlier," she said nervously. "Is everything alright?"

Carter slipped out of his New England Patriots jacket, and the bulging dressing on his right arm was immediately obvious beneath his shirt sleeve. His wife noticed the lump right away and she reached for him gingerly. "What did they do?" she cried, hesitant to touch him. "It's that growth on top of your arm, isn't it? Did they lance it?"

He patted her on the shoulder, and reached for two wine glasses from a kitchen cabinet. "Meili Song decided to take it out," Carter said. "She was available all afternoon...so was I... and that was that. No more basal cell."

He took an open bottle of Shiraz from the same cabinet and poured two half-glasses of the dry, red wine. "Are you sure you should...did you take any medication earlier?" Elizabeth Banning asked, draping her husband's jacket over the back of a kitchen chair, and she continued to question him. "Have you eaten anything?"

Carter sat at the table, raised his glass, and said with a deep sigh of relief, "Yes ma'am, I ate lunch...just like you instructed...the Doc said the wine's okay. So you be a good girl...have a seat... and I'll tell you everything that happened."

"Do you want an ice pack for your arm?"

"Not necessary...just have to change the dressing tomorrow... apply pressure continuously for twenty minutes if it bleeds... keep the wound moist with Vaseline...that's about it."

"Did the Dermatologist say the canc...?" Elizabeth pressed her knuckles to her lips, hesitant to use the dreaded word.

"You can say it, Sweetheart," Carter smiled. "Yes. It appears your beloved sun bum of a husband is officially a cancer survivor." He took a healthy swallow of the Shiraz and said ruefully, "Not that I deserve to be."

"Don't say that, Carter. You haven't spent any more time in the sun than the average..." she searched for an appropriate term, "...the typical outdoor type. And you certainly never encouraged the children to sunbathe unduly."

"Don't make excuses for me, Dear. I never gave a damn about the consequences during all those years of burning up in the sun. As for the kids, they'd have been cooked to a crisp all summer long if it hadn't been for you."

"Children burn more easily, Cart..."

"I know…I know. And big, tough career soldiers like yours truly are fireproof, right? Or so we thought." He rolled his shirtsleeve to his elbow and pressed lightly on the thick, gauze bandage. "But it does occur to me that it might be wiser to take a rain check on Midnight Mass this year." Carter gave his worried wife a sidelong, sheepish glance. "Could prevent some unwanted complications if I can keep this thing dry as long as possible."

Elizabeth Banning leaped to her feet. "Absolutely!" she cried. "You are not going out of this house for one minute!" She marched to the stove, wine glass in hand, and turned on the burner under the kettle for the fourth or fifth time today. "St. Stephen's will have to do without us for once."

Carter poured himself another half-glass of wine from the magnum. "Well, that doesn't sound like equivocation to me." He brought the glass to the living room, sat in his oversized rocker, and turned on the television set. Immediately the wide screen was filled with scenes of yesterday's carnage in downtown Istanbul…half a world away.

Elizabeth entered the room and stood watching the news report in front of her favorite easy chair. Apparently the Hotel Cadiz had been specifically targeted in this latest bombing. All the victims except one were American students. The lone Muslim casualty was an Iraqi college professor. The bomb had exploded some ten hours earlier. About the same time as it was now, here in Massachusetts.

She placed her wine glass on a small round table and walked across the living room to kiss her husband on the forehead. "It's terrible what the world has come to," she said. "I thank God every day that you're no longer involved in that military business."

Carter Banning squeezed his wife's hand and she walked to her upholstered chair. He narrowed his eyes and peered at the rubble that had been the Hotel Cadiz. Elizabeth was unaware, of course, that Sergeant Carter Banning, ostensibly of the Third Infantry, U.S. Army, had in fact been Major Carter Banning… Senior decoding expert assigned to the Army's twelve-man First

Encryption Platoon. Nor had Elizabeth Banning ever known that the Hotel Cadiz had been the elite squad's headquarters so many years earlier.

That, obviously, was during the latter stages of the Cold War. It was before the proliferation of Improvised Explosive Devices… prior to the Arab Spring…and long before the radicalization of misguided young men like Peter Wilkinson. In those days, Americans were safe in their own homes. The country's cities were beyond the range of intercontinental ballistic missiles. And installations like the huge Veteran's Administration Hospital at Southwick would never have been considered vulnerable targets by Islamic militants.

But as Elizabeth Banning had said…the world was a different place now…and none of those old assurances any longer applied.

Chapter Fifteen

MAJOR AMANDA BRAGG'S HEAD was pounding like the legendary 'Hammers of Hell,' the nickname for the 800-member antiaircraft artillery battalion her Brigadier General grandfather had commanded in World War II. She dry-gulped two more aspirins…her fifth and sixth since arriving home at her studio apartment on the edge of Slater's Lake…and she imagined that the acetylsalicylic acid was already burning a hole in her stomach.

But now that seemed the least of her worries.

A career Army officer and first-rate administrator, she had graduated from The Point ninth in her class and risen steadily through the ranks in near-record time. 'Mandy' was unmarried… only forty…and rumor had it that the statuesque blond was a virtual shoo-in to be named a Lieutenant Colonel any day. Furthermore, 'Mandy' was still young enough to picture herself wearing a star, just as her Grandad 'Boomer' Bragg had, if things continued to go her way.

Of course, those dreams had all vanished a little over three hours ago. Now she faced arrest at the very least…and possibly long imprisonment. There was no acceptable reason for leaving the scene of an accident involving personal injury…she shuddered in recollection of the youth who lay twisted and unconscious on the road in front of her new convertible.

Personal injury, she repeated inwardly. Then she reiterated *Personal injury...or worse!* And the words caught in her constricted throat.

She belched the astringent aspirin and the caustic taste on the base of her tongue made her gag.

What could you have been thinking? Amanda Bragg asked herself as she lay on the rumpled bed in her darkened room, eyes pinched shut, a soaking facecloth on her forehead dripping onto her feverish cheeks and throbbing ears. But there was no remedy for the images and sounds that swarmed in her head; no relief from the guilt that clogged her cluttered mind.

Should she turn on the radio? What if the worst had happened? She wasn't sure she could handle a situation of that gravity...not here alone...not sweating, retching, and sobbing in the dark.

Perhaps she should try to contact the jogger—the young man who lived over in The Landing. Peter was his name...Peter Wilkinson. Surely he would know. He had seen the whole sudden accident. And he had seemed to understand her confusion. It was the Wilkinson boy—the jogger—who had suggested she go right home...relax...there was nothing she could do..."Leave it to me," he'd said. "I'll get somebody over here right away."

What a level-headed fellow! What a godsend!

It's possible the youth wasn't seriously hurt at all, she tried to tell herself.

Maybe he hadn't even required an ambulance, for heaven's sake.

What I need is a few minutes of sleep.

Amanda lifted the sodden cloth from her forehead and dropped it on the floor beside her narrow bed.

This whole unfortunate business won't seem nearly as awful in the morning, she thought.

And exhausted 'Mandy' Bragg permitted herself to sleep... because at this point there was little else she could do. She had already committed a serious crime, and the Chief of the Southwick VA Hospital's ID Department was about to discover how unpleasant life can be...on the run from one's own conscience.

* * * * *

LIEUTENANT FRANK BROGAN STOOD in the overcast fifty-five degree Christmas Eve weather and pretended to sing with the other carolers. But try as he might, his heart just wasn't in it. The teenaged Renaldo Vega had died, the apparent victim of a hit-and-run MVA, the first ever in Frank's normally peaceful precinct, and it appeared that Roseanne Turbish, one of Southwick's most upstanding citizens, was in a lot of trouble.

Up in the North Ward, in the less affluent section of town where the poor, but respectable Vega family lived, young Renaldo's relatives were experiencing grief almost beyond measure. Theirs was a test of faith that was bound only to intensify during the next few days...the woeful duration of the pitiful wake at the Vega household. There, the Christmas Vigil regularly followed with such happiness and religious fervor by these devout people under normal circumstances, was going to become a nightmare.

To make matters worse, it had been reported that a group of American students had been massacred in Turkey and at that very moment their bodies were being flown home to Dulles International outside Washington D.C. Incredibly, one of the sixteen academics was reported to be a young woman from nearby Springfield.

Perhaps he could be forgiven, Frank Brogan thought, if just this once he mouthed the words, 'Joy to the World.' Because try as he might, he honestly lacked the Christmas spirit to sing them. Finally, Lieutenant Brogan handed his borrowed hymnal to Frank, Jr., patted his daughter Nora on the shoulder, and trudged in the direction of his home two blocks away. Something was prompting him to question Peter Wilkinson further...now...

while the boy's amazingly detailed memory of the accident on Middleville Road was still acute.

He speed-dialed his wife, Colleen and told her not to be alarmed. He'd be taking the unmarked police car from its regular place in the driveway where it was pointed toward the street. Something had come up at headquarters, he said.

"Do you have to, Frankie? It's Christmas Eve. I'm making hot toddies for us and punch for the kids."

"I'll probably be back before they are," he lied. "You need anything from 7-Eleven?"

"Just try not to be too late, okay?" And she hung up. How often had Colleen Brogan been through this frustrating routine in their twenty years together…a hundred?…easily! She tasted the cranberry punch. Maybe a touch of brandy. At seventeen and eighteen, the kids were old enough. Besides, she was tired of drinking alone.

Chapter Sixteen

MEILI SONG KEPT CHECKING the big clock on the wall. She had returned to her office from the cafeteria after exchanging holiday pleasantries with her friend and patient, Carter. She watched him vanish into the near-deserted parking lot, then climbed the stairs alone to the female staff rest room. It was located in the dim corridor adjacent to the atrium where she'd nearly been knocked cold by the over-exuberant Banning. She shook her head in recollection and sheepishly fingered the torn shoulder seam of her lab coat.

Once the sun had gone down at a little after 4:30, it was impossible to tell the time by looking through the single window of her examining room. Technically, she didn't have to be physically *in* the Emergency Room at six o'clock, she was required merely to be on the hospital grounds and continually available within a five-minute response time…from 1800 hours to midnight…or until her relieving physician arrived at approximately 2400 hours.

Still, she had a reputation for punctuality to live up to. Her notable standing was best upheld by appearing at the attending doctor's elbow within thirty seconds if and when summoned, and that had always been the case with Meili.

Carter Banning's extracted tumor had been embalmed, packed, and labeled. She would bring it to the Laboratory herself on the way to the ER. It was 5:50 PM.

Time to go.

The Dermatologist decided to leave her coat, pocketbook, and medium-heeled shoes in her office closet for the next six hours. They would be safer there than in the always-hectic Emergency Room wardrobe, where things were forever getting lost or damaged. Meili would retrieve them when she finished the shift and came back to lock-up the last open clinic, before departing for the long weekend.

She parted the slats of the Venetian blind and looked for her car in the Staff Parking Area. The new, black Mercedes was vaguely visible there, along with two other vehicles. One of them an improvised golf cart that held an assortment of gardening tools in the rear compartments where golf clubs normally were kept.

That's strange, she thought. Doctor Song donned a pair of white Nike sneakers and turned off the lights…leaving the office illuminated only by the opaque glow from the computer monitor.

*****

WHEN CARTER BANNING answered the front door at 7:15, the deliveryman held a tall box containing a coral-colored poinsettia plant that was in full bloom. Its lush green leaves and variegated pinkish blossoms were covered with perforated cellophane and the gift card stapled to the red and green wrapping around the pot identified the sender as a 'General Karol Ladka, U.S. Army.' Carter took the plant, accepted the courier's apology for not coming in for a Christmas drink, and after returning the civilian clad man's crisp salute, set the gift on the kitchen table.

"Who is it, Dear?" Elizabeth called from the living room.

"Present for you," Carter called back. He unpinned the small, attached envelope that bore his name, and he read its tiny calling card. 'Greetings from a friend in need,' was the only inscription…

and the six words were followed by a telephone number. The area code was 202…Washington D.C.

Carter slipped the card into his shirt pocket and called to his wife, "This'll make your Christmas, m'dear."

Whereupon Elizabeth Banning appeared in the kitchen archway, her eyes suddenly huge, round, and smiling. "Oh, it's lovely. Is it from the girls? Oh how beautiful!"

"It's from Karol Ladka," said Carter…but what he didn't say was that General Ladka, Chief of Encryption Services, U.S. Army, had long been known to cloak his bizarre requests in the most delightful floral gifts. And usually the more challenging the ensuing assignment…the lovelier the flowers!

Elizabeth removed the cellophane from the plant and dug a forefinger into the soil. Its dampness met her satisfaction and she fussed with the big gold bow. "You'll have to tell General Ladka I think it's just gorgeous!" she gushed.

"Good idea," said Carter. "His number's upstairs. I'll call him now." At the base of the stairway he turned and asked his bustling wife, "That's a poinsettia, right?"

She was busily placing the gift in the middle of the dining table. "Of course it's a poinsettia," she said. "And tell The General it's simply beautiful."

* * * * *

"SHE SAYS IT'S 'SIMPLY BEAUTIFUL,' Karol. Now why don't you make *my* holiday beautiful and give me a hint about what's going on?"

"There's no sense in beating around the bush," said the 68-year-old Chief of Encryption Services. "We've had a communiqué dumped in our lap by our Consul General in Istanbul. An obviously encoded message to a radical cell in England. It originated with an Islamist recruiter up your way… New Haven…a college professor at Yale. He goes by the name Mujab Baghdadi…Iraqi national. It appears that one Hamid al-

Jamil, another Iraqi, relayed the transmission from Istanbul to Stonehenge in the U.K. We can't find al-Jamil."

Carter Banning removed the telephone receiver from beside his head, looked at it quizzically, and frowned. He returned the handset to his ear and waited several beats to determine that Elizabeth hadn't picked up the phone in the kitchen. Finally, "Is the Encryption Service so hard-up that you're reduced to exhuming septuagenarians, General?"

Karol Ladka laughed. "You're the only sober code-buster we could find on Christmas Eve,"

Carter took a quick sip of the wine he'd brought upstairs with him. "Well, if your guy had shown-up an hour later, you'd have been shit out of luck here, too."

"Come on, Banning," Ladka joshed, "...you've broken more ciphers with half a snootful than the average cryptosleuth ever did cold sober."

"If you're determined to stroke me, Karol, the next time I'd prefer chocolates."

"Milk or dark?"

"Mixed."

"Done," said General Ladka. "They're on the way as we speak. Meanwhile, our New Haven mystery message is waiting on your laptop. Welcome home, Major Banning. Buzz me when you're ready." And he hung up.

Once again, Carter looked dully at the silent handset. "And a Merry Christmas to you too, you old Polack!"

* * * * *

ENCODING AND DE-CODING requires such intense concentration that members of the military's Encryption Service have been known to compose and solve some of the most complex coded messages aloud...and even in their sleep. In one notorious World War II case, a fledgling decoder...a snoozing Lieutenant...was overheard mumbling the solution to a code he'd recently solved involving Luftwaffe tactical strategy. The man had been sleeping in an English manor house appropriated as a barracks for the USES when the incident occurred. The poor fellow was summarily flown to Fort Leavenworth, Kansas, where he was confined in the federal prison under maximum security until the conclusion of German-American hostilities. Even the six-man cadre that attended to him had been held in isolation for the duration of the war.

Carter Banning knew that members of the U.S. Encryption Service never really left the military completely. He and his former colleagues comprised a special breed. The country had spent a fortune finding these uniquely gifted people, testing them for months, training them for years...and all USES personnel knew from the outset that the same qualities with which they were endowed by nature, would always be traits deep-rooted in their personae...until the day they died. Thus, these exceptional people had all sworn that they would never reveal their true wartime duties to another living soul. Not their spouses—their offspring—no one. They simply knew too much, and there was always a chance that they might be inadvertently compromised by loved ones...or in a worst case scenario...blackmailed!

Carter had been on pins and needles following his phone call to Karol Ladka. He was eager to see this mysterious communiqué from New Haven to Istanbul...the cipher he knew was waiting as an email attachment on his computer...the message that needed decoding so quickly that the head of USES felt it had to be tended to on Christmas Eve!

He'd trimmed the tree in record time after his talk with Ladka, and hadn't even finished his last glass of Shiraz. "Why don't you drink this, Dear," he'd suggested to his wife, knowing the extra wine would make her tired and hasten her departure to bed. "I'm going to watch the news we missed when I was talking with your secret admirer 'The General.'" He pointed to his bandaged arm..."I'll sleep in the guest room...if I can."

Of course, Elizabeth was aware that her husband had worked for the Army man she knew simply as 'The General.' But Carter had always been hesitant to discuss his role in the war, referring to it with the catch-all term 'Intelligence.'

"Try not to stay up too late," she said. "The girls will be here by one, I'm sure. Goodnight, Dear."

In five minutes flat, Carter had closeted himself in the den, fired up his computer, and accessed General Ladka's email. He opened the attachment and the printing on his flat-screen monitor read:

> one Period in life surpasses four eternities.
> three Will be as three kinsmen…nay…three sons.
> two heroes out of five shall all five serve.
> after the four, then shall three die in allah's bosom.
> when the last two, at two mystical moments know him…
> …then the major seven commandments will be fulfilled.

The first thing the former code-breaker noticed (with relief) was that the message was in English. Given that it had originated with an Iraqi national in Connecticut…was sent from there to Istanbul…and was forwarded to England by an Islamist recruiter in Turkey…the use of English was gratifying in itself. The six-line dispatch might easily have been prepared in Mesopotamian Arabic, Kurdish, or Standard Arabic; all were official languages of Iraq, Carter knew. For that matter, the message could have just as logically been composed in Turkish.

Yes, the use of English was indeed a plus. Working with his native language would be significantly easier for Carter.

After reading the six lines twice more, Banning noted another odd characteristic of the missive's construction: The entire message was a mere fifty-two words in length…and thirteen of the words were numbers—not Arabic numerals, but the English words representing thirteen single-digit numbers...a lone 'one'—three 'twos'—four 'threes'—two 'fours'—two 'fives'—and a 'seven.' Carter could not remember ever seeing such a brief encryption with so many numbers spelled out. Thus, he drew the first conclusion that was going to prove vital in the cracking of Mujab Baghdadi's cipher: *It's an alpha-numeric code*, he said to himself.

Very clever, Mujab, you're using numbers disguised as plain words, aren't you? And he leaned toward his computer monitor... his elbows on his desk...hands clasped beneath his chin.

But what do the numbers signify? Carter wondered. Certainly not times or geographic coordinates. Most times-of-day involved hours and minutes that were identified by three or four combined numbers...like 1:25 or 12:38. But these numbers were all single digits.

They could hardly represent latitudinal or longitudinal designations on a map, either.

As he stared at the encrypted note, he was soon struck by the fact that only two of the words were capitalized...and without apparently needing to be. The first was the simple noun 'Period'...a word not even at the beginning of a sentence.

A country? A City? Somebody's name?

The second such word was the auxiliary verb 'Will.'

And both of them were preceded by a number modifier...'one' and 'three.'

Strangely, Carter thought, *the words beginning the five different sentences are not capitalized...and even more oddly, neither is the phrase 'Allah's Bosom.'*

Unheard of if this is actually an Islamic creation, as Karol seems to think, he reflected.

The fact that the two words 'Period' and 'Will' are singled out for emphasis has to tell us something, Carter Banning concluded...and he quickly visualized the terms connected to the 'number' words that preceded them.

Perhaps the word 'one' refers to the first letter of the following word—Period, the former Cryptologist mused. *In that event, the modifying word 'three' would turn its following capitalized word 'Will' into—Wil.*

Carter felt he was making significant progress.

He got up from the computer and walked into the kitchen. It was time for a Shiraz nightcap. *Definitely someone's name*, he said under his breath.

But whose?

He poured half a glass of wine and brought it back to the desk that held the glowing computer. *Don't you worry. I'm gonna' find out soon enough,* he said inwardly. *Maybe you can't teach an old dog new tricks...but well-trained dogs don't forget the old tricks they've learned, either.*

Chapter Seventeen

FOR THE THIRD TIME in his adult life Frank Brogan wished he were in another line of work. The first time had been ten years ago, when his service weapon misfired during an armed robbery at the Chicopee Savings & Loan on Depot Street, and the other instance was the day he'd had to tell the wife of a new recruit that her 25-year-old patrolman husband wasn't coming home anymore.

The Chicopee S&L incident had turned out well, because against all odds, the perpetrator's illegal gun had jammed too, and he was now doing twelve years in Concord. But the emotional trauma resulting from the death of young Barry Probst in a high speed Granville Road car chase was something that he knew would haunt him forever.

Of course, Frank's training at the Hamden County Police Academy had prepared him for problems…even tragedies…that inevitably arose in the conduct of police work, but he'd never in his wildest imagination pictured himself arresting a woman eighty-some years of age on suspicion of Vehicular Homicide.

Still, a VH victim was dead, and the family of Renaldo Vega was entitled to whatever justice was appropriate in an unfortunate situation like the one that had taken place today on Middleville

Road. It wasn't Lieutenant Frank Brogan's role to establish the science, study, and theory of the law, but it *was* his sworn duty to enforce it.

He turned his unmarked cruiser onto Point Grove Road and drove toward The Landing. It was a little after nine-thirty. *If Roseanne's house is dark*, he began to rationalize…*I'm not going to wake her*…but once on Stony Path…nearing Caleb's Creek, he saw that Roseanne Turbish was obviously still up. Lights were on in the kitchen and dining room areas.

In fact, the whole sparsely populated neighborhood seemed to be awake. Judging from the dim first-floor light, Carter Banning was still downstairs, probably at his computer, Frank figured… and both floors of the Wilkinson house showed light in at least half a dozen rooms. Those three were the only houses he could see in this part of The Landing.

Lieutenant Brogan had little choice. If he didn't make the arrest and impound the Turbish's blue Chevy tonight, he would have to do it either tomorrow—Christmas Day—or Saturday or Sunday…he couldn't imagine waiting until Monday.

Furthermore, proper police procedure dictated that he would have to be accompanied by a Matron when apprehending Roseanne…probably one of Springfield's three female police officers, he thought. And in the case of a woman in her mid-eighties, shouldn't he arrange to have a doctor or at least an EMT at headquarters when he brought her in? What if she had a heart attack? Would he be held liable if no medical person was on hand to administer to her?

And there was the matter of bringing in the blue Impala and securing it properly.

Frank Brogan pulled onto the shoulder of Stony Path to think…and he killed his lights.

Behind him a new Buick convertible came into view…one of its headlight beams shining at an awkward angle into the night sky. Amanda Bragg was at the wheel, and she was proceeding very slowly.

Looking for a name on a mailbox, the Lieutenant speculated.

And she stopped to ask the man parked in front of the Turbish house…tentatively…falteringly…lowering her passenger side window only a few inches…if he knew where Peter Wilkinson lived.

* * * * *

BEFORE HE'D FINISHED HIS WINE, Carter Banning had broken Mujab Baghdadi's alpha-numeric code, and he sat tapping the decrypted cipher on the monitor with his fingertip. Even Carter was stunned that he'd solved the puzzle without employing a single arithmetic formula, grapheme, or syllabary… all devices he'd employed decades ago as a military cryptologist. Incredibly, he had made not one written notation on the alphabet grid pattern that lay atop the desk where he sat. Nor had he even created a 'frequency of use' chart—a stratagem considered vital in determining a passage's probable scheme and content.

Most codes he'd ever worked on depended on complexity to insure their security, but this one was so simple that that feature in itself apparently made it effective.

Still, he wondered how his intuitive, but hardly Einsteinesque 'Baghdadi Solution' could have evaded his old friend and colleague, Karol Ladka. The General would never have risked leaving an encrypted message to the vulnerability of cyberspace had he not been convinced of its rock-solid impenetrability.

Hell, maybe old Carter Banning had a few good years left in him yet.

He went to the kitchen, poured another self-congratulatory few ounces of Shiraz, and returned to the Christmas Eve news on WHDH-TV.

The Bombing in Turkey was now the lead story, and Carter wondered if General Ladka's intercepted message had anything to do with the deaths of the sixteen American students…and a college professor…at Istanbul's old Hotel Cadiz.

Of course, he knew full well that it must have.

And he was equally certain that Karol must have already cracked the Yale Professor's homespun code himself.

He knows, alright, Carter pondered. *Why else would he be exposing me to my next-door neighbor's apparent involvement in an international terrorist conspiracy?*

But regardless of the reason, the former Major Banning would have been lying were he to deny his profound interest in Peter Wilkinson's association with this Baghdadi fellow. Clearly Mary Wilkinson's son was sympathetic to the radical Islamist's cause.

"He shall serve," the cipher had said.

But in what way? Carter wondered...*and to whose peril?*

"...then die at my command."

When?...Where?...How?...

"Damn you, Ladka!"

But Banning recanted the condemnation as soon as he had uttered it.

The television screen was filled with the videotaped images of teenaged urchins clawing like so many vultures at the broken bodies of their prey. The scavengers were actually turning out the pockets of bloodied men and women alike...ripping away the contents and jamming them under their own filthy shirts. Some fought viciously over wallets and prized wristwatches. Others were pounding out the teeth of victims with pieces of shattered brick...frenzied in the apparent hope of finding gold. The earliest arriving foragers were already running away, lest the Turkish police strip them of their loot and keep it for themselves. These were the zealots who five times daily fell to their knees and implored their generous god to grant them the good fortune of another massacre to race to...and sift through...maybe as soon as the following day.

Had Carter not been refreshing his wineglass in the kitchen moments before, he might have seen a grubby boy on the television screen, a squalid but exuberant lad named Abdul Sanzir, who snatched a folded, eight-inch-square letter from the pocket of a dark-skinned Iraqi. The man, when alive, had been known as Professor Hamid al Jamil. With youthful curiosity, the barefoot Abdul had quickly read the note…and dashed eagerly over the rubble toward an ultimately violent rendezvous where he too would join al Jamil in Paradise.

But there was no way that the former Major Banning could have detected all that from the dusty scene of carnage that was the ruined Hotel Cadiz.

Carter decided to call Karol Ladka…right away. He was confident The General was still awake…and no doubt watching televised footage of the same devastating scene.

Chapter Eighteen

THE SCREEN ON PETER WILKINSON'S computer posed a provocative question. It was the third entry in the 20-question test that Peter was required to answer correctly before he could qualify for his Signing Certificate.

Is fingerspelling a popular way to communicate in American Sign Language?

The 'Document of Completion' would be automatically printed only when he had answered all the 'Yes or No' or multiple-choice questions correctly during a single online session. He moved the cursor to the 'No' box and clicked the mouse. Immediately the word 'Correct' flashed, and continued to do so once every half-second for five full seconds…before being replaced by the command words, 'Support Answer in 20 Words or Fewer.'

Peter typed his validation:

Only 15% of a conversation between Deaf people uses fingerspelling!

Again the word 'Correct' flashed ten times before being replaced by the fourth query on the test. This one was a multiple choice question:

In what Shakespearian play are the similarities between a character's words and American Sign Language evident?
A Julius Caesar
B Othello
C The Tempest
D King Lear

Peter Wilkinson selected 'C The Tempest…'Correct' flashed… and again the 'Support Answer' prompt appeared. Accordingly, Peter typed the fourteen-word justification:

In The Tempest, a slave is forced to learn a master's language through Signing.

Another 'Correct' glimmered.

A grinning Peter put the test on Pause…and he went downstairs to make himself a sandwich. He was pleased that he'd be returning to Yale next week armed with an additional set of credentials. And wouldn't his friend and mentor the profoundly deaf Professor Baghdadi be so pleased!

* * * * *

BACK AT HIS COMPUTER, Peter Wilkinson successfully completed the 20-question quiz and his laser printer automatically produced a handsome 'Signing Certificate of Achievement.'

Eager to show the document to his mentor, Peter hurriedly hid his thick ham sandwich in the small refrigerator in his room, and dialed Professor Baghdadi's Skype address.

In his plush apartment on the Yale campus overlooking Farnam Memorial Gardens Mujab Baghdadi identified his correspondent on the monitor's caller ID line, and he activated the computer's camera and microphone.

"Good Evening," said a smiling Baghdadi...and he added in a congenial tone, *"Ah sah LAHM ah LAY koom."*

"Wa ah LAY koom as Alam," said Peter, simultaneously fingerspelling the English words, *Peace be with you.*

"I have something to show you," Peter signed...and he held the certificate before the camera lens built into the frame of his computer.

"Aha!" said the professor approvingly. "I see you have learned quickly, my young friend."

"I have a fine teacher," Peter signed.

Baghdadi pressed the palms of his hands together and touched the upward-pointed fingers to his forehead.

At that moment, Mary Wilkinson knocked on her son's bedroom door and called. "Peter, this is your mother. There's someone here to see you. She's waiting in the living room."

Alarmed, Peter dashed to his bedroom window and searched the long driveway with an apprehensive sweep of his eyes. Amanda Bragg's white convertible was parked midway between the garage and Stony Path.

"That bitch," he groaned. "How dare she?"

He returned to his desk and with fumbling fingers he signed for Mujab Baghdadi's benefit. *Forgive me...I must go...a friend is waiting...* and he circled his heart with his hand in apology.

"Understood," said the professor, and in the time-honored fashion of a Yale man, he added, "Always obey your mother."

And the screen went blank.

* * * * *

IN SOUTHWICK ONLY TWO LOCATIONS were open for business at ten o'clock on Christmas Eve. One was Walgreen's, which planned to close at eleven, and the other was the 24-hour Boston Market on College Road. The eatery was a beehive of activity, but virtually all the goings on involved behind-the-counter preparation of take-out orders that would be picked up between ten and noon tomorrow.

At a rear table near the rest room doors Peter Wilkinson sat glaring at Amanda Bragg over his steaming coffee mug. She, in turn, merely stared at the tabletop, red-eyed and sniffling, as she idly stirred a bowl of clam chowder and gnawed at her bottom lip.

"I don't think you fully understand the position you've put yourself in," the scowling Peter said in a monotone. He paused, sipped the coffee, and asked softly but severely, "Did you hear what I said?"

"I know," the forlorn young woman whimpered.

"You should never have left your place. That was idiotic!"

"I know."

"And you certainly should never have come to my house. You know that too, don't you?"

She nodded, and without looking up said almost inaudibly, "Yes."

"Then why did you?"

"Why did I what?"

"Come to my house, you stupid bitch!" He leaned to his left and looked past her toward the front of the otherwise empty restaurant. Peter Wilkinson fired Amanda a withering glance from beneath half-closed eyelids and said bitterly, "Eat some soup; you're drawing attention from the help."

"I...I can't...it's...too hot." She stirred the chowder faster, and visored her eyes with her other hand.

"If you don't stop acting like a petulant child," Peter threatened, "...I'm going to throw that soup in your goddam face."

She slid her chair an inch closer to the small table, and the spoon juddered in her quivering hand as she ladled an ounce of the milky broth into her mouth. An errant drop slid down her chin and left its creamy stain on the dark blue blazer that she wore. She dabbed at it apologetically as Wilkinson glowered at her in disgust.

Wadding the Kleenex and slipping it into her pocketbook, Amanda Bragg managed to consume an ounce or two of the chowder and she actually found it somewhat rejuvenating.

"Did anyone see you?"

"No," she lied…and blew on another spoonful of the soup without looking up.

"How do you know?"

"The roads were…were empty. There was…no traffic."

"All the more reason you should have stayed put," he growled. "Didn't you see the way that headlight was shining, for Christ's sake?"

"I didn't see anything unus…"

"No, of course you didn't," Wilkinson muttered. He tossed her a scornful look and added, "How the VA ever chose you to head up the Southwick ID Department is…"

"Please don't bring up the hospital," she begged him. "They have nothing to do with this."

"Oh, is that a fact?" Peter glared at her. "Do you have any idea how long that cushy job of yours would last if your moron bosses knew their Director of Identification is a felon?"

'Mandy' Bragg dropped her spoon and the utensil fell to the floor with a clang that resounded in the near-empty room. In seconds a young waitress was at her side. With an understanding grin the aproned girl picked up the wayward spoon and handed her patron a fresh one. The blushing woman accepted it with an embarrassed half-smile…before Peter waved the waitress away.

"Don't you dare call me a felon," Amanda hissed. "It was an accident and you know it." She pushed the bowl of chowder to one side and fished in her purse for her car keys.

Wilkinson reached across the table and grabbed her wrist. He recited evenly and in a menacing tone. "Leaving the scene of any accident is a crime. When a personal injury occurs, the fleeing driver is subject to 'Felony Hit and Run' charges. Is that clear? The vehicle has become a weapon…you understand?"

She smothered a wail with the large cotton napkin from her lap.

Peter snatched the napkin from in front of her face. "Listen to me. Now that you've put your 'weapon' out in the open for everyone to see, the only way out of this mess is to cover up for that damaged headlight."

"I think I should…"

"Shut the fuck up and listen to me." He leaned forward on the table and pulled her aching wrist toward him. "We've got to smash that right front fender for real!" he whispered.

Peter stood and yanked Amanda to her feet. He pulled the car keys from her hand. "Come on…I'll drive. And you don't say a word…is that clear?"

Chapter Nineteen

NICOLAI DOUNIAT QUICKLY BECAME a very busy man. After immediately arranging for a tail that would follow and protect Evrim Yildiz day and night, and having relayed the man's decryption on to General Ladka in The Pentagon, he now wired Commander Whitmore at Scotland Yard. Douniat's request was brief and straightforward. He required their participation in what he had innocuously designated 'The Southwick Incident.' More explicit details would follow.

With the addition within the hour of the FBI…and by dawn in Stonehenge, the British Censor's Bureau…the net that the Deputy Consul General in Istanbul was preparing for Yale Professor Baghdadi and his target, Peter Wilkinson, would soon broaden significantly. With even a modicum of good fortune, Douniat calculated, the multi-bureau effort would ultimately enmesh the entire cast of characters in a conspiracy that bore all the earmarks of an incipient terrorist cabal.

These Islamists are clever in choosing their targets, and radicalizing recruits to destroy them, Douniat theorized, *but it is a rare faction that can evade five determined counter-terrorist agencies.*

The Deputy's next communiqué went directly to Miles Plumber, Chief Inspector of the Censor's Bureau in London. It was 2:00 in the morning...4:00 AM Istanbul time. For three out of every one thousand Turks, today was Christmas...for the other nine hundred and ninety-seven, the vast majority of them Sunni Muslims, it was just another Friday.

Still, although he was a Christian, and a Greek Orthodox one at that, Nicholai Douniat was singularly suspicious of 'Jummah' (Friday) when it came to terrorist activity. For was it not known throughout the Islamic world that, *"Any Muslim who dies during the day or night of 'Jummah' will be protected by Allah from the trial of the grave?"*

Douniat wasn't sure whether that meant 'Jummah' locally, or in Mecca. At any rate, Friday, like every other day, dawned earlier in the Holy City than it did in time zones west of it. Accordingly, if it was midday 'Jummah' in Europe, Africa, or the Americas... it had to be Friday in Mecca too.

The best day of the week to meet Allah, and remind Him of His promise.

* * * * *

IN SOUTHWICK, MASSACHUSETTS, Carter Banning was brooding over exactly the same thing, as he stared at the television screen in his den...reflecting on those days more than forty years ago in Istanbul...and he fell asleep wishing this spring-like Christmas season were over and done with.

* * * * *

PETER WILKINSON KNEW what he had to do...not only to maintain Amanda Bragg's integrity and keep her secure in the position that would soon become so valuable to him...but also to support his fabricated eye-witness account implicating Roseanne Turbish. The ploy was known as 'distraction,' and it seldom failed to divert the attention of even the most meticulous investigator.

The crash needn't be a bad one—Amanda had to be able to drive the car home, after all, and even a blown tire could thwart his plan. Peter, in turn, would walk to his house in the darkness that was typical of The Landing area at this hour. As for the specific location of the collision—any stout tree on Stony Path would do if it was close enough to the shoulder. All that would be needed was damage sufficient to mask that sustained when Amanda had struck Renaldo Vega.

The frightened woman had insisted that she wait on the side of the road while Peter inflicted the required damage, but he wouldn't hear of it. What if she ran away? No. He couldn't risk letting her out of his sight. As an alternative she begged that she be permitted to huddle in the backseat, and he acquiesced.

At a point roughly equidistant from the Banning and Turbish houses, Peter chose a mature oak that protruded somewhat onto the sloping shoulder of Stony Path, and gauging the speed required to smash the Buick's headlight, while keeping the convertible drivable, he struck the tree a glancing blow with the passenger-side fender.

While glass from the headlight flew amid the sound of wrenching metal, Amanda Bragg screamed and covered her head with her arms. Instantly Wilkinson applied the brakes, and then quickly doused the headlights. In the utter darkness, he backed the car onto the road surface and shifted it into 'park.' "Out!" he ordered.

He exited the still-running car and held the driver's seat bent forward. "Now get in and drive," he instructed, "…and get out of here fast."

As 'Mandy' Bragg climbed weeping behind the wheel, Peter reached and turned on the lights. Only the left headlight shone. "If you so much as mention my name," he seethed, "…you'll go to jail for the rest of your life. Check the Internet. That Mexican you ran over is dead."

Amanda's hand went to her chest and she choked back an agonized cry.

"I'll be at your office on Tuesday," Peter barked. "At noon. Have a full set of photo ID ready for me."

He slammed the door of the new Buick and gave the side window a 'get going' slap. Then Amanda sped north…the narrow road illuminated by just one of her headlights.

* * * * *

LIEUTENANT FRANK BROGAN HAD LEFT Stony Path ten minutes before the contrived 'accident' and he sat at his desk at headquarters reviewing once again Peter Wilkinson's perfectly detailed description of Roseanne Turbish's Chevy sedan, and its departure from the Middleville Road accident scene.

Two things bothered Brogan about the account.

First, was the fact that young Wilkinson had reported no erratic driving on the part of the car's operator…that, despite the unlikely presence of the empty brandy bottle Frank had seen on the Impala's front floor.

The other thing gnawing at the Lieutenant was that although Peter had clearly noted the vehicle's make and model—a two-door Chevrolet…recalled its color—blue, specifically light blue…and correctly indicated its approximate vintage—an 'older model maybe 15 years'…he had been unable to supply any information whatsoever about the license plate. He could not recall if the plate was one of the current red, white, and blue 'Spirit of America' types…whether it was a so-called 'vanity' tag purchased from the Motor Vehicle Registry for a premium… or for that matter, if it was a Massachusetts plate at all!

The reason all this bothered Frank Brogan was that Herman Turbish's old sedan bore an easily recognizable license plate if ever there was one; Herman had bought the 'legacy' plate that still adorned Roseanne's car when the patriotic versions first were offered back in 1987. It bore the loyalist imprint USA 4ME.

The Lieutenant withdrew the three-by-five-inch notepad from his shirt pocket and flipped a few pages to the entry he'd jotted after driving Wilkinson home from police headquarters. It read:

"Nine out of ten people in this country are assholes"

He tapped the spiral pad on his cluttered desk and stared at the image of a supremely confident Peter Wilkinson reciting on the Dash Cam. Brogan clenched his teeth and thought, *It must have been annoying for a superior intellectual like you to live next door to such an ignorant patriot as Herman Turbish...right Mister Yale Man?*

Then he said aloud to the image on the camera, "Well, let's see how well you do on cross-examination." He left headquarters and drove back toward Stony Path. He wanted another Christmas Eve chat with Wilkinson...the cool wiseguy with such an eye for detail.

Chapter Twenty

THE FIRST THING EVRIM YILDIZ DID when he left the Consul General's office was take a taxi to the teeming Bayrampasa section in old Istanbul. That was where a *clean* Beretta (well oiled…its serial number obliterated…test fired) and a box of reliable American-made ammunition, could be had for twelve-hundred Turkish Lira. The ten thousand lira in modest, easily negotiable notes taped to his chest was not only the most money Evrim had ever possessed, it was the most cash he had ever *seen* in all his thirty-eight years combined.

Yildiz knew that his chances of arriving safely at his slovenly quarters beneath the Bosphorus Bridge were slim if he should attempt the trip home from the Consulate unarmed. Thus, he had persuaded Deputy Nicholai Douniat to provide a trustworthy taxi to West Istanbul's black market district where he would make his purchase. Once armed with the beautiful .38 caliber automatic he'd long yearned for, the likelihood of his being robbed during the remainder of his trip home would be greatly reduced.

'Benito,' his faithful Corso guard dog would protect him thereafter.

Douniat's two assigned tails followed the one-armed Yildiz in distinctly different vehicles. One was a decrepit, 20-year-old

Fiat…the other a nondescript but somewhat newer Renault. Both types of Italian and French imports were commonly found on the streets of Istanbul. They might as well have been invisible, changing locations and intervals erratically as they did to avoid detection on the city's crowded roads and highways.

The elder of the assigned shadows was a middle-aged woman, the other, a scruffy looking agent in his late twenties. Once Evrim Yildiz had made his purchase, arrived at the bridge, and isolated himself in his hovel, his followers continued their surveillance trading cars every hour or so. One of the tails made non-stop back and forth crossings on the always-busy Bosphorus span, while the other parked in a nearby 24-hour shopping mall, making sure to change locations frequently.

Had Douniat thought for one minute that General Ladka's old Cold War colleague would so easily solve the code that supposedly existed only within the mind of the opportunistic Yildiz, the Deputy might have saved the Consulate the trouble of following and protecting the man. Indeed, the Consulate could have disposed of him before he'd ever left the five-story complex.

The unfortunate fact was that by mid-day on Christmas, Istanbul time, Nicholai was in possession of Carter Banning's decryption…and Evrim had outlived his usefulness. Alive, Douniat knew, the severely disabled informant might reveal what US authorities in America and Turkey now knew…that a radicalized Islamist named Peter Wilkinson was a threat to his country's security. Possession of this information made Yildiz a potential double agent, of course…a man perhaps to be waterboarded at least…or even, should he become suspect, suffered the severing of his remaining arm during interrogation by his fellow Islamists. It would be a fate worse than death. Any man would capitulate under such a threat…and Nicholai Douniat knew it.

Accordingly, by late-afternoon, both Evrim Yildiz and his trustworthy dog were dead, their bodies washing south toward the Mediterranean as the sun lowered over the swift-flowing flood tide of Turkey's Bosphorus Strait.

* * * * *

DOCTOR MEILI SONG SAT in a straightback chair behind the ER Receiving Desk. She was reading the December issue of JAAD, the Journal of the American Academy of Dermatology. The nurse to her right was making entries in a loose-leaf log book. Two trauma patients had been brought in about seven… assault victims who had seen fit to celebrate the upcoming holiday by pummeling one another in a drunken brawl. Both had been treated and released in the custody of their furious wives. The four principals were no strangers to the Southwick VA Emergency Room.

Thankfully, at a little after nine, that had been the extent of the unusually slow Christmas Eve activity, and Meili, having cleansed and bandaged the fists and faces of the combatants, had taken advantage of the ensuing lull to catch up on her reading of a particularly interesting article on *Acne Vulgaris*. The feature addressed in detail the long-term skin disease that occurs when hair follicles…particularly those of adolescents… become clogged with dead cells and oil from the skin. The heartbreaking affliction was the most common problem that Meili Song was called upon to treat, and though not as physically problematic as severe psoriasis, or certainly melanoma, it could be psychologically devastating.

The emergency phone at the nurse's station jangled at 2115 hours military time. Charge Nurse Jean Gustavson promptly pressed the speakerphone. "VA Emergency…Gustavson."

The Southwick Police medical technician identified himself and announced that their ambulance would be arriving at 2125 hours…ten minutes hence…with an Adult Female…approximate Age Forty…condition Stable…vital signs Normal…the victim of a Barbiturate Overdose…apparently Self-administered.

Nurse Gustavson noted the information on a form attached to a plastic clipboard, acknowledged receipt of the transmitted information, and used a desk microphone to broadcast an announcement of the incipient arrival throughout the ward.

Meili Song quickly replaced the JAAD magazine in its rack to her left, and lifted her stethoscope from the desk. She suspended it from her neck and hurried toward the automatic doors at the end of the ER's wide corridor, careful not to stand in the area where the heavy doors would swing inward. As she waited, a burly male nurse joined her…and she heard the Police EMT advise over a speakerphone, "Victim is regaining consciousness…advises she is a VAMC employee…name, Amanda Bragg. Medical records should be on file with the hospital. Patient indicates the consumed substance is known as 'Easy Off'…Over."

Doctor James Briley the attending physician turned a corner and approached Doctor Song. "What have we got, Millie?"

The intermittent blaring of the ambulance's backup horn could be clearly heard outside, and the doors of the emergency entrance flew open.

"Sounds like attempted suicide," said a businesslike Meili Song…"It's Amanda…from Identification…she ingested oven cleaner."

With one attendant on each side, the rolling stretcher that bore the twitching victim was swiftly wheeled out of the ambulance, over the floor-level exterior ramp, and through the double-wide doorway of the Emergency Suite. A broad-shouldered nurse named Ryan, who had been the first to reach the semi-conscious woman's side, shone a penlight in one of Amanda Bragg's wildly darting eyes as he ran along the corridor beside her. He produced a syringe from his pocket, and was prepared to plunge the needle into her flailing arm, injecting its 5-milligram dose of Diazepam into her bloodstream, but Meili Song abruptly seized his arm as she ran with him toward the treatment room. "No! she ordered. "Not yet, Ryan. We need to empty her…let her rinse herself out…then we can ease the reverse peristalsis."

The nurse nodded and grabbed a bedpan from an aide who was standing with it at the ready by the open treatment room door. The husky nurse handed her his Valium-filled syringe in return and she stepped aside with it.

"Let's get her on her stomach," commanded Doctor Briley, and the two men joined Meili in turning the Bragg woman over in a single, well-practiced motion. "Is she pregnant, Doctor?" Briley asked Meili, sensing that Song knew the patient.

"Not that I'm aware of," Doctor Song replied, and she took the bedpan and held it beneath a narrow slot in the end of the padded stretcher. Amanda vomited profusely, producing a frothy mix of green and yellow slime that seemed to simmer in the oval-shaped receptacle. "Good girl," said Meili. "Again, Honey." She snapped her fingers for a cool, damp cloth the Charge Nurse held, and she used it to massage the back of Amanda's sweating neck. "Get it all up, Dear," she said soothingly. "I know it burns. Just a little more."

Soon the retching produced less and less mucus, and as her spasms diminished in intensity...and ultimately ran their course...the exhausted woman finally fell asleep.

"Bring me that Diazepam," Doctor Song said to the young aide. "She's a tough one, but right now she deserves some sleep."

The strapping nurse stood at the deep sink washing stray splashes of ejaculate from his hands and forearms. "I wonder what possessed her to do it?" he murmured shaking his head.

"That's for a different kind of doctor to determine," said Meili Song. "Hopefully one who can find out who this 'Peter' person is that she seems so terrified of."

Chapter Twenty-one

THE SUPPOSEDLY PROFOUNDLY DEAF Professor Mujab Baghdadi realized his mistake as soon as he'd made it. What's more, he was sure that his newly radicalized student, Peter Wilkinson, would come to recognize the slipup too. What had seemed at the time a simple, innocently uttered colloquialism, *'Always obey your mother,'* was a fatal error on Baghdadi's part, and it could not help but ultimately reveal the deception involving his feigned auditory impairment.

True, Peter's mother had summoned him to come and greet his guest, but there had been no mention of her on Peter's part… either spoken or signed. Indeed the woman had not even entered the room where Baghdadi might have seen her on the Skype camera; she had merely identified herself by calling through the closed bedroom door.

And obviously the 'deaf' professor had heard her.

Peter was a bright boy…a superb student…that, after all, is why the Islamic terrorist recruiter who called himself Mujab Baghdadi had singled him out from a group of Yale non-patriots that numbered in the hundreds. Thus it was a near-certainty that Wilkinson would soon realize his mentor's duplicity.

This was a grievous error, committed in the conduct of a cutthroat enterprise that brooked no such foolish mistakes. Baghdadi knew that the punishment for such a lapse was beheading...not in public, of course, that would only focus the attention of Infidel enemies on Mujab's stupidity. He would be brought home to be executed...in the flat, rocky Syrian Desert on the southern perimeter of his native land. There, dead men's flesh was known to turn to dust in a matter of weeks, such were the harsh elements of the unforgiving region known as al-Hamad.

The commonly held notion in The West: that all Islamists welcome death in the service of Allah, is a gross misconception. Groups like Al Qaeda and ISIS encourage that perception among their enemies because they believe it makes terrorists seem noble and invincible in their zealotry...fearing nothing—not even death. But the truth is that more Americans kill themselves violently in a week (as Amanda Bragg had attempted to) than do all Muslim terrorists in a year. Not that the statistic in and of itself makes America's collective death-wishers any more admirable than Islam's...it merely puts the lie to the so-called universal fearlessness of Muhammed's followers.

But Mujab Baghdadi had no wish to die, thank you. And if that was considered straying from the ISIS script, so be it. He had even been known to enjoy both alcohol and women in New Haven's naughtier neighborhoods near the Quinnipiac River. Baghdadi's justification for this seeming abuse of Islamic law lay in his rationalizing of an ancient Persian legend that tells of one King Jamshid.

Jamshid was a grape-loving ruler, who stored ripe grapes grown in the Shiraz region in a deep cellar so that he might consume them at his pleasure throughout the year. One day he craved grapes and sent slaves to fetch some. When they failed to return, the annoyed Jamshid went to the cellar himself...where he found that carbon dioxide gas coming from his now-fermenting grapes had rendered his slaves unconscious. Accordingly the king ordered that the wine be labeled 'Poison.'

Subsequently however, one of the king's rejected mistresses, deciding to kill herself, went to the cellar and drank a copious amount of this 'lethal' potion...but in actuality, the giddy young lady left the cellar singing and dancing merrily. Thus, the amazed ruler realized that his fruity grape-liquid actually had a wonderful power...it could make sad people happy!

Mujab Baghdadi decided that what was good enough for King Jamshid's concubine (peace be upon her) was, like life itself, surely good enough for him.

* * * * *

GENERAL KAROL LADKA ANSWERED Carter Banning's call on the second ring. He too had been watching ongoing rescue efforts at the Hotel Cadiz in downtown Istanbul. The bodies of the sixteen American students had been identified and removed early on, and only in the last few minutes had Hamid al-Jamil's identity been established.

"You got my email?" Carter asked. He'd awakened moments earlier and his bloodshot eyes were fixed on the television screen as he spoke on his cell phone.

"Just got it," said General Ladka as, from his desk in The Pentagon, he too watched the NBC Special Report. "You haven't lost a step, Carter."

"And you're as close-mouthed as ever," Banning said, "...aren't you?"

"Meaning?"

"Meaning...the only reason you're ringing me in on this deal, is because you already cracked the goddam code yourself, didn't you? The CIA found out this mystery man Wilkinson is my neighbor...and you want me to tail him...report on his every move." He took a sip of wine. "Isn't that about the size of it, Karol?"

"Weeeelll," Ladka responded lightly, "That's roughly what I had..."

"For Christ's sake, I'm seventy years old, Karol!"

There was a five-second pause on the line. "Then Wilkinson would never suspect you, right? No one would."

Carter Banning couldn't argue with that.

In addition to his advanced years, the retired Army veteran was a constant fixture in the Southwick area, as familiar a figure as anyone in town. So long as Ladka didn't expect him to provide accounts of Wilkinson's doings outside the region where he and Peter both lived…southeastern Massachusetts, and more specifically, The Landing…getting a line on the Yale student's activities when home from school shouldn't be difficult. Not for a man with Carter's training in Military Intelligence. Furthermore, despite the current incidence of a minor basal cell carcinoma removal, he was a surprisingly healthy specimen…easily up to the physical demands that such a mission would likely call for.

But before the former Major Banning could accept his friend's proposed assignment, he wanted answers to some important questions. In short, if he were going to follow and keep tabs on an individual that an authority like The Pentagon considered suspicious, he needed to meet with Karol Ladka.

"We have to talk further," said Carter, "…face to face."

"When?" said Ladka.

"It's your show," Carter said dismissively. "You tell me."

"Tomorrow."

Carter removed the cell phone from the side of his head and stared at it…puzzled…unbelieving. He returned the device to his ear. "Tomorrow's Christmas, General…December 25th… remember?"

"This isn't something I've dreamed up to pass the time of day, Carter. I know damn well what tomorrow is. Listen, the brass here in Arlington doesn't enjoy the luxury of pursuing America's enemies only at times that fit comfortably into our schedules."

A chastened Carter Banning responded meekly, "I didn't mean to suggest…"

"No explanation necessary, my friend." Karol Ladka's voice took on a sterner tone. "Are you still watching the NBC feed from Istanbul?"

"Yes."

"You see our soldiers surrounding the Consulate?"

"Yes."

"We have reason to believe they might soon be called upon to defend against an attack they can't possibly win. Our Intelligence operatives anticipate a series of terrorist attacks between now and New Year's. Some seem scheduled here in the US...others at our properties abroad. It appears the explosion at the Hotel Cadiz is merely the first in a series of planned assaults on buildings where Americans congregate." The General's voice became more conversational. "I needn't tell you, our agents take terrible risks to learn the clandestine activities of foreign adversaries. We'd be nuts to take their discoveries lightly, Carter. Someone once said 'Haters can't hurt you unless you let them.' Well trust me; I personally have no intention of letting Islamic terrorists eliminate Christmas and every other Christian observance from our calendars forever—you there, Carter?"

"Where do you want to meet?" said Carter Banning. "And what time?"

Karol Ladka didn't miss a beat. "Take the 10:30 ferry from Bridgeport to Long Island...Port Jefferson...tomorrow morning. Be at the Bridgeport departure dock at 10:00. You can leave your car there...just don't park in a conspicuous place. Crossing time is an hour and fifteen minutes. Once you disembark at Port Jeff, it's a four or five minute walk to The Steamroom restaurant on the south side of Main Street. I'll be inside...at the counter... eating Little Neck clams and drinking lemonade."

"What's the occasion supposed to be...or is this a blind date?"

"If anybody asks, I'm a Broadway producer, James Weiss... you're an angel...an investor, Brian Parsons. We're there to make a business proposal to Hugh Harmwell. He's the major domo of Theatre Three on North Main Street. For your ears only,

Hugh's also one of our counterterrorism agents. It could become important that you know one another. There's no performance at the theater tomorrow, so Harmwell's office will be a secure place to talk."

"Is that what I'm supposed to tell Elizabeth?—that I'm leaving my wife and my visiting daughters on Christmas to meet with a Counterterrorism Team member…in an empty Long Island playhouse? Sounds pretty Ludlumesque, old friend."

General Ladka laughed aloud in his cell phone. "Remind me to tell 'Scrooge' you said that."

"Who's 'Scrooge'?"

That's Harmwell's Homeland Security code name. Hugh plays 'Ebenezer Scrooge' in Theatre Three's annual performance of 'A Christmas Carol.' But to answer your question, I suggest you tell the family you're seeing an oncologist about today's surgery on your arm. A specialist who's doing a JAMA paper on prompt 'Skin Cancer Detection Among Seniors'…something like that. Use your imagination."

Carter paused and frowned. "How the hell did you know about my skin cancer?"

"Really, Major Banning, come on!" Ladka then feigned concern. "How *does* your incision feel, by the way?"

"Peachy," said Carter. "And how's that penile enhancement of yours doing?"

The General's eruption of laughter stung Carter's ear. "Good one, my man." Then he added, "But promise you won't tell Hugh Harmwell that joke when you meet him…we happen to know he's recently had the procedure done at a private lab in Stony Brook. You understand."

Carter Banning grinned and looked at his watch. He guessed he'd better get some sleep. "Okay…10:30 ferry to Port Jeff…Steamroom restaurant…eating clams at the counter…see you at noon."

"Clams and *lemonade*," Karol Ladka quickly corrected. "If I'm drinking anything else, it means I'm being watched...*and you get out of there fast!*

"Oh...and Carter...use cash for the ferry. That was Ebenezer's mistake...he paid for his implant with VISA. Now the whole espionage industry knows...poor bastard!"

Chapter Twenty-two

LIEUTENANT FRANK BROGAN doused his lights as he pulled into the Wilkinsons' long driveway. The electrical Christmas decorations that adorned the interiors of the home's sixteen windows had been turned off, but light still shone from one bedroom upstairs and another room…probably the den… on the main floor. By the illumination of an outside pole lamp midway between the house and its large detached garage, Brogan eased his unmarked sedan to a stop near the slate front walkway.

Inside, Peter Wilkinson was happily watching the NBC Special Report that now showed the United States Consulate in Istanbul. It was ringed by dozens of armed American troops, and encircling them were ten times that many ragged civilians. They were clearly taunting the soldiers…eager to provoke the camouflage clad men.

Peter was recording the broadcast. The video would be only the latest in a stack of DVDs that he kept in his dorm room at Yale and reviewed time and time again. With any kind of luck, he'd concluded, tonight's episode would end in the sort of massacre the American invaders deserved.

Wilkinson had grown to despise his country's colonialist behavior. Who was the almighty United States to impose its will on helpless countries in Africa, Asia, and South America? Professor Mujab Baghdadi was right: the bloodsucking pillagers that had arrived on America's shores...then ripped a fertile land from its peace-loving natives...they were the epitome of evil. They deserved the condemnation of Allah...and Peter Wilkinson was virtually drooling as he watched the tension building in faraway Turkey.

There was a knock at the front door.

Startled, Peter walked cautiously through the living room and into the center hall.

Peter hadn't heard the Lieutenant's sedan in the driveway. He'd been so engrossed by what he still hoped would be a bloody mêlée at the Istanbul Consulate that the prospect had riveted his full attention. Now, however, he could clearly see the unmarked car between the house and the oversized garage. It was illuminated by the rear pole light's modest 60-watt bulb.

Shit!

Peter hastened to open the door after Brogan's second series of raps. If the policeman decided to ring the bell, the Westminster chimes would echo throughout the house and surely alert Peter's mother and his insufferable adoptive father. That was a prospect best avoided, he concluded...who knew what Frank Brogan had in mind?

Wilkinson opened the door and smiled through clenched teeth. "Hi. Still hard at work, I see."

"Never stops," said Brogan. "Got a minute?"

"Sure," said Peter, bobbing his head toward the den where the television screen flickered with scenes hurriedly recorded by hand-held news cameras. He held a perpendicular finger to his lips. "The folks just went to bed." He ushered the Lieutenant into the den and closed the door behind them.

The first thing Frank Brogan's trained eye noticed was a small red light on the television cable box. It indicated that the program on the large screen above it was being recorded. "Have a seat," said Peter. "Want a drink...a beer?"

Brogan didn't answer right away. He merely shifted his eyes lazily from Peter to the digital 'Record' light and back again.

Young Wilkinson noticed instantly what was going on. He dropped into one of two large armchairs and motioned for the Lieutenant to take the other. "Quite something…that accident in Istanbul," he said, gesturing toward the flat screen TV monitor mounted above a low cabinet.

Frank Brogan sat, but again was slow to respond. When he did, he regarded Peter Wilkinson through disdainful, half closed eyes. "Accident?"

"Yeah," said Peter. "Didn't you hear? Sixteen American students." He snapped his fingers. "Gone…just like that."

Brogan continued to play the waiting game. He didn't know exactly what he was looking for, but he suspected that the insensitive young fellow sitting opposite him would do or say something to incriminate himself. He nodded toward the ongoing audio display that showed a crowd of Turks gathering and becoming more frenetic as dawn broke over Istanbul. "Who told you the explosion was an accident," he said.

"That's what the announcer…the Lester Holt guy said," Wilkinson lied…and he shrugged.

Brogan gave him another lingering look. "Well, since you're recording this whole program, maybe you wouldn't mind playing it back for me. I'd like to see that 'accident' part."

Peter Wilkinson squirmed and smiled weakly. "I just started recording the disc a few minutes ago," he lied again.

Frank Brogan cocked his head and gazed at the fellow who had now become his adversary on several different levels. "The Elapsed-Time Indicator, Peter, the gauge on the left of the cable box. It reads 92.51. You've been making a record of this carnage for an hour and a half!"

The announcer was droning on in a somber tone of voice, the sound emanating from the Panasonic flat screen television had been lowered to a barely audible level. Brogan assumed correctly the purpose was to avoid disturbing the elder Wilkinsons upstairs. Frank Brogan decided to make his move. He reached for the remote on the coffee table between him and Peter, and muted the broadcast. "An accident," he said reproachfully, "...is an unintended event. It's something that happens by chance...accidents are unplanned...fortuitous."

"I know the definition of an accident, Lieutenant," Peter said, reddening.

"I should hope so," the policeman shot back sarcastically, "...after spending the last six years in a New Haven university."

"Is that why you barged in here at ten o'clock on Christmas Eve...to remind me that I'm a Yale graduate student?"

"You're confusing your terms again," Brogan said with a faux smile. "I knocked on your door...three times lightly...you opened it...invited me inside. That's hardly barging in."

Peter glared at the plainclothes officer. "That's *your* version."

Frank Brogan shifted in his chair. "It's also the version that's recorded on the Dash Cam in my car."

"Well, I had nothing to do with that crash down the road, if that's what you're wondering."

The Lieutenant hadn't the slightest idea what young Wilkinson was talking about, but he said nothing...merely folded his arms...and waited.

"Drunks run into trees regularly in this neighborhood. Especially on holidays. Residents call you guys if the road's blocked...usually the asshole drivers just take off. Don't want to get involved with the cops." Peter picked up the TV remote, cancelled the mute, and turned up the volume. "You know where the door is."

Insolent little bastard, thought Brogan. But he exited the den and walked silently to the door through which he'd been admitted to the house. He left, and quietly closed the heavy oak door behind him. The camera on the dash of his unmarked cruiser recorded his departure...as it had every detail of his unspectacular arrival and entry ten minutes earlier.

Lieutenant Brogan backed discreetly out of the Wilkinson driveway guided only by the illumination of his back-up lights. On Stony Path he soon found a scarred tree, broken glass, and a twisted headlight rim…clear indicators of a recent accident. Also…lying upside-down near the base of the scraped twelve-inch-diameter oak…was the front license plate of Amanda Bragg's new Buick convertible.

Chapter Twenty-three

IN A MATTER OF HOURS after Istanbul's Hotel Cadiz had been destroyed, Homeland Security increased its TAL, or Terrorism Alert Level, to 'High.' The new Obama system had done away with the color-code scheme established in 2002. That advisory under Director Tom Ridge, ranged from Green (normal) to Red (severe). Recently the Terror Alert Level nationwide, had been described in everyday English as 'Elevated.' In other words, equivalent to the relatively mild 'Yellow.'

Whenever alert levels changed, among the first agencies scheduled to be placed on increased alert status were the country's Veteran's Administration Hospitals, and in particular the Emergency Rooms of those Medical Centers.

When Doctor Meili Song answered the phone at the Southwick VAMC Emergency Desk it was ten after ten…2210 hours in military time…and she heard the following recorded announcement:

'By order of the President of the United States, all US Military installations are hereby placed on 'High' alert for terrorist activity until advised otherwise by the Director of Homeland Security.

All formerly authorized leaves for both Commissioned Officers and Enlisted Personnel are hereby cancelled.

Uniformed personnel already traveling off-base are instructed to return to their assigned stations forthwith.

All Civilian Employees of the United States Military are hereby placed on 24-hour call by their Unit Supervisors.

Medical Personnel already in attendance at Military Medical Centers are to remain on duty until relieved by Unit Commanders.

I say again: By order of the President of the United States, all US Military installations are hereby placed on 'High' alert for terrorist activity. This advisory remains...'

The recorded message was obviously on a loop, and Meili handed the phone to the Attending Physician, who listened carefully to the advisory. "At least the TAL isn't 'Severe,'" he said passing the phone to the Charge Nurse. "...but it doesn't look like we're going anyplace for Christmas, ladies."

Doctor Song's first thought was of Amanda Bragg. The Director of Southwick's Identification Department had responded well to treatment for her brush with catastrophe and she was weak, but at lease she was on the way home in a taxi. Meili knew Amanda lived alone, and she'd promised to stop by her flat at the end of her shift. Now, of course, that would be out of the question.

The only person Meili Song knew who lived in the same general area as the Bragg woman was Carter Banning. He wasn't affected by the Homeland Security directive...and surely he wouldn't mind looking in on Amanda if Meili called him right away. He would understand why doctors were enjoined from leaving the hospital, and Meili was equally confident Carter would see to it, if he knew the circumstances, that Amanda didn't attempt to report to the hospital.

The Bannings' number was unlisted, the doctor assumed, but Carter's cell phone would be on file in the computer system along with his other personal information. Besides, the Dermatologist rationalized, it'll be good to know whether there's been any problem with his incision.

Meili opened Carter Banning's file and it appeared on the computer monitor behind the Emergency Room Desk. There it was...the 'Contact' entry...Carter's Stony Path address...the area code...and the number 278-5100.

She tapped it out on her own cell phone, and hoped Carter hadn't muted his device for the evening.

But he had.

* * * * *

LIEUTENANT BROGAN GOT INTO HIS CAR. He prepared to call-in the combination of numbers and letters on the dislodged license plate he'd retrieved from the base of the tree on Stony Path. But before he could do so, the squad car's dash-mounted scanner squawked its emergency message. It was similar to the one received minutes earlier by Meili Song...but this notice was broadcast on 155.6...the frequency used to alert all Law Enforcement facilities throughout Hamden County:

'By order of the Director of Homeland Security, all State, County and Municipal Police personnel are hereby placed on 'High' alert for terrorist activity until further notice.

All formerly authorized holiday schedules for both Uniformed and Plainclothes Personnel are hereby rescinded until advised otherwise. Extended attendance at stations countywide are in effect for the next twenty-four hours

Law Enforcement Personnel preparing to leave or in the process of departing Hamden County are instructed to return to their domiciles forthwith and await further...

Frank Brogan returned the hand-held microphone to its cradle and made a U-turn on Stony Path. In his rearview mirror he saw the first-floor light go out at the Wilkinson residence.

News of the upgraded Terrorist Alert had interrupted NBC's coverage of the bombing in Istanbul…and an animated Peter Wilkinson was eager to get upstairs and contact his no doubt equally joyous mentor, Mujab Baghdadi, at Yale's Farnam Gardens apartment. He would call him on Skype once again… after all, what use was a land line phone to a deaf man?

* * * * *

AT A LITTLE AFTER FIVE on Christmas morning, Nicholai Douniat emerged from an emergency meeting with the Consul General and his several deputies. All of the Consulate's American nationals in residence lived in bomb-proof apartments in the five-story building's steel-walled interior…said to be the most heavily fortified building in Istanbul. That is where this morning's ultra-secure session was conducted.

The recently constructed fortress had been fashioned in this way with good reason. The fact was that the Consulate happened to be where the most sensitive transcripts, electronic records, and other files concerning Turkish-American relations, were stored. Indeed, while the United States Embassy is commonly thought to be the most important American address in any friendly city, those posh buildings are merely the elegant residences where ambassadors and their families live, and of course entertain. The real daily political posturing takes place at the Consulate…the 'Pentagon-away-from-home.'

Since the capitulation of the Administration in Washington to Iranian demands, the U.S. Consulate had become a more chaotic managerial center than ever before. Confusion reigned supreme. No one was really sure who could be relied upon any longer. No individual's word was truly trusted. Informants were confused, and thus mistrusted. Rumors abounded…most of them scoffed at...including one that Secretary of State John Kerry's daughter, of all people, had married an Islamic man. Only to be confirmed as fact by none other than *The New York Times*! What the hell was going on? It was in this helter-skelter atmosphere that sixteen seemingly innocent American students had been murdered, along with an Iraqi professor, whom no one seemed to know.

* * * * *

PROFESSOR MUJAB BAGHDADI SAT in his Yale apartment watching...and listening to...the Iraqi Media Television Network. The IMTN was a public broadcasting station in his homeland similar to America's PBS. Professor Baghdadi was convinced that like its American equivalent, the IMTN was nothing more than a mouthpiece for the failed Iraqi government that authorized, funded, and controlled it...the unforgivable group of cowards in Baghdad who had reneged on their promise to litter the streets of every Iraqi town with the corpses of United Nations troops.

There was little viewing choice on Iraqi television. The despised regime in Baghdad...which was nothing but a UN-fearing puppet, Mujab was sad to admit...had reined-in all electronic media and subjected them to the dictates of Iraq's International Telecommunication Union, clearly a United Nations treaty sympathizer in disguise. All Iraqi television stations sanctioned by the ITU merely mouthed the same tepid, accommodation of the US and its crony allies.

The announcer spoke in Arabic, as a heavily edited series of still photos flashed on a screen to his left. The images appeared, and replaced one another, too rapidly to be examined in any significant detail.

> *IMTN has learned that US officials declared a state of extreme national emergency in their country after American students were injured in an Istanbul hotel yesterday.*

It is not known what the unidentified group, consisting of both men and women, were doing in the hotel.

An unidentified Iraqi college professor was killed while attempting to assist the Americans.

Turkish security authorities have declared a state of heightened surveillance in Istanbul, said Brigadier. General, Saad Tarmann, a Turkish military spokesman.

All gates that lead to Istanbul are closed. No one is allowed to enter the city, but those who wish to leave Istanbul may do so.

Protesters objecting to the presence of American intelligence operatives in Turkey, have gathered peacefully outside the heavily fortified US Consulate and...

Mujab Baghdadi leaned forward and squinted as one of the photographs showed a victim of the bomb blast being hurriedly covered and rushed on a stretcher from the rubble of the Hotel Cadiz. His bloodied face made him difficult to recognize...but he wore a familiar looking taqiyah, and for a fraction of a second the Yale professor could have sworn the green and white skull cap with the single word embroidered in black looked...Could it be?

He turned to his computer and dashed off an email to his old classmate...his fellow terrorist, Hamid al Jamil, who had been living across the Boulevard of Martyrs from the University of Istanbul

Hamid:
Please let me know by return mail that you are well.
I suggest you destroy your hard drive after doing so.
Burning is the most effective means, as you know.
I will then abstain from corresponding until project is complete.
You should do likewise.
Ah sah lahm ah lay koom.

Mujab.

But, Hamid had been in the arms of Allah for at least an hour. Furthermore it was Baghdadi's fellow jihadists and one of their improvised explosive devices that had sent al Jamil to Paradise... as a precautionary measure, of course.

The same fate awaited Mujab Baghdadi, naturally...and his pawn, Peter Wilkinson, though not until they had contributed their fair share to the planned Great Massachusetts Massacre... the murder of six thousand despised American military veterans at five VA facilities in Bedford, Brockton, Leeds, and Roxbury... but first—Southwick.

Thanks to the carelessness of Hamid al Jamil however, the once tightly-knit plot was beginning to unravel. Because along with Shelby Whitmore of Scotland Yard and the BCB's Miles Plumber in London, Nicholai Douniat now knew about the Yale connection, and he'd informed both the FBI and the CIA. It was the latter agency that had sought the assistance of General Karol Ladka...and tomorrow the noted Army Cryptologist, Carter Banning would be brought into the picture.

If the radicalized Islamist Peter Wilkinson and his mentor *'Wif. en.poof'* only knew what Allah had in store for them! They were going to be hunted down like dogs...whether they succeeded in their nefarious scheme...or not!

Achieving the latter result would depend, Karol Ladka knew, on the nimble mind of his usually dependable associate, the elderly, but still crafty, retired Major Banning up in Southwick.

General Ladka went to bed. He had a long helicopter ride ahead of him in the morning.

Chapter Twenty-four

THE FERRY RIDE from Bridgeport to Port Jefferson was a predictably uncomfortable one. All of Long Island and Connecticut had been affected by a persistent low pressure system centered south of Montauk Point for nearly a week, and a choppy sea marked by three-foot, white-capped waves had built up in the deeper parts of The Sound.

Still, the huge ferry bearing Carter and his seventy fellow passengers (and thirty cars) had negotiated the twenty-mile voyage in the normal hour and fifteen minutes. A stiff following breeze from the north had created the rough surface, but it also compensated for any delay the restricting waves might normally have caused. Thus, a somewhat windblown, but otherwise unaffected Carter Banning strode into the busy Steamroom restaurant at precisely eleven-fifty as planned.

He spotted Karol Ladka immediately. The husky career Army officer, tall, broad through the shoulders, his complexion ruddy even in winter, was seated in casual civilian clothes where he'd said he would be…alone at the counter…and in front of him was a large oval dish containing a dozen opened Little Neck clams on shaved ice. He was sipping a tall glass of lemonade.

Carter approached Ladka from behind, and when he was still five feet away, The General lowered his glass and said without looking over his shoulder, "Merry Christmas, Brian."

Carter Banning sat on the upholstered stool next to his old friend and responded, "Same to you...Jimmy. How are the clams?"

"This is my second helping," said Karol, alias James Weiss. "That should tell you something." He slurped one of the ice-cold Little Necks and followed it with a crisp Oysterette.

The 70-year-old from Southwick, who was posing as theatrical investor, Brian Parsons, signaled to the counterman approaching from the noisy kitchen. "My friend recommends the clams. Any left?"

"Sure thing," said the aproned waiter. "Dozen?"

"Please."

"Lemonade? Beer? Iced tea?"

"Iced tea," said Carter, "...with Sweet 'n Low and lemon." He turned toward The General, who held another clam to his mouth and was preparing to suck it from the shallow shell. "So how was your trip?"

Karol Ladka gulped the tender Little Neck and assumed a pained expression. "Pain in the ass," he said as he chewed. "This is lousy weather for helicopter travel. What about you?"

Banning shrugged. "Boring. No newspapers. The boat's concession stand was closed."

"Well, look at it this way. It can only get better when we meet with Harmwell. He's never boring."

"Let's hope not."

The waiter returned, reached across the counter, and set a paper placemat, a tiny three-tined fork, and a large tented napkin in front of Carter. He added a small bowl of Oysterettes, a silver eggcup filled with horseradish, and an open bottle of Tabasco. "Cocktail sauce comes along with the clams," he said. "Be right out with the iced tea. That was Sweet 'n Low, right?"

Carter Banning nodded…and General Karol Ladka held up his near-empty glass. "Better refill my lemonade while you're at it," he said, "…and how's the cherry pie?" The waiter winked his recommendation and took 'James Weiss's' glass into the noisy kitchen.

Carter munched on one of the crisp, round crackers and said to Ladka, "This is a busy little town. Where does one park one's helicopter in a joint like this?"

Karol finished the last of his Little Necks and grinned. "In the only available parking spot you'll ever find in Port Jefferson. And it's right around the corner from Harmwell's office…the Fire Department parking lot."

"What?"

"Made a deal with the Chief," said Ladka. "He lets us use his lot…my pilot flies Santa Clause in from Macy's at two o'clock." Karol smiled coyly, leaned toward Carter, and murmured, "Nobody thinks for a minute there's a CIA operative hitchhiking with Jolly Old Saint Nick."

* * * * *

BANNING AND LADKA LEFT The Steamroom at twelve-thirty. The men trudged south on Main Street for five minutes, and soon saw the well-lighted marquee of Theatre Three ahead on the west side of the road. Noting Carter's surprised expression, Karol Ladka explained that the landmark playhouse, a one-hundred-year-old operating fixture in the waterside village, was lit-up seven days a week…even when, as today, there was no performance scheduled. "Hugh Harmwell knows the power of advertising," he said.

Around the corner from Theatre Three was the largest building in town…a two-story brick edifice that housed the proud Port Jefferson Fire Department, founded in 1887. Four double bays on the cubic structure's ground floor held the PJFD's fleet of gleaming red pumpers, rescue vehicles, a tanker, and a ladder truck whose reach was easily twice the height of any building in the three-hundred-year-old community.

On the department's high-ceilinged second level were the meeting, training, and recreation rooms that served the 107-member organization. Lined up at the ready on the east side of the building...and prepared to roll at a moment's notice... were three gold-leafed, predominantly white, SUV Chiefs' Cars. Virtually every Port Jefferson child longed to command one of the brightly lighted vehicles one day, but on this Christmas afternoon, the main attraction for a group consisting primarily of a few dozen men and boys, was General Ladka's ride in from Reagan National Airport.

The all-black helicopter sat grandly in the middle of the Fire Department's broad parking lot, its five long rotor blades drooping and turning lazily in the breeze that blew steadily from the Long Island Sound. Soon the chopper would make the brief trip to pick up Santa at Macy's in the Smith Haven Mall.

Carter and Karol crossed Main Street, and entered the Theatre Three lobby through one of the long, wood-framed glass doors. A cardboard sign pinned to the curtain inside the box office window read:

Open Sat. Dec. 26
10:00 AM
Merry Christmas To All!

"That's our cue," Ladka said. "In we go." And he knocked three times on the locked interior door.

Like the theater's box office window, the row of tall, glass-paneled doors that separated the beautifully restored playhouse from the unpretentious lobby, were each lined with a pair of pleated, opaque curtains. The semitransparent draperies were gathered top and bottom on three-foot rods, effectively permitting anyone inside the darkened mezzanine to observe those in the vestibule, while remaining obscured themselves.

After a ten-second wait, Karol Ladka was preparing to knock on the center beveled glass door once again, when the curtains lining its interior slowly parted…revealing the distinctive, rosy face of five-foot-nine Hugh Harmwell.

Carter Banning had not been prepared for the apparition that appeared in the narrow space where the man's thumbs held the curtains eight or nine inches apart. The square-visaged fellow sported as unlikely an image as any Carter might have expected…it was not at all the plain look he'd supposed a secret agent would wear. Indeed, Hugh Harmwell's appearance was just the opposite of ordinary…his face was downright unforgettable! From the fluffy, four-inch muttonchops that framed his sculpted cheeks and jaw…to the aquiline nose pointing down menacingly toward his narrow lips and determined chin…the man with the dusky brows and even darker, unblinking eyes presented an almost haunting mask of a face.

On further reflection, however, the septuagenarian from Southwick immediately revised his estimate of the man peering out from the darkened theater—the quiet, hallowed place that was his sanctuary. Yes, Carter could understand how this fellow with the chiseled features…this esteemed actor/writer/director… might well successfully assume any role assigned to him.

Even by the CIA.

The door opened halfway. "Inside!" Harmwell ordered with a sweep of his hand, projecting his resonant, confident voice out of habit. The man was obviously accustomed to being instantly obeyed. "I saw your interesting aircraft," he said, re-locking the lobby door, adjusting the curtain, and ushering his visitors along one of two aisles sloping toward the dim-lit stage. "A clever touch, the helicopter, if I do say so, Karol." He stopped at the sixth row and led his guests into the approximate center of the orchestra section…where they all sat side-by-side…Harmwell in the middle.

"Perhaps you could assist our Props Manager in securing one of those impressive birds to open our modern dress version of 'Macbeth.' We're doing it outdoors…in June."

Harmwell's perfect diction bespoke refinement and civility, Carter Banning thought. And he looked every inch the 19th Century *bon vivant*. But there was an indefinable something about the barrel-chested man that disturbed him. Was it the vest he wore?…the arm-garters at his biceps that bloused those loose-fitting shirtsleeves? The severe black satin ascot? Carter had always associated men thus attired with saloon musicians, poker dealers, or snake oil salesmen. Individuals of less than sterling reputation. That must be it, Banning decided. Hugh Harmwell was so accustomed to performing in 19th Century roles that even the appearance common to the eighteen hundreds had become a part of his artistic persona.

* * * * *

ALONE IN THE DARKNESS of the empty theater…all of its five hundred upholstered seats empty except for the three that the men occupied…Ladka, Banning, and Harmwell had an unobstructed view forty feet in every direction. Clearly, they were alone. A single, 100-watt lightbulb burning atop a six-foot wooden pole in the middle of the stage was the principal source of illumination in the old playhouse…that, and two red 'Exit' signs over doors left and right of the elevated stage. A little ambient light seeped through the curtained doors that defined the lobby behind them.

They spoke in hushed tones, continually scanning the dim surroundings as they did so.

Harmwell turned to his right. "Have you told Carter of his neighbor friend's involvement in this incident?"

Carter answered for him. "Yes. The General and I discussed it at lunch."

The director turned toward him. "And have you any reason to suspect this Wilkinson chap of untoward activity...terrorist activity, to be specific?"

"I suspect everybody," said Banning. "All the time."

"How long have you known the young man?" Harmwell asked.

"Since he was born," Carter answered. "Twenty five...twenty-six years."

"Then you probably know he has no criminal record," said Hugh Harmwell. "His college career appears to be an exemplary one."

"So I'm told," said Banning.

Harmwell frowned and folded his arms. "You decoded the Istanbul letter, Major. What's your interpretation of our friend Mujab Baghdadi's statement that he plans to 'use' Peter Wilkinson...and then order his death?"

"I haven't the foggiest," said Carter. "I'm a cryptologist...not a mind reader."

"But you're also one of only three living persons—Mrs. Banning, Mary Wilkinson, and yourself—who have been in a position to observe Peter's development over the years."

"You're forgetting his father, Carter said. "Maynard Price. He deserted the family in 2009...when Peter was in high school."

Hugh Harmwell glanced at Karol Ladka, and turned back to Carter. "We know about Price," he said. "He was murdered three years ago...in Bimini...while Peter was on spring break...in Fort Lauderdale."

Carter Banning chewed his lip, mulling the new information in silence. Ten seconds later he said, "And of course authorities in The Bahamas have no clue."

"None," said Harmwell.

"And you think I should look into the matter."

"Might help if we knew the details. Don't you agree?"

Banning looked to his old friend Karol Ladka, who was studying his fingernails. "Okay, Karol, give it to me straight. Do you really expect me to untangle a three-year-old murder…in Bimini…one that may or may not be connected with suspected Iraqi terrorists…in New Haven…and Istanbul…and God knows where else?"

General Ladka spoke for the first time since they'd entered the theater. "Take as long as you want," he shrugged. "But we have reason to think this needs to be wrapped up by New Year's."

"That's seven days, Karol! Jesus!"

Harmwell looked at his watch. "Six and a half, Major Banning…today's half over."

Chapter Twenty-five

AT THE CONCLUSION of the two-hour meeting with Hugh Harmwell...as soon as Ladka's pilot had ostentatiously delivered Santa to the Chief and the assembled Port Jefferson citizenry in the crowded Fire Department parking lot...The General and Carter Banning climbed virtually unseen aboard the Sikorsky helicopter...and the big bird took off over The Sound.

Carter had turned in an Academy Award-winning performance this morning, telling his wife that he and his Basal Cell Carcinoma removal procedure were to be featured in an obscure medical journal published by Stony Brook University Hospital. To his profound amazement, Elizabeth had approved of his contribution wholeheartedly...even on Christmas Day. He would never... ever...understand women!

The twenty-minute flight to Bridgeport's Sikorsky Memorial Airport would enable Carter to retrieve his car from the ferry lot about a mile from the field and be home in time for dinner with the girls...grown bachelorettes of 44...if they didn't mind waiting for him until six o'clock. Of course Elizabeth said they would happily do so.

The brief trip would also provide ample time, and above all a private venue, for Banning's debriefing. And as far as Carter was concerned, there was some serious debriefing to be done.

First and foremost, he wanted to know more about this strange fellow at Theatre Three in Port Jefferson. His sterling credentials relative to writing, performing, and directing drama were beyond questioning. The former Army cryptologist fully accepted that. But how did those attributes qualify him for clandestine participation as a CIA operative? No two professions could be more dissimilar, he'd suggested to Ladka.

"Not really," Karol Ladka hollered above the annoying high frequency blare of the Sikorsky's tail rotor. He leaned closer to Carter's ear and made a megaphone of his cupped hands. "All of us in this business are actors if you stop to think about it."

"But where did he come from?" Carter yelled.

"Actor's Studio," Ladka bellowed. "Father was a friend of Lee Strasberg."

"Then he was successful on the Broadway stage."

"No. He hated it."

"I don't get it."

Karol raised his voice half an octave. "He hated so-called 'Method Acting.'"

"So he wound up here in the suburbs."

"Right. Hugh's a drama purist. He made Theatre Three what it is."

Carter Banning frowned and he gazed out the reinforced side window of the sturdy military aircraft. Both men seemed in deep thought as the black MH-65 skimmed low over the whitecaps of Long Island Sound.

"You don't like him," yelled Ladka.

"Don't necessarily dislike him," Carter responded.

"What, then?"

"Dunno," shouted Carter. "Lemme sleep on it."

But by the time they'd touched down at Memorial Airport's asphalt Helipad Number One, Carter Banning had pinpointed what it was about celebrated thespian Hugh Harmwell that bothered him.

The two old friends debarked from the multi-million-dollar Dolphin helicopter. They would meet here at the airport terminal again in the morning. Karol Ladka was booked into the Hampton Inn in nearby Milford. If Carter had to contact him beforehand, he'd be registered under the name Harry Iniduoh. "Easy to remember, it's…"

"I know," said Carter, "…it's Houdini…spelled backwards." He gave Ladka a look. "You don't have to be much of a cryptologist to figure that one, General."

"See you at ten," Karol said.

"Ten," said Carter. "Merry Christmas." And he climbed into a taxi that the pilot had called for while in flight. The cab would take him to the Bridgeport Ferry slip, and from there, he'd have an hour's drive home for Christmas dinner.

Chapter Twenty-six

IT WAS NINE AM ON SATURDAY, traditionally one of the slowest days of the year. Regardless of one's age, occupation, or interests, it seems the day after Christmas is a time to sleep late, kick back, and dine on leftovers if and when the spirit moves you.

But in the Emergency Room of the Southwick VA Hospital, Doctor Meili Song was worried…frustrated…and contrary to her long held religious beliefs, even angry.

These past few days had become particularly irritating for the conscientious Dermatologist. Granted, she was unmarried, and thus not terribly inconvenienced by the restrictions imposed by the elevated Terrorism Alert Level she was now working under. None of her relatives lived in the United States, so they would certainly not be affected by America's heightened TAL. Her mother, father, and her only sibling…a sister…still lived in coastal Shandong Province, south of Beijing. There, her parents both worked as government clerks, and 37-year-old Ling taught at the Shandong University of Traditional Chinese Medicine, in Jinan.

They would know of Meili's situation only when they viewed China Central TV news reports. Like Meili, the family was

Buddhist. For them, and their 400 million fellow believers, it would not be as if a major holiday…like Vesakha, the birthday of Buddha…was being disrupted by this Radical Islam threat. Indeed, the sad truth was that people the world over were becoming inured to such international coercion by merchants of disaster. From Oklahoma City…to Beirut…to Paris…and Orlando…the world's inhabitants were growing hardened to the prospect of sudden catastrophe. Even those gentlest of all people, the Mahayana Buddhists, wondered on occasion if they might have misjudged the adherents of Islam.

Still, it was annoying to be so isolated…so helpless.

Meili had been unable to get in touch with Carter Banning Thursday night…apparently he'd turned off his cell phone as soon as Karol Ladka had told him the specifics of the morning's Port Jefferson rendezvous. Then, on Friday, Christmas, all non-emergency outgoing calls from the Southwick VAMC had been embargoed…as had discretionary departures from the complex, either vehicular or on foot.

As far as Doctor Song knew, Carter would be spending the day a mere couple of miles distant as the crow flies, blissfully luxuriating in the consumption of roast turkey and dressing… egg nog and mincemeat pie.

As for Amanda Bragg, she was understandably incommunicado…probably still sound asleep at this hour… undoubtedly just happy to be alive. Surely someone would be looking out for her.

Maybe I worry too much, Meili Song thought. And she returned to her reading of the Academy of Dermatology Journal.

* * * * *

BY TEN O'CLOCK on Saturday morning, Carter was seated inconspicuously inside quiet Memorial Airport's modest terminal in Bridgeport. As Ladka had suggested, Banning had parked his Volvo within a stone's throw of the little facility's main door, and there, the US Chief of Cryptology now exited a taxi and discreetly entered the long, low building.

Both men were dressed in unspectacular, casual clothing. Carter wore denim pants and a five-year-old red, white, and blue New York Giants football jacket...one that Ladka had once given the inveterate Patriots fan as a joke...and Karol sported a plaid woolen shirt, padded nylon vest, and khaki chino slacks. Neither man had shaved today.

The pilot of their MH-65 helicopter had arrived an hour earlier, and had long since conducted his meticulous pre-flight examination of the sleek Dolphin. He had also filed his flight plan which indicated that the MH-65 would be flying under Visual Flight Rules to Bader Field in Atlantic City. There, he would refuel and proceed, also VFR, to Savannah/Hilton Head International Airport. From Savannah, the chopper would continue to Jacksonville, then West Palm Beach...and finally, Grand Bahama International Airport, in Freeport.

This projected itinerary information was required of all non-military pilots flying civilian aircraft in US airspace...but the operator of General Ladka's helicopter was, in fact, an Air Force Lieutenant Colonel, and he was commanding a USAF version of the Sikorsky Dolphin. The craft was equipped with the latest and most exotic avionics available...and was valued overall at a cool $19 Million.

Banning and Ladka weren't going anywhere near Atlantic City, Florida, or The Bahamas, of course. That was merely diversion for Hugh Harmwell's benefit. No covert agent of the CIA worth his salt would announce his proposed whereabouts in advance. "I'm taking you back to college," said Karol Ladka. "Specifically to Yale, my friend." He grinned coyly. "How's your knowledge of 'Historic Preservation' these days, Carter?"

* * * * *

LIKE MANY AIRPORTS on the east coast, Tweed-New Haven Regional occupies a neck of land that juts well out into the adjacent coastal water. In the case of HVN, the main runway, two-zero, points almost directly south toward the widest part of Long Island Sound. There, the hundred-foot-deep, thirty-mile-wide span separates the Connecticut coastline from The Island's rocky North Shore.

It was over this broad salt water estuary that General Karol Ladka's Dolphin, after departing Memorial Airport in Bridgeport, approached southern Connecticut. The chopper was bearing down on Tweed-New Haven on a low trajectory…unannounced… well aware that, like hot air balloons and gliders, helicopters have right-of-way priority over fixed wing aircraft. Any plane overtaking the slower moving Dolphin would be required to bear to starboard and remain well clear of the helicopter.

Ladka and Banning sat on opposite sides of the MH-65's fuselage. Both men peered in opposite directions through their side windows, ready to inform the pilot instantly of any approaching traffic. Actually the Dolphin's 'wrap around' radar feature would automatically detect aircraft oncoming from any angle, and its GPS advisory would instantly suggest the most appropriate course alterations available.

Still, sneaking into an airport where the tower doesn't expect you is a nerve wracking business. Air traffic controllers are called that for a reason. When their controlling role is overridden, safety is always compromised.

Karol Ladka and Carter Banning had discussed all of this in the virtually empty terminal at Sikorsky Municipal before leaving Bridgeport. The diversionary maneuver that involved filing the bogus flight plan to The Bahamas…the Dolphin's initial takeoff headed south toward Atlantic City…and the aerial U-turn over Fire Island that aimed the big black bird toward its true destination, Connecticut's sleepy little NHV Regional—two miles from Yale University.

Ladka had also informed Carter of the reason for the clandestine maneuvering: Hugh Harmwell was not to be trusted!

The Pentagon had known for some time that he was what is commonly known as a double agent. The renowned theater impresario was perfectly willing to accept the CIA's off-the-books $200,000 per year—his fee for ostensibly keeping tabs on Islamic zealots attending nearby Stony Brook University... but Harmwell was also on the ISIS payroll—to the tune of $1 Million annually!

Karol Ladka had long been aware of Maynard Price's murder in Bimini, though he had only recently learned that Peter Wilkinson was the assassinated man's son. The significance of that connection became apparent when CIA operatives at Yale intercepted a communiqué from Harmwell to his fellow ISIS mole, Professor Mujab Baghdadi. The FBI had an agent-Internet repair technician...posing as a student...make a copy of Baghdadi's hard drive.

Thus the Wilkinson-Baghdadi-Harmwell connection quickly became apparent, and a thorough background check of young Peter's friends, family, associates...and most notably, his neighbors...fortuitously produced the name: Carter Banning.

Army records were consulted, and Banning's old boss Karol Ladka was brought into the picture.

"So Harmwell thinks we're headed for Bimini," Carter said.

"Right," Ladka responded. "We're supposed to be following a meaningless lead about a killing that means nothing to us."

"Why did your 'Basil Rathbone' friend set us up that way?"

"Hugh knows we smell a rat with Wilkinson...I literally told him so. He also knows we're onto Baghdadi...I as much as told him that, too. So he wants us out of town. Probably until he and his raghead buddy can pull off whatever it is they're putting the Wilkinson kid up to."

"And then Peter gets his ticket to Paradise," said Carter

"That's what the email says, if our decoding's correct."

"And what about us?"

"We get fed to the sharks in Bimini, naturally."

"Nice," said Carter morosely.

"Except we're not in Bimini…we're comfy cozy right up here in good old New Haven, Connecticut."

Carter nodded and looked at his old friend knowingly. "Not to be a smartass or anything, but I think I had that Harmwell prick figured from the beginning."

"Really? Was it the ascot…or the muttonchops?"

"Neither one. It was Macbeth."

"Macbeth?"

Banning crossed his arms contentedly and smiled as he bobbed his head. "Yeah…it was when Mister Show Business expert, Harmwell, sat right in the middle of his vintage old theater and said, *'our modern dress version of…Macbeth…'*"

Karol Ladka frowned. "And…?"

"It's just not done," said Carter. "That particular Shakespeare play is supposed to be cursed. Actors never pronounce its title inside a theater. Never. They might refer to it as 'The Scottish Play,' or some other euphemism…but they never call it 'Macbeth.'"

"Hadn't heard that," said Ladka. "What happens if somebody slips like our pal Hugh did?"

"Legend has it you're supposed to leave the building, spin around three times, spit, curse, then knock on the door to get back in."

"Giddouddahere!"

"No lie. You can't wish someone 'Good luck' in a theater, either. Gotta say, 'Break a leg.'"

"Damn," said Karol Ladka. "And we think these Muslims are weird!"

Chapter Twenty-seven

FRANK BROGAN HAD GONE against his better judgement on Thursday night, Christmas Eve. The Lieutenant had decided to wait until Saturday to call Motor Vehicles and determine the owner of the banged-up license plate he'd retrieved from Stony Path. At first, he wondered if failing to return the plate immediately to the owner of the vehicle might potentially constitute contributing to a misdemeanor. It was a violation to drive without proper registration affixed to one's automobile, after all. But on further reflection, and considering the communication restrictions in place due to the heightened terror alert, Brogan decided that he could always vouch for the driver in Traffic Court, should a related issue arise before the 26th.

Now it was nearly mid-morning on the day after Christmas, and the Lieutenant had obtained Major Amanda Bragg's name and address from the Motor Vehicle Bureau. At 9:40 he approached her garden apartment building in the Slater's Lake section of Southwick; the residential area opposite The Landing. Bragg's front license plate was in a large brown envelope under the policeman's arm.

As soon as he'd pulled up to the curb at suburban Shirley Court and Sanford Street, Brogan had spotted the rear of the white Buick convertible. It was clearly the same automobile whose driver had asked him for directions to the Wilkinson house on Christmas Eve. He walked to the front of the vehicle and confirmed from the absence of the plate and the condition of the right fender that it must be the car that had sideswiped the tree on Stony Path. The policeman withdrew his small notebook and made an entry.

Gripping the envelope that held 'Mandy' Bragg's dented front plate, Frank Brogan rang the doorbell of Apartment 12-B. A bustling sound inside told him that the occupant must be somewhat indisposed…but at least Amanda Bragg was at home.

"Major Bragg?" Frank Brogan called through the wooden front door, "It's about your accident on Thursday…we've retrieved something from the scene, ma'am."

The Lieutenant heard more activity as apparently a heavy object was pushed across a wooden floor…and shoved against the door with a thud.

Brogan stepped to one side of the doorway and unbuttoned his sport jacket. "Amanda Bragg…Southwick Police…open up, please."

Inside, there was a scraping sound. A drawer was drawn open, Brogan estimated, and the concerned policeman knocked on the door four times rapidly. "Major Bra…"

But before Lieutenant Frank Brogan could say her name, 'Mandy' Bragg was dead…a bullet in her brain…fired from her Army issued nine-millimeter sidearm. The woman had died instantly. The weapon involved was one she'd never fired for effect in fifteen years of military service.

Brogan heard her corpse strike the floor. It was an all-too-familiar sound. One unlike any other in the world, he thought.

He called headquarters for an ambulance…and thrust his shoulder against the barricaded wooden door.

* * * * *

NICOLAI DOUNIAT KNEW ABOUT Amanda Bragg's suicide before Ladka and Banning did. Such was the speed with which non-classified internal military matters were electronically transmitted and made known throughout the world.

Bragg's death was instantly treated as more than just another depressed soldier's way of finding relief in a turbulent world. Everyone these days was interested in details surrounding the rash of suicides that had erupted among American servicemen since the turn of the 21st Century. The sad fact, and one that had driven US armed forces commanders to distraction, was that a tragic milestone had been reached in 2015.

In the twelve months of that year, 185 Army soldiers on active duty had taken their own lives…a number that eclipsed the 176 battle fatalities sustained on the bleak killing fields of Afghanistan during the same period. International communication lines had become abuzz with news of the phenomenon. For whatever reason, the Army's suicide rate had tripled since the year 2000. Major Bragg's was only the most recent in the horrific trend, and to everyone but Peter Wilkinson her case was also the most puzzling.

No one in the chain of command that included Major Amanda Bragg, knew about the insidious game that the radicalized Yale scholar had subjected the field grade officer to. She alone had borne the secret weight of the hit-and-run crime she'd committed at Wilkinson's instigation…and she'd taken that transgression with her to the grave.

At the American Consulate in Istanbul, Douniat regarded the communiqué concerning Bragg's death with suspicion. Granted, suicides among American military personnel had been on the rise, but they were confined almost exclusively to victims of Post-Traumatic Stress Disorder, or soldiers in combat situations. The Deputy Consul General knew that such a high-level officer's taking her own life would be cause for deep concern, and would generate considerable speculation all up and down the line of covert activity...on both sides of the Western/Islamic intelligence front.

Nor was the unease confined to diplomats and the military. Lieutenant Frank Brogan was beginning to sense some sort of strange connection here. The name of Peter Wilkinson appeared all too frequently in the policeman's little notebook, he felt. Its presence could not be merely shrugged off as coincidental involvement in the activities of quiet little Southwick on December 24th, 2015.

Why? First, of course, Peter had been the only witness to a felony.

Then, incredibly, he had clearly identified his own next-door neighbor's vehicle as the 'weapon' now assumed to be that used in a vehicular homicide.

Furthermore, Peter Wilkinson had somehow known the identity of the victim in that tragic accident.

For whatever reason, he'd been implausibly insensitive about the deaths of sixteen students in Istanbul...what's more, he'd lied to Brogan about the maudlin video recording he made... referring to the slaughter in Turkey as 'an accident.'

And finally, Amanda Bragg had been searching for Peter on Christmas Eve...two days before killing herself with a single gunshot wound to the head.

Frank Brogan knew that not one of these factors constituted a crime on Peter Wilkinson's part in and of itself. Indeed, taken individually, none of them could be considered probative of the young man's connection to any wrongdoing. But Lieutenant Francis Xavier Brogan had been a sworn law enforcement officer too long, to discount the weight of accumulated circumstantial evidence. The cop in Frank Brogan told him the smart aleck Ivy League student was up to something, and the Lieutenant was determined to find out what it was.

He was too old a cat to be taught by kittens.

* * * * *

DOCTOR SONG WAS understandably distraught. Even with the limited communication restriction recently imposed on both civilian and military personnel, news of Mandy Bragg's suicide had circulated throughout the Southwick VAMC family like wildfire. Announcement of her advancement to Lieutenant Colonel would have come as no particular surprise, but this…? Shot…? With her own Army-issued handgun…? God! It was unthinkable.

Millie and the other medical personnel who'd treated Amanda for what had already been written up accurately, but euphemistically as, *"Unexplained Ingestion of a Foreign Substance,"* were now on the hot seat. The fatal gunshot would be considered by the medical higher ups an obvious extension of Bragg's earlier attempt to harm herself, and everyone involved in her emergency treatment would have a shitpot full of explaining to do.

One person in the whole convoluted matter seemed to be off the hook, however. It was Peter Wilkinson. Like everyone in town, he had heard almost immediately of Southwick's first suicide in recent memory. Oh, he was disappointed, but his only real regret was the loss of an insider to help expedite the forthcoming attack on the Southwick VA Hospital.

Perhaps he should put off informing Professor Baghdadi of matters with the bitch Major Bragg, Peter thought. Who knew? Cleverly handled this turn of events might even prove fortuitous. Maybe he could manage to find out who Amanda Bragg's replacement as head of the Identification Department would likely be. With a day or two to wheedle his way into his (or her) good graces, it shouldn't be hard to establish himself as the friendly, reliable, local resident that any new appointee would give their right arm to befriend when assigned to an unfamiliar location. Especially in provincial, standoffish New England.

What the radicalized Yale man should have figured, but didn't, was that the 'stone deaf' Mujab Baghdadi, like everyone else in the international Islamic cabal, already knew every detail of Bragg's death…the so-called 'setback' to their scheme. And they too had seen the sudden occurrence as quite possibly representing a fortunate scenario.

With that in mind, and praising Allah effusively, the Islamic collaborators had swiftly decided on two key courses of action: One had to do with selection of a hand-picked double agent to replace the unlucky Major Amanda Bragg…the other involved immediately terminating the increasingly bothersome…and no longer necessary…Peter Wilkinson.

Chapter Twenty-eight

THE CITY OF NEW HAVEN, home to Yale University, sits like a half-circle on the western bank of broad New Haven Harbor, an inlet extending north from Long Island sound. At the approximate center of the west-fanning semi-circle are the several buildings of the vast Ivy League school itself; it is the city's largest employer, taxpayer, and tourist attraction. On the harbor's east bank, and a mile farther south, is tiny Tweed-New Haven regional airport. There, General Karol Ladka and Carter Banning now climbed into an orange and white Metro taxi. Their pilot would wait in the new Sikorsky helicopter for the men's return some four hours hence.

Banning and Ladka had no intention of meeting with Professor Mujab Baghdadi today, or otherwise exposing their presence in the area to him. As far as the radical Islamist knew, the men had been sent by Hugh Harmwell on a wild goose chase and were on their way to far-off Bimini.

Actually, CIA operative Ladka and his old friend were in New Haven merely to familiarize themselves with the city…and in particular the several Mosques where Baghdadi was likely to worship, and which might be expected to provide him with sanctuary in the event he ever required it.

Both men carried credentials that identified them as inspectors with 'Habitat for Diversity,' a non-existent organization, supposedly headquartered in Washington, DC. The group's function was purportedly to assure that all sanctioned religious edifices met government safety standards. A bogus telephone number on the pair's authorization documents would be answered by a trained 'HFD' representative in the Pentagon. One who spoke fluent Arabic.

The first Mosque that Banning and Ladka visited was Masjid Al-Salam on George Street, three blocks west of the manicured Yale campus. It was the nearest Islamic establishment to Baghdadi's Farnam Gardens apartment, thus it was the place he would most likely worship. And to put it bluntly, the place was a dump!

As the taxi pulled to a stop in front of the old, two-story, white clapboard house that served as Mosque Al-Salam, Carter raised his eyebrows and gave his old friend beside him a sidelong look. The place stood on a steep, overgrown, fourteen-foot-high hill close to the street, and was surrounded by a rusting fence that had once been painted a sickly green. Brown fabric blinds were drawn inside all of the peeling structure's long, double-hung windows, and a shallow front porch crammed with outdoor furniture and broken toys ran the width of the place. To one side of the shabby house was a similar structure that appeared to be vacant…on the other side was a long narrow parking lot that was more like a series of potholes separated by strips of cracked asphalt. A dozen cars were parked close to a side storm door; none of the vehicles appeared to be less than ten years old.

"Wonder if we're in time for Vespers?" said Karol. And he handed the cabbie a ten-dollar bill.

"Maybe we should have him wait," Carter murmured. "This doesn't look exactly like the Mosques I remember in Istanbul."

Karol Ladka winked and opened his door. "Islam's come a long way since then, my friend."

Carter shrugged. "If you say so." He got out of the cab. "Can hardly wait for the Christmas Carols."

Karol led the way up the severely sloping driveway that rose and broadened into the Masjid Al-Salam parking lot. Fifteen or sixteen apparent worshipers were exiting the side door of the Mosque and hastening toward their cars. Carter Banning wondered if the man whose communiqué he'd decrypted was one of them. If indeed Mujab Baghdadi was among the faithful departing the mid-morning *Salat*, or Muslim worship, he was a far cry from Carter's image of a typical Yale professor.

Based on the little he knew of Middle Eastern historians... and Iraqis in particular, the former Army cryptologist had drawn a mental image of Baghdadi as a tall, densely bearded scholar...a well-dressed man, probably in his fifties...of ruddy complexion...with dark brown eyes, black hair, and dazzling white teeth.

But no such person emerged from the Mosque on George Street following this Saturday's 10:30 *Salat*. Of the roughly twelve men and four women departing the ramshackle building, no one was taller than five-foot-six, the men sported only light, spotty beards, and none of the worshipers was older than thirty-five.

Additionally...though all were brown-eyed, flashed typically brilliant smiles, and had dark skin and hair...these congregants were hardly what might be termed 'middle class.' The men wore patched trousers for the most part, and dark, high-neck sweaters under wrinkled woolen jackets. The only splashes of color in the group were the rose and green hijab, or head scarves that two young girls wore. Their mothers were dressed all in black.

As Banning and Ladka neared the Mosque's side door, Carter looked at Karol and rolled his eyes. *No Professor Mujab Baghdadi here!* his skeptical glance seemed to say.

However, Karol Ladka was not so sure.

CIA Identification had provided The General with a recent photograph of Baghdadi secretly taken in Yale's *Mat'am*, or

Islam-correct cafeteria, where, the bizarre dietary restrictions of mostly slovenly visiting academics from a dozen different Islamist countries could be accommodated. The man in the photograph appeared to be in his early forties, bore a short, scruffy beard, and had bad teeth. His plain cotton *taqiyah* skull cap failed to conceal the fact that the professor was bald. He was standing in line at the *Mat'am's* steam table, and if the photo was any indication, Baghdadi was about five-foot-six. He wore loose-fitting trousers, sandals, and a white shirt with long, bloused sleeves and a modified Nehru collar. It was buttoned at the neck, and like the pants, the shirt badly needed pressing.

"I've got a feeling our man might prefer this environment," Ladka muttered looking left and right. And with that, the door on which he had knocked was slowly eased open.

In the doorway a smiling young man stood before the two Americans. He was obviously Mosque Al-Salam's *Imam*. The fellow was a good six feet tall, and wore a long black *Dishdasha*—the equivalent of a priest's cassock, Banning noted—but with accented white stripes around the sleeve's cuffs and biceps. His head was thick with tight black curls and he wore no cap. The cleric placed his palms together, and holding his fingertips to his chin, bowed slightly and said, *"Salam marhaba."*

Karol nodded and reached into his back pocket for the document that identified Carter and him as 'Habitat for Diversity' agents. "Hello," he said. "We'd like to speak with the *Imam*," and he held his ID card at eye level.

The tall man stepped to one side immediately and he swept a hand toward the interior of the Mosque. "Come in...please... welcome. I am *Imam* Ali Aziz."

Banning and Ladka stepped inside the building's musty kitchen where a pre-pubescent girl was busily washing several pairs of plastic flip-flops in the sink. The *Iman* snapped his fingers, and the child quickly dried two pairs of the thongs with a filthy towel. She held them in front of Carter and Karol, her head bowed submissively.

With a smile, Karol accepted two of the sandals, and Carter followed suit. They slipped off their shoes as the *Imam* nodded his approval, and they gingerly replaced them with the still-damp flip-flops.

"It is customary to first pay homage to Allah when initially entering Masjid Al-Salam," said *Imam* Ali Aziz. "Kindly follow me."

The inside of the Mosque wasn't much of an improvement over the outer façade. The house's inner walls and ceilings had been torn out, reducing it, with the exception of the kitchen, an adjoining bathroom, and an overhead bedroom, to one large, single-story room fifteen feet high. Only four fat candles illuminated the dim interior of the building. The heavy candlesticks were positioned at what Carter assumed were the four points of the compass because the largest and highest candle was green…Mohammed's favorite color…and it was glowing at the point that Carter had calculated must be east—the direction of Mecca from New Haven.

The tall cleric dropped to his knees and lowered his head until his brow touched the floor. Apparently *Imams* were exempt from removing their shoes.

The floors of the Mosque were covered with a crazyquilt pattern of different sized faux Persian carpets, and extending from the wall separating the Prayer Room from the kitchen, was a large porcelain tub with a working spigot and drain. This was for the convenience of the more diligent faithful who followed the dictum that washing the body should always precede prayer.

As with every religion in the second millennium, Banning figured, there must be those who rationalized matters and claimed justified exceptions. The tub looked like a toilet in a roadside gas station that hadn't been scrubbed in months. Surely Allah would understand one's taking a pass on submitting to ritual washing… *wudu*…prior to prayer in such circumstances.

In front of the Mecca Candle was a foot-high plywood platform the size of a twin bed. There *Imam* Ali Aziz held forth leading the congregation five times a day in prayer. As with the Roman Catholic Church until the mid-twentieth century, the Iman prayed with his back to his devout followers. He couldn't very well turn it on the Holy City in Saudi Arabia.

Carter made a 360-degree scan of the dilapidated place dominated by its two rows of tall windows, upper, and lower. *Come to think of it,* He said inwardly...*this place reminds me a lot of the Sistine Chapel.* He'd seen the famous old barn of a room in Rome when assigned to military duty in Italy, and had been singularly disappointed in the place where Michelangelo had painted some of his finest works. Sacrilegious though it may be to observe, except for its size and fancy frescos, the dark hall where the Cardinals met to elect popes wasn't a far cry from Masjid Al-Salam!

Banning and Ladka stood in their damp flip-flops waiting for *Imam* Ali Aziz to finish the compulsory preface to speaking with them. Finally, he stood and they followed him back to the kitchen. The pre-teen had finished rinsing the sinkful of sandals and they were lined-up on a drain board to dry. She speedily arranged three plastic chairs in a triangle for her father and his guests, and at his command dashed outside to sweep the steps.

The *Imam* offered Carter and Karol tea, which they declined, then he asked Ladka what he could do for them.

"'Habitat' is aware of Islam's rapid growth in the area," he began.

Ali Aziz smiled and nodded approvingly. "Praise be to Allah," he said.

"But our organization is concerned about the possibility of over-crowding in your people's many Mosques."

The cleric frowned and held up his hands as if in surrender. "I can assure the great United States gover..."

"Not at all," Ladka purred with a reassuring waggle of his head. "It would appear that Mosque Al-Salam presents no problem. But your membership roster, *Imam*. We must examine it, and then we can leave. Please hurry."

Imam Ali Aziz dashed up a narrow wooden staircase and into a similarly slender open doorway, where he disappeared from view. Banning and Ladka clearly heard him scurrying across the floor overhead. After a brief pause, the man could be heard retracing his hurried steps, and he soon darted back down the stairs.

The *Imam* grinned and waved two pages of names stapled together; each name was handwritten in both Arabic and English. "Our members," he announced proudly…and extended the list toward Karol.

"Aha," said Ladka. He took the roster and scanned first one page, then the other. He noted that the names, each of which was numbered, totaled thirty-three…they were not in alphabetical order…and all were men.

Number thirty on the list was 'Mujab Baghdadi.'

Karol Ladka handed the list back to Ali Aziz and feigned concern. "The women," he said, "…when they are included… and also the children over the age of seven…how many believers might then be in the Prayer Room at any given time?"

The *Imam* nodded that he understood his questioner's apprehension. "Our *Mullah* at the great university," he answered in a lilting, reassuring tone "…the wise Karim el Mofti…may Allah be pleased with him…he has anticipated the question— and solved it." Ali Aziz waved his arm in a wide arc. "The women and girls pray here in the comfort of the kitchen. The door to the Prayer Room is kept open for their convenience." He folded his arms as if to say, *'There…that settles the matter,'* and he added, shaking his head solemnly, "There are never more than fifty worshipers within the Prayer Room."

Karol was incredulous. "All the women and children fit in this kitchen?" he asked.

"It is a fact that during the holy month of Ramadan, some of the younger women may prefer to kneel outside in the parking area. The great *Mullah*…may his name outlive the stars…he has proclaimed it is their choice."

Ladka looked at Carter Banning, shrugged, and stood up.

Carter clapped his knees with his hands and did likewise. He smiled sweetly and said to the *Imam*, "Thanks for the Ull-bay It-shay," he said. "Your place is darling."

Karol Ladka hustled his old friend out of the grungy Mosque, down the driveway, and to the street. "Jesus!" he whispered "…even a Muslim cleric might recognize pig Latin…ever think of that?" They turned east at the cracked sidewalk. "A career cryptologist should know better!"

"Don't be an Ain-pay in the Alls-bay," said Carter.

The men strode in the direction of Yale's distinctive Sterling Library…home of fifteen million volumes! Mujab Baghdadi might be using the massive facility when they got there General Ladka realized, but so what? He and Carter had the advantage on the Islamist. They knew what he looked like, for instance…had a fair idea of his intentions…even had learned where he went to church…and soon they would know what books and other documents he had most recently read.

Furthermore, the Pentagon was already embarked on the hacking of Baghdadi's email and other online accounts…and Nicholai Douniat in Istanbul had the Brits and his double agents closing in on the professor's friends in the UK and Iraq.

But most importantly, the identity of Baghdadi's main contact in Massachusetts, Peter Wilkinson, had been virtually compromised by the deaf professor's easily decoded message…the one that bore his accomplice's name. Now both insurgent moles figured to be undone by…of all people…Peter's 70-year-old neighbor in Southwick.

Ladka had come to New Haven well prepared. With CIA-forged identification in the name 'Mujab Baghdadi,' and clutching a perfectly falsified Borrowing Pass with up-to-date holograph, The General and his long-retired colleague walked quickly along George, to High Street. There they turned left and proceeded three blocks north on the narrow, immaculate, one-way road. In a few minutes they found themselves in a cobblestoned courtyard where the immense fieldstone façade of Sterling Memorial Library dominated the eastern quadrant.

"Wow!" said Branning as he took in the massive Gothic structure. "To think that I've lived a stone's throw from this place for thirty years, and never seen it. Incredible!"

"What's incredible," said Ladka, "…is that some people detest this country so much that they can't wait to destroy institutions like this."

Carter's eyes roamed the vast lawn with its huge granite 'Women's Table,' a fountain in the exact center of the Yale campus. He elbowed Carter and nodded toward the distinctive, low disc that weighed several tons. It was sculptor Maya Lin's tribute to the females who had brought the institution kicking and screaming into the 19th century, when the first women students were admitted to the School of Art in 1837.

"Wonder if our friend Mujab appreciates *this* artistic rendering," said Banning.

"One thing's for sure," Ladka answered. "Like it or not, he'll never be able to blow it up. A hydrogen bomb could go off, and that baby will stay right where it is!"

Carter Banning gritted his teeth at the mention of the unthinkable. As he continued scanning the stately buildings that comprised renowned Yale University, he tried to picture the seared stone skeletons that might survive an atomic blast, but the man simply could not envision such desecration. *Maybe Yale should have a legend like 'Macbeth,' does,* Carter thought. *Perhaps it should be considered bad luck even to mention the uncomfortable words, 'Hydrogen Bomb' within the confines of this majestic old enclave.*

But it would probably take more than an improvised myth to save the imposing institution from Mujab Baghdadi's wrath.

Chapter Twenty-nine

E SPIONAGE IS AN INTERESTING SCIENCE, but an inexact one at best. True, General Karol Ladka and his associates at the Pentagon were adept at keeping tabs on the insurgents that peopled their 'Bad Guys' list, but following the day-to-day activities of counterintelligence operatives was understandably tricky. These moles had to be given a certain amount of discretionary time, or 'slack,' if they were expected to be trusted by the enemy. After all, that misplaced confidence was the glue that held a double agent's sub-rosa operation together.

Thus, on Saturday morning, with no performance of 'A Christmas Carol' scheduled until 8:00 that night, Hugh Harmwell found himself free to spend a private hour in Theatre Three's backstage make-up room. There, having expertly altered his appearance, the newly created Islamic merchant, Adnil Yam, slipped through a side door of the old theater and sauntered down to the Long Island Ferry dock at the foot of Port Jefferson's Main Street. There, he purchased a round-trip ticket to Bridgeport (with cash) and, under the name Yerffej Leznas, made arrangements for a taxi. It would be waiting for him an hour later in Connecticut, and would drive him to New Haven...where he was to meet with Mujab Baghdadi…at, of all places, the threadbare Mosque Masjid Al-Salam on George Street.

As far as the CIA knew, actor/director Hugh Harmwell was still tucked away in his Theatre Three office preparing for his eight-hundredth performance as Ebenezer Scrooge before a sold-out Long Island audience. In actuality however, the radical Islamist was seated on the open rear deck of the ferry, *Grand Republic*, watching the pretty little town of Port Jefferson slowly slip away behind the big, white boat's boiling wake.

* * * * *

NORMALLY, MAJOR AMANDA BRAGG'S FUNERAL would have been a well-coordinated affair involving full military honors, invariably with an Honor Guard salute provided by The Army. Amanda's family and any clergy that the Braggs might deem appropriate would typically have been contacted, and their wishes accommodated…at least to the extent that the Military could provide them. That is what ordinarily would be the case.

But Major Bragg's was far from a typical situation.

In the first place, Amanda had never been married, and had no living next-of-kin on record. Adopted as a child of three, she had no known siblings, and her parents, the last survivors of their line, had perished in a common automobile accident in 1990.

As for her religious persuasion, Bragg was a declared Atheist whose service record indicated her preference for immediate cremation upon her death. There was to be no ceremony, save for any low-key tribute that the military might wish to bestow in the routine conduct of Army practice. In short, Amanda Bragg would simply be gone…her body consumed in a standard Army crematorium…her service record sent to join millions of others at the National Personnel Records Center in St. Louis, Missouri… and her personal possessions divided among any friends and associates who might want them, and could persuade LAS— Legal Assistance Services—of their right to claim them.

To put it plainly, there simply would be no more Amanda Bragg.

But there was one other component in poor Amanda's brief, sad legacy, and it was owned exclusively by Doctor Meili Song. It was the persistent, lingering memory of a name...the name the terrified Major had repeated over and over in her near-catatonic state on Christmas Eve...when she'd tried to kill herself and failed. The first name was Peter—of that Meili was certain—and the second sounded to her like, 'Wilkes.' For some reason, Amanda had been obsessed with this 'Peter Wilkes,' and Meili Song felt it her duty at least to make an attempt to locate the person.

If, indeed, he still lived. He could have been a relative...or a former lover.

She would look into it as soon as the heightened terror alert was lifted. Obviously there was nothing to be done for poor, dead Major Bragg now...except to see her off.

* * * * *

YALE'S STERLING MEMORIAL LIBRARY was operating with a skeleton crew, most of the regular staff having been granted half-pay vacation days during this week between Christmas and New Year's. Even so, many of the librarians and custodians on the job found little to keep them busy on this lazy Saturday in New Haven. Some sat with bag lunches, taking in the balmy, spring-like weather on the half-dozen permanent benches that flanked the Women's Table monument; others took their brisk constitutionals along the restricted Rose Walk between High and Wall Streets.

Karol Ladka and Carter Banning sat at a strategically located bench watching as a steady flow of students and townspeople entered, then left the ornate building. The splendid structure had been built in 1918 with a seventeen million dollar bequest from New York lawyer and Yale alumnus John Sterling. His only proviso was that the library be "...an enduring, useful, and architecturally beautiful edifice." Accordingly, by most accounts, it is Yale's finest landmark.

Banning and Ladka had studied the various computer-enhanced images of Mujab Baghdadi's face and physique provided by the FBI. They knew who they were looking for, and normally, he would have been impossible to miss, his dark, middle-eastern features and requisite beard setting him apart from the mostly pink-cheeked members of the student body. But Yale, like all of the Ivy League universities, was undergoing a virtual sea change of diversity. Both its faculty and its curriculum were taking on the characteristic of a semi-Islamic institution. Everywhere one looked these days there were knots of uncharacteristically shabbily dressed students listening in rapt attention to the urgent and animated pronouncements of some self-proclaimed *Imam*. Still, Ladka and Banning were confident they would spot their man if and when he showed up at the school's academic hub... the Sterling Library.

And at one minute before twelve...he did.

Carter and The General could have staked out Baghdadi at his apartment, but it was situated in a relatively low traffic area of the Yale campus. They would have been much easier to detect positioned outside the single-story complex, they knew. There had been a few drug-related break-ins of late, and residents of Farman Gardens had recently been advised to remain vigilant. Besides, the immediate mission of the two operatives was merely to watch the deaf professor leave the Sterling Library, which he was known to visit once daily...usually at midday. Once the Iraqi spy had departed the building, they would be free to enter and check on his history of book and document use. In no time the CIA, FBI, and Scotland Yard would have an up-to-date profile of Baghdadi's 'academic' interests to mull over.

As Karol Ladka was fond of saying, "You can tell a lot about a man by the things that make him laugh...and even more, by the books he chooses to read."

It was high noon, and as he neared the library it was clear that Mujab Baghdadi was in a hurry. He approached the building from High Street almost at a trot, and he hurried up the ten granite steps while looking at his watch. As their quarry disappeared through one of two arched gothic doorways, Carter looked knowingly at his friend Ladka and said, "Can't be that he's late for class, can it?...school's out 'til January second."

"Mmmm," Karol responded, "Maybe he's late for his sign language lesson...though it's a bit surprising that a profoundly deaf individual should suddenly look at his watch the instant that bell tower started tolling the hour."

"You think he's faking?"

"I do."

"We've got his cell number. We could go in and call him... watch what he does."

"Won't work," said Ladka. "Five'll get you ten he keeps his phone on 'tone' and 'vibrate'...just like I do. I'll bet you do, too."

"Good point," said Banning.

"Better not to spook him. The important thing is we know our friend may be able to hear every word we say. Let him assume we think he's stone deaf. When push comes to shove, that could prove useful, partner."

The two men moved to a different bench. Karol removed his cap...Carter took off his jacket and donned sunglasses.

In a few minutes, Baghdadi emerged through the door he'd entered. He visored his eyes against the midday sun and scanned the parklike quadrangle. Banning and Ladka engaged one another in animated, waggish banter.

Satisfied that the coast was clear, the academic tucked two thin volumes under one arm and strode south on High Street...in the direction of the grubby Masjid Al-Salam mosque.

Immediately, his two observers sprang into action.

In less than ten minutes...with Carter standing watch at the door...General Karol Ladka had presented his credentials to the Head Librarian...taken her to one side...and learned that Professor Mujab Baghdadi had checked out two obscure volumes. Neither had been taken on loan since the end of the Vietnam War. One involved *"...safe transportation and storage of the general purpose explosive, Semtex."* The other was a treatise on *"...detection and concealment of the chemical compound Phosgene..."* the colorless gas that smells innocently like new-mown hay...and which killed a hundred thousand men during World War I.

Chapter Thirty

MASTER SPY AND DOUBLE AGENT Hugh Harmwell exited his taxi in front of Mosque Masjid Al-Salam on George Street just as his underling Mujab Baghdadi arrived at the dilapidated building on foot. The professor crossed the street hurriedly and the two men embraced in a manner typical of Muslim males, and indeed most Middle Eastern men of Islamic faith. *"As-Salaam-Alaikum,"* said Baghdadi.

"And with you," Harmwell answered grudgingly, as he wiped Mujab's kiss from his cheek. "Come. I have no time to waste. Have you obtained the documents?"

Baghdadi grinned and extended the two slender volumes, one in either hand.

"Idiot!" Harmwell snapped. He seized the books and placed them atop one another, their titled covers facing each other. "Inside!" he ordered, and he jerked his head toward Masjid Al-Salam's now-vacant parking lot.

The chastened Baghdadi blushed noticeably and quick-stepped toward the entrance to the mosque, where the young *Imam* held the door ajar. *"As-Salaam-Alaikum,"* the nervous cleric intoned, holding his palms together and bowing.

"Peace be upon you," Harmwell growled, and he added rancorously, "Speak English, for Christ's sake!"

The two insurrectionists swept past the *Imam* into the dim interior of the makeshift prayer room and the tense host quickly closed the exterior door and locked it. "Will you have tea?" he said with an uneasy smile. "Or perhaps Turkish coffee. My wife takes great pride in preparing it to my exacting standards."

"I did not come here to dine," the double agent from Long Island snorted. He turned to Baghdadi. "Are you aware your miserable identity is compromised? Well, are you?"

Baghdadi's breath caught in his throat and his disbelieving eyes grew large and round. "Compr…how compro…?"

"Because of your idiotic code, you reckless ass."

The professor narrowed his eyes, and the *Imam* hastily departed the Prayer Room, leaving the two antagonists to what promised to be a heated confrontation.

"The code was unique," Mujab Baghdadi sniffed. "It combined letters and numbers in such a way as to render the message indecipherable."

"You are an insufferable fool," Harmwell hissed. "Worse still," he thundered, "…you are an overbearing egotist."

Baghdadi averted his eyes. It would be futile to challenge the counterintelligence agent's authority, he knew. The success of ISIS and its recruitment of so-called 'Home Grown' radicals depended entirely on strict adherence to the decrees set forth by the *Mullahs* in Mosul and Tehran. There was no room in the inflexible organization for pardon or forgiveness when mistakes had been made. He lifted his gaze from the frayed Persian carpet on the floor between them, and looking toward Mecca he mumbled the prayer that had been whispered in his ear as a newborn infant:

There is no God but Allah…
And Muhammad is His Messenger

With that, Baghdadi removed his sandals and walked stoically to the rust-stained bathtub that served as the mosque's ablution facility. Slowly, he removed his clothing, piled everything neatly in a plastic basket beside the tub, and climbed into the porcelain purification appliance. As Hugh Harmwell watched patiently, the academic knelt, removed a razor-sharp penknife from the loincloth that modesty dictated he wear…and with it, Mujab Baghdadi quietly cut his own throat in two swift slashes.

The young *Imam* returned carrying two small cups of hot tea from the kitchen. He handed one of the decorative teacups to Harmwell and keeping the other for himself, he sat in the chair that had been Baghdadi's. "Peace be upon you," he said in English, and raised his cup in salute to his guest.

"See that the body is disposed of," muttered the double agent. "Dismember it…and burn it."

The *Imam* sipped his tea. "There is a stone hearth behind the mosque that will suffice. It shall be accomplished as you command."

"See to it!" said Harmwell glancing at his watch. "But first, you will call a taxi."

Chapter Thirty-one

PETER WILKINSON CONSIDERED it strange that his neighbor Carter Banning had found it necessary to be away from home on Christmas Day...and also the day after. Odd! In all his years living in The Landing, Peter had never known the man to be out of town on Christmas...Easter...Mother's Day. Really weird! But then again, the past few days had been replete with oddities, he thought. The most unnerving of them from Peter's standpoint was the intolerable Lieutenant Frank Brogan's constant patrolling of the area since Amanda Bragg's suicide.

Equally unusual...or nearly so...was the fact that Professor Baghdadi had failed to maintain contact with him during the critical past two days. Peter was eager to report to his mentor that everything was in readiness for the day after New Year's... and the annihilation of the VA hospital's returning medical staff. As planned, Peter had thoroughly scouted the vast facility on the past week's daily jogging treks. He had reconnoitered every available route in and out of the exposed HVAC array where huge ventilation and air conditioning units occupied much of Building 200. Access to their constantly rotating intake fans from the golf course had been a snap!

As directed, he'd stacked the two hundred pounds of Phosgene pellets, the size and shape of golf balls in their thin plastic containers, adjacent to the six-foot-high fan housing. That structure was practically obscured behind the seventh fairway maintenance shed, which, in turn, was alongside the fairway's grassy expanse where everything smelled like new-mown hay...even in early winter. Perfect! All that was left for young Wilkinson to do was to inform Dr. Mujab Baghdadi...wherever he was...that the plan had been set in motion: The Phosgene had been delivered...Peter had placed it as directed...the pellets would ultimately disintegrate when and where anticipated...and the residue would trickle into the HVAC system on schedule.

Peter checked the time: 7:30. He got out of bed and looked toward the lake. There was that goddam Brogan cruising down Stony Path again. *Doesn't he ever take a day off?*

A few hundred yards away, Elizabeth Banning was preparing to depart with her daughters for Sunday Mass at St. Stephen's. For the third successive day Carter would be leaving to meet with the cancer research people on Long Island, and his wife was thankful that at least she'd had the girls for company. Carter was to be the guest lecturer at today's meeting, which was scheduled for early afternoon at the Stony Brook Oncology Center. Had it not been for the fact the girls were returning to Saratoga and Philadelphia in the afternoon, she would love to have attended.

Of course the 'event' at the famed teaching hospital was still another innocent ruse. Under no circumstance was Elizabeth to be burdened with the true knowledge of her husband's deep involvement in what was, at best, a dangerous counter-espionage project. That was Carter's proviso. His only other stipulation was that his wife of forty years, though she was a healthy 65-year-old with all her faculties intact, would not be required to spend more than two successive nights alone.

General Karol Ladka had given his word. In view of the fact that the Baghdadi communiqué had been decoded, revealing that the Wilkinson boy was involved with the Iraqi somehow,

Karol had also arranged for round-the-clock surveillance of the Banning home on Stony Path…and constant observation of the nearby Wilkinson and Turbish residences as well.

To that end, a three-member squad of seasoned Navy SEALS disguised as vacationing fishermen was already on-site at Slater Lake. Equipped with Federal Conservation Department credentials should they be needed, they occupied a less-than-elaborate camper near the *cul-de-sac* at the southern perimeter of Stony Path. Lieutenant Brogan and his staff had been notified that the out-of-town landowner and his friends would be visiting his property temporarily. If Brogan suspected any sort of clandestine activity, he didn't say so. Had the local boys in blue known the electronic reconnaissance capacity of the innocent looking vehicle, they would have been stunned; had they any idea of the team's combined firepower capability, the Southwick cops would have been envious in the extreme!

One of the SEALS posed as a uniformed Special Delivery mailman with a motorbike. His function was to bring daily messages replete with apologies and humorous anecdotes from Carter on The Island. The agent had been advised by Banning as to the exact time of day when Elizabeth should receive the notes. Any indication of irregularity in her normal daily routine was to be instantly conveyed to her husband and he himself would telephone to verify her safety.

Few private citizens had ever been afforded such thorough security. Elizabeth Banning was as safe as a baby in a cradle.

* * * * *

AT ONE O'CLOCK MUJAB BAGHDADI hadn't returned from wherever it was he had gone after leaving the Sterling Library. Units from Bradley Airport's military drone reconnaissance team at the Windsor Locks facility were positive…he had not been anywhere near his apartment since eleven-thirty. It was time, a skeptical Karol Ladka thought, to find out what Hugh Harmwell was up to. And Banning and Ladka were in luck as they met in Tweed-New Haven Airport's modest coffee shop. There, The General received an urgent tweet.

One of Ladka's occasional informants, an itinerant Digital Technician whiz named Albert Tremaine, had observed Harmwell on the return trip to Long Island from Bridgeport on the *Grand Republic*. The twentysomething fellow had been homeward bound from a conference with one of his clients in Hartford—the Wadsworth Atheneum. He had recently developed an App for use by the Wadsworth...the nation's oldest public art museum. The clever Application's sole function was to trigger a flashing

"REWARD...STOLEN...REWARD"

alert on any user's ordinary smart phone when an item containing an embedded, constantly oscillating 'Swipe Chip' (also of Tremaine's invention) was detected within seventy yards. The message then flashed:

"REWARD...CONTACT LAW ENFORCEMENT...REWARD"

The need for such an app on phones carried by the famed museum's guards was obvious. Small art works had been concealed from view and stolen by professional thieves despite the fact that each of the Wadsworth's fifty thousand art objects bore one of Albert's microscopic chips. Clearly, the concealed 'Swipe Chip' was only as effective as the ability to detect it. And young Tremaine's new supplemental invention provided the answer to the Atheneum's dilemma. Parenthetically, it was going to make Albert very rich indeed.

Unknown to Hugh Harmwell and his cabal, a few thousand of the vast Sterling Memorial Library's books...chosen at random without regard to subject, age, or value...had been outfitted with the sensitive chip by Yale curators on a trial basis. By pure happenstance, one such equipped volume was titled *"...detection and concealment of the chemical compound Phosgene..."* and Hugh Harmwell had been reading it as the *Grand Republic* churned from its berth in doughty old Bridgeport...headed for Long Island's charming Port Jefferson harbor.

It was precisely then that Albert Tremaine received an alert on his Samsung Galaxy phone and arranged 'accidentally' to brush against the oblivious Harmwell. In doing so Albert noted the book's interesting title, and decided to call his Army friend. Tremaine excused himself profusely for jostling the man with the two old musty-looking volumes...and he made his way to the rest room in the big ferry's bow. He locked the door behind him...and sent his message to aakkddaall@aol.com:

unknown party—heavily disguised—modest stature
carries interesting book
subject: Phosgene
arriving Port Jeff 2:10—Cross-Sound Ferry
advise

General Ladka had been engaged in espionage long enough to get the picture instantly.

NFIA

he returned the communication. The acronym meant, 'No Further Immediate Action.' The last thing Karol wanted to chance now was to alert Harmwell that he might be under suspicion.

It was apparent to Ladka what must have happened. Baghdadi had checked out two books at Sterling Memorial—Ladka and Banning already knew that. The professor had no doubt taken the contraband volumes in question to the Masjid Al-Salam mosque on George Street...the direction he'd walked when leaving the Yale campus. The only scenario under which the Phosgene book could have found its way into the possession of a 'heavily disguised' party...of 'modest stature'...heading to Port

Jefferson...was if Baghdadi had given it to such an individual... and that person had to be Hugh Harmwell!

For obvious reasons, Harmwell had conducted this transfer of the damning documents without notifying Ladka. No indication of the dramatist's duplicity could have been more compelling. It appeared that Agent Harmwell wasn't as smart as he was cracked up to be.

Karol's conviction was sealed in his already suspecting mind immediately. Furthermore, the element of surprise was now his entirely...and as The General was well aware, it could be a powerful tool. Ladka and Banning would surprise 'Scrooge' as he'd never been shocked before. The bombshell would take place where and when Hugh Harmwell least expected it—inside Theatre Three—during the Sunday matinee of 'A Christmas Carol.'

But the timing was critical.

Harmwell would be arriving at the North Shore ferry dock with plenty of opportunity to get to Theatre Three and change into his 'Ebenezer Scrooge' costume. It might be close, but the show would certainly not begin without its star. At any rate, performances...particularly matinees...never started exactly on schedule, especially during holidays. The double agent had planned this whole situation very well indeed.

The timely arrival of Ladka and Banning in Port Jefferson might present more of a problem, however.

Ideally, Karol's helicopter should fly across Long Island Sound on a course well east of Tweed/New Haven so as not to be observed from the Bridgeport ferry. Once over Lake Ronkonkoma near the geographical center of The Island, the MH-65 Dolphin should turn 180 degrees and approach Port Jeff undetected from the south.

But it was a strategy easier conceived than executed. In the first place, the big Fire Department parking lot was out of the question as a destination. It was virtually in the side yard of Theatre Three, and arriving there could not possibly go unnoticed. Also, any prospective landing north of the Main Street playhouse would be similarly unacceptable.

At nearly one-thirty…time was running out…the sit-down site would have to be decided upon after Ladka and Banning had taken to the air.

As they buckled themselves into the big Sikorsky's jump seats, Carter volunteered what he thought was a feasible alternative. "Why not land in the parking area of that Catholic church just south of the theater?"

Karol looked at him with narrowed eyes. "You think?"

"I *know*," said Banning. "There's nothing in the world deader than a Catholic church on Sunday afternoon. They have the occasional Christening, but not two days after Christmas…trust me."

Ladka keyed his mic and intoned instructions to the pilot who had just fired up the MH-65's two synchronized rotors. "Roger," came the crisp response. "That would be Infant Jesus, General." There was a pause. "What do I tell 'em, Sir?"

Karol Ladka looked at Carter inquiringly. The septuagenarian pushed the mouthpiece on his helmet close to his lips. "They don't need to know we're coming," he said. "But once we're down, if anybody inquires…tell them it's official Knights of Columbus business…tell 'em the pope's on the way…tell 'em anything."

Karol grinned. "You're a brave man, Major Banning. Unless I miss my guess, there's a school at that church. Hope the Pastor doesn't sic Mother Superior on you." He keyed the foam-covered microphone again. "Pedro…one more thing…there's a riding stable nearby…Terryville Equestrian, I believe. Get them on the radio. We'll need two bales of hay delivered to the Theatre Three stage door promptly at 3:30." He looked at a startled Carter Banning and flashed a devilish grin.

"Say again?" said Colonel Avila from the Dolphin's cockpit. "Was that 'hay' as in 'haystack' General?"

"Correct," said Ladka. "Hay…as in 'new-mown hay!'"

Carter looked sidelong at his old friend and covered his microphone with one hand. He mouthed the single word, 'Phosgene?'

Ladka nodded slowly and peered contentedly through the starboard window of the Sikorsky MH-65. Soon the rocky shore of Miller Place came into view, and after that, Lake Ronkonkoma off to the west. From there, the chopper turned on a descending course for the near-empty parking lot of Infant Jesus church in Port Jefferson.

Chapter Thirty-two

PETER WILKINSON DONNED his flannel sweatsuit...the blue and gray one with the large Y on the chest, and the words 'Yale University' in azure blue letters extending down one leg. In the middle of the fourteen-inch-wide chest logo was the profile of a scowling, white bulldog, ironically named 'Handsome Dan.'

Wilkinson was tired of waiting for final instructions from Professor Baghdadi. The man hadn't contacted him since before Christmas, and now that the VA Medical Center had re-opened, albeit with a limited staff, Peter was eager to get the Phosgene project rolling.

He left the house by a side door and jogged down the driveway...onto quiet Stony Path...and there he ran west all the way to Point Grove Road before he'd even begun to breathe hard. Turning north on Point Grove, Wilkinson jogged at a noticeably slower pace along the asphalt surface that bordered Edgewood Golf Links, and in ten or fifteen minutes the tractor shed near where he'd stashed the solidified Phosgene compound came into view.

The golf course had been closed until after New Year's, thus Peter had the green expanse to himself, as he'd assured Mujab

Baghdadi would be the case, and today, he'd decided, was to be a dry run.

The insurrectionist professor had supplied Wilkinson with the cleverly disguised Phosgene 'golf balls' in a number of shipments to his home from operatives at a dummy insecticide facility—Plymouth Rock Chemical—in western Massachusetts. Peter had then concealed the poison alongside Edgewood Links' seventh fairway.

Key to the deadly Phosgene plot, of course, was the huge exterior air conditioning unit scant yards from the Edgewood Links perimeter. Partially obscured by tall oaks interspersed with evergreens, the installation circulated fresh air sucked from the open, grassy area, and fed it through a series of broad, yellow intake tubes into the various buildings of the Southwick VAMC.

The intake unit consisted of four generators housed in a single enclosure, and arrayed along its metal topside were eight flat, rapidly spinning fans covered only with stout wire cages. They protected against invasion by rodents, birds, and predatory creatures. It was into these intake ducts that the crushed, innocent-smelling, Phosgene powder would trickle not long after the bags were finally positioned…ultimately killing most of the Center's patients, medical personnel, and support staff on the day Professor Baghdadi had designated.

Unsurprisingly, the radicalized Peter Wilkinson had no way of knowing that his mentor had recently chosen, unannounced, to cut his own throat in a dirty New Haven mosque.

It couldn't hurt, Peter decided, to place half the calcified Phosgene balls in their ultimate destination atop the big air conditioning unit…even before Baghdadi had ordered the go-ahead. The Edgewood Links greens keepers would not be cutting grass or otherwise attending to the adjacent hospital grounds until sometime in early May. They certainly wouldn't be mowing now, in late December, the lovely weather notwithstanding. And an impatient Peter had decided it would be best to have the transport and positioning segment of the operation over with... or most of it at any rate.

The total shipment of the poisonous compound was twice that needed to circulate throughout the VAMC, infiltrating each of the buildings sufficiently to eradicate, or at the very least mutilate its inhabitants. Thus, Peter could leave half of the delivery next to the old equipment shed as a backup...just in case. There, the packaged Phosgene would be adequately protected from the elements...first, by the plastic bags in which it had been delivered...and additionally, by the generous overhang of the shed's roof.

In the improbable event that some trespasser should come upon the 'golf balls' before the time for their macabre use, the printed warning on the red, white, and blue sacks would surely deter them:

GOVERNMENT PROPERTY DO NOT TOUCH!

...after all, it would hardly be worth risking a year or two in federal prison to nose around five 20-pound bags of lumpy, seemingly innocent material.

Peter made the transfer in a little over fifteen minutes. The intake ducts had to remain free from obstructions, of course, but so long as the bags did not interfere with the fans, they were unlikely to provoke an investigation. He'd hoisted the Phosgene from the high grass onto the roof of the fan housing. Should there be an unanticipated snowfall or some other interruption, at least that part of the plan would be accomplished.

Only a stark-still herd of twelve curious deer watched—and waited—as the man in the gray sweatsuit dusted himself off... then departed the otherwise uninhabited golf course.

* * * * *

DILIGENT DOCTORS take their lunch breaks at times unlikely to inconvenience their patients, and Dermatologist Meili Song had been tied up tending to a young man with a stubborn Poison Ivy rash. The Marine vet had been clearing brush at his Granville home five miles west of Southwick, and foolishly burned a pile of the crimson-tinted vines. More unwisely still, he'd gotten downwind of the dense smoke, and the residue from the burning leaves had clung to his sweating face and arms. A few days later he was a swollen, blistered mess, and Doctor Song had been called in.

At 2:00 PM on Sunday the 27th, Meili had finished coating the patient's inflamed and seeping exposures with lotion that would cake, and absorb much of the oily product oozing from the blisters on his skin. Corporal Murray would be an uncomfortable fellow for a few weeks, but at least he hadn't inhaled a significant amount of the permeating smoke.

With the emergency treatment completed, Doctor Song washed up, grabbed a bowl of vegetable soup at the Countryman's Café, and set out on her usual mile-long lunchtime walk along the curving hill that led from Building 200 to the east gatehouse on Middleville Road.

The balmy weather had lingered past Christmas, and native New Englanders were wondering if indeed they were going to 'dodge the bullet' altogether this winter. So far, some had observed, it had been a winter "...to die for!"

From the base of the winding, descending roadway that terminated at a sentry enclosure, the shortest way back to the hospital's main building was diagonally across fairway seven of the Edgewood Links. That return route would be the preferred one for Meili now that the golf course was temporarily closed; as was standard procedure during periods of elevated terror warnings.

Doctor Song waved to the two policemen at the Middleville gatehouse, left the sidewalk, and headed smartly across the seventh fairway expanse in the general direction from which she'd come. The short-cut would take the petite woman past a maintenance shed that she assumed was closed for the winter, and alongside the nearby air conditioning units that had always intrigued her when viewed from her office window. Today, for some reason, there were dozens of squawking crows circling the enclosure that held those huge, rapidly rotating fans. *Maybe they've seen a dead squirrel,* she thought. *Possibly a raccoon.*

At any rate, the Dermatologist would just as soon not inspect an animal carcass so soon after lunch. She veered back to the semi-circular roadway and trudged along the sidewalk leading to Building 200.

Chapter Thirty-three

IT WAS EIGHT PM IN STONEHENGE…nine, in bleak, moonless Istanbul…and ten o'clock in Mosul and Teheran. In his London office, a melancholy Inspector Miles Plumber of the British Censor's Bureau was finishing dinner and examining the week's summary of suspect correspondence intercepted by the BCB. An untouched glass of sherry sat on the table before him. He had ordered stepped-up vigilance for any and all communiqués that originated with Professor Mujab Baghdadi in the United States, and were relayed from Salisbury's Woodstock Café to twin destinations in Iraq and Iran.

Miles had hoped that Father Christmas would bring him such a Yule gift, primarily because the Inspector would love to have presented a second wire of this significance to Scotland Yard's high-reaching Shelby Whitmore. It would have ensured a smashing Christmas for Inspector Plumber as well as his associate, the ambitious Scotland Yard Commander. They'd be making progress, at least…and that would look quite impressive indeed on the performance sheets of both men.

But no such luck…not a bloody word from *'Wif.en.poof.'*

However, in the radical Islamic outposts of Mosul, Salisbury, New Haven, and Port Jefferson, the word was already being widely circulated that Mujab Baghdadi had become the latest casualty in a war of attrition that was not going well for the Islamic extremists. One by one, key members of the insurrectionist movement were being killed...or were killing themselves.

There is no Arabic term for 'bad luck'...indeed it is forbidden for Muslims to believe in 'luck' of any kind (since one must not attribute to another, that which belongs only to Allah)...but if a belief in misfortune were possible, it would be termed '*mahzuz.*' Euphemistically put, Allah seemed not to be smiling on His people for the time being.

The jihadists, normally loath to meet in the highly visible venues of downtown Teheran, now gathered in a locked and guarded room of the Azari Teahouse. The popular restaurant was located on Avenue Valiasr, one block from Vah Ahan Square. A sign on each of the eatery's three entrances read: 'No Admission—Alterations Within.'

A dozen heavily armed guards posing as protectors of workmen inside the building, glared silently at curious passersby. The intimidation was effective. There was no indication that violence was imminent. Still, men passed with only a modest reduction in their pace...and veiled women in hijab and burqa scurried quickly by the shuttered Teahouse, their eyes modestly averted, their daughters running in tow alongside. Only young boys danced and taunted the sentinels in the manner of precocious lads everywhere. The guards reacted as if the young males were somehow entitled to this rite of passage.

Inside Azari, eight men sat at a low, round table. The obvious leader was the renowned jihadist, Jahan al Shaheetz, a 50-year-old one-time *Imam* from Pakistan. In 1985, al Shaheetz had become the husband of an Iraqi girl, and the former cleric, having received a handmade gift tunic from his bride, is said to have found it unacceptable. The garment had failed Sharia Law on three levels—it contained a few threads of 14-carat gold...bore two small insets made of silk...and its lower hem terminated an inch above his knees.

The Holy Quran clearly states that Muslim males may not wear any gold…neither are they permitted to adorn themselves in silk…and a male's *'Awrah,'* the intimate part of his body, must be covered in public from his navel to his knees. Accordingly, the ultra-observant Jahan immediately had his young wife buried in sand to her neck…summoned his Pakistani neighbors…and led them in her ritualistic stoning. Two years later, his reputation for ruthlessness having spread throughout the Middle East, al Shaheetz directed the infamous Iraqi attack on the Kurdish town of Halabjah.

His weapon of choice…the deadly gas, Phosgene.

Al Shaheetz had decided that all in his party would dine on the same fare—his favorite, *'Dizi—the meal of warriors.'* His selection was more than a palate pleaser; there was serious symbolism in the *'Siyasi Jahan's'* choice. In Iran and surrounding nations, *Dizi* is more than a dish to be shared; it is a ritual complete with its own progression of special rites. These suggest good humor, comradeship, even brotherhood. On the walls of the Azari Teahouse where al Shaheetz and his entourage sat, there were large 19th century paintings depicting tired but jovial laborers dining on *Dizi* almost two hundred years ago. Others showed Middle Eastern clerical leaders and Dervishes happily stuffing themselves with the traditional fare in an almost Bacchanalian (if un-Islamlike) display of gluttony. All of the frescoed banquet scenes were charming and colorful; hardly like the frequently bombed-out landscapes that currently dot Muslim-held cities… the sad towns that date back to once-pleasant and prosperous times.

Jahan al Shaheetz held out his arms and said, *"Bismillahi wa 'ala baraka-tillah."* It was the prayer he had recited before his meals for forty-five years: *"With Allah's name and upon the blessings granted by Allah…we eat."*

"Bismillahi," the others responded.

A squad of five bustling waiters, two assigned to al Shaheetz alone, delivered a stainless steel spoon and fork to each of the eight diners. Each set of silverware was encased in a clear plastic tube whose access end was sealed shut. Jahan's men waited until their leader had pried open the taped flap on his utensils, then they did likewise.

Soon the table was groaning with plates, cups, saucers, glasses, and bowls. In front of each diner was a shallow dish piled high with chicken glazed in an orange sauce, and a mound of rice liberally sprinkled with pineapple and raisins. A small plate of shaved cabbage and carrots drenched in olive oil and honey was beside each entrée. Next to that interesting salad was a three-inch-deep cup containing green and yellow peppers swimming in vinegar. In front of every patron there was placed a bowl of stewed apples covered with chopped walnuts and drizzled with a clear, sugary marinade. Next to it, in a matching white bowl, was what looked like borsht...a steaming cabbage soup in whose broth swam parsley and several round carrot slices. In the center of the table, a platter overloaded with crisp baked *Barbari* bread held the place of honor...each thin slice bearing uneven, scorched marks from the oven. Caraway seeds were randomly sprinkled and baked into the lumpy, brown surface.

A bottle of water was brought to every guest...Jahan al Shaheetz providing the only departure from Iranian tradition. Beside his oversized, blue mug was a sweating bottle of Pepsi-Cola.

When the servers had completed their delivery work, al Shaheetz snapped his fingers for the head waiter, then brusquely waved all the servers away with a backward flip of his hand. They disappeared through two padded doors as if sucked into a vacuum. He took a piece of the *Barbari* bread...the customary signal that the meal had officially begun...and with that, all the members of the cadre were free to dig in.

"We have a serious obligation to resolve," said *'Siyasi Jahan.'* "The Infidel has designed against Allah...*May peace and blessings be His eternally*...a great sin." He placed his spoon slowly, silently, on the table. His associates stopped eating as their leader idly broke his piece of brittle bread in two.

"It appears that the American government has enlisted a most traitorous agent in an attempt to disrupt our plans of many months." The seven jihadists murmured and leaned forward, eager to learn the identity of their new adversary. "He is a despicable man familiar with our homeland…and hateful of our ways." The insurgents glanced at one another inquiringly. "Furthermore, this devil is equipped to unleash upon Allah's people the acquired wisdom of many years." There was a collective mumble that became an annoyed muttering, and al Shaheetz impatiently rang his water glass with his spoon.

"The Infidel is a cryptologist. It was he who caused the death of Mujab Baghdadi"

Amid a sudden grumbling, the jihadist, Omar Inbula…at eighty-two the senior member of the group…stood and waited for quiet. "I know him," said the old man. "He killed my family in Turkey. I respectfully beg that I be permitted to return the favor."

Chapter Thirty-four

'A CHRISTMAS CAROL' had reached its fifteen-minute intermission and Ladka and Banning repaired to the step-down bar fronting in the theater's lobby and extending to the area beneath the orchestra pit. Neither had eaten lunch, so they ordered Bloody Mary cocktails as a substitute, wolfed down the substantial celery stalks, and chewed the pulp from their lemon wedges as well.

Thus fortified, Carter laid a folded twenty-dollar bill on the mahogany and asked Scott the bartender for the nearest doorway where they might get a breath of the cool December air. He waved a hand signaling *'no change'* from the twenty, and Scott nodded toward an Exit sign adjacent to the men's washroom. He glanced at his watch. "Show resumes in nine minutes gents," he said.

The casually dressed men left the bar through the fire exit and, as expected, found themselves a dozen or so paces from the stage door. At a little after 4:00 o'clock, twilight had already begun to descend on dim-lit Port Jefferson, but Ladka and Banning could see that positioned tight against the building's barn-red, wooden exterior were two medium sized bales of newly cut, sweet-smelling hay.

Beside the stage door were two ducts that served the fog machines used in the famed scene where Ebenezer Scrooge is confronted by the ghost of Jacob Marley. One of the ducts sucked air onto the stage from the alleyway…the other was an exhaust vent that blew out the smoky looking but non-toxic 'fog.'

Ladka twirled his index finger in a 'hurry up' gesture and Carter rushed to help him manhandle one of the damp hay bales, turning it end-over-end until it covered the ground-level intake duct. A recorded announcement at the beginning of the show had advised patrons that use of sometimes alarming strobe lights and fog machines should not be mistaken for symptoms of emergencies. Of course, few if any members of the cast and audience were aware that a telltale sign of the lethal gas Phosgene's presence was the disarmingly pleasant odor of new-mown hay.

But Ladka and Banning were sure Hugh Harmwell knew it.

At any rate, when the fog machine was engaged late in 'A Christmas Carol's' second act, not only would the artificial fog usher in 'The Ghost of Christmas Future'…it would also fill the stage with the sweet smell of Phosgene. If Harmwell reacted as Karol Ladka estimated he might, the double agent would have implicated himself…and his on-stage apprehensiveness would result in a melodramatic first for grand old Theatre Three.

The two army friends re-entered the split-level bar, winked at Scott the bartender, and hurried to their Row L orchestra seats. There, practically invisible beyond the glow from the proscenium, they would sit back…enjoy the play…and wait for the revealing aroma of 'Phosgene.'

Then…self-styled actors in a real-life drama…they would add to the theatrics by coughing in fitful spasms.

* * * * *

L'HAD (SUNDAY) WAS JUST ANOTHER DAY in the almost entirely Muslim city of Teheran. Nothing of great significance to

Islamists had historically happened on *L'had*. It was a day best given to leisurely planting one's garden and decorating one's home. According to the Holy Quran, Sunday was something of an insignificant day, this was the principal reason for Jahan al Shaheetz's choosing it for his evening meeting in the Azari Teahouse.

The following day—*L'itnayn*—would have been a different story. After all, the great and powerful Prophet Muhammed (*May eternal blessings descend upon him*) was born on Monday, and He left the temporary world to enter the eternal on Monday. Similarly, the great Hazrat Idrees had gone to the sky and entered Paradise (in other words, he died) on Monday...the supreme Hazrat Moosa ascended the Mount Tur on a Monday...and most significantly of all, the definitive proof of Allah's *Oneness* had been revealed on a Monday. To dine on *Dizi* during such a day would have been highly inappropriate, though hardly forbidden given the nature of the threat to Islam posed by the insufferable Infidel, General Ladka...and especially the murderous Carter Banning.

By the time al Shaheetz and his inner circle had finished their *Dizi*, the old man, Omar Inbula, had relayed the story of his family's 'slaughter' at the hands of Banning. It was a seriously flawed tale recognizable as truth only in the addled mind of Inbula himself. In the summer of 1970 Istanbul had been in the throes of a cholera epidemic and Army Major Carter Banning, a US cryptologist impersonating a British national customs inspector, had been issued a dozen bottles of drinking water by a Royal Air Force helicopter relief unit. When Omar Inbula's 6-year-old son begged Banning to share his ration of potable water with him and his infected mother, Carter did so willingly...but mother and child were already beyond help. They perished two days later. The grief stricken Inbula, returning home from Cyprus, had heard neighbors' accounts of his family's death and immediate burial, and he had inwardly accused Banning of intentionally infecting them with tainted water.

For forty-six years the heartbroken Omar had vowed Jihad against the homeland of the man he had later been informed was the retired American cryptologist, Major Carter Banning…and when, during the *Dizi*, Jahan al Shaheetz had identified him as the agent responsible for Baghdadi's death, Inbula considered the coincidence a clear signal from Allah.

"You will abide under my roof until *Lah-ta*," said a receptive Jahan al Shaheetz, indicating Tuesday, "You will depart for Canada late that day…and proceed to Boston without difficulty on *Lahrba* (Wednesday)." He smiled at the frail man in the purple *jubbah*. "You will play the role of a crippled old man. The airline fools will treat you with great care and love. Poisonous assassination darts for our use will be hidden in your bandaged legs. If it is the will of Allah, you will be vindicated upon our unspeakable American enemies by *Zhima* (Friday)."

Inbula nodded without emotion.

Their business over…the jihadist council concluded its meal and the members kissed. They paired up, and left the empty restaurant going their separate ways. Al Shaheetz and Omar Inbula walked arm-in-arm along Avenue Valiasr to Vah Ahan Square. Behind them a busboy was busily removing the 'No Admission' notices from the three doors of the re-opened Azari Teahouse.

* * * * *

THE HOUSE LIGHTS DIMMED, and Theatre Three's orchestra struck up a gavotte. It was not difficult for Carter Banning and Karol Ladka to keep track of Hugh Harmwell during the performance. As the central character, Scrooge was on stage virtually all of the time. There weren't many changes of costume requiring Harmwell's absence from the spotlight, because the miserly Scrooge basically owned only one suit of clothes and a frayed nightgown. At the point in the show when the 'Ghost of Christmas Future' prepared to take the stage, and the miserly

Ebenezer Scrooge's epiphany was at hand, Karol Ladka nudged Carter Banning with his elbow. Slowly the floor of the dim-lit stage became engulfed in a shallow fog that began to waft almost imperceptibly upward. From their orchestra seats neither Ladka nor Banning could detect the odor of the damp hay they had jammed against the exterior intake duct.

Carter gave his friend a cautious, sidelong look and folded his arms across his chest. The General held up a hand unobtrusively. *Any moment*, his cautioning finger seemed to say. The stone-silent audience focused on Scrooge as he commanded their rapt attention at center stage. The milky-gray vapor created by the fog machine began to obscure Scrooge's slippered feet…then ankles…and build upward over the hem of his tattered robe. Actor James Schultz playing 'Christmas Future' seemed to float toward Harmwell from stage right on the billowing mist. "Ebenezer Scrrrooooge," he moaned.

Appropriately, Hugh Harmwell peered at the ghost, startled… then, inexplicably, he extended his arms out from his sides and gaped down toward his no longer visible feet. It was as if they'd suddenly become numb…or perhaps they were burning… paining him. The audience gasped, expecting the star of the play to lunge away from some unexplained discomfort.

What Harmwell did next was incomprehensible to everyone save Banning and Ladka. In abject terror, he seized the skirt of his nightgown and wadding it in a muslin ball, brought it up to his wheezing mouth. It would not be necessary for Banning and The General to embellish matters by faking a coughing fit… Ebenezer Scrooge was already convinced that he had somehow become a victim of his own malevolence. Immersed in mist and the unmistakable scent of freshly cut hay, he was positive that Phosgene poisoning was about to claim him.

As he burst, flushed and sweating, from the stage, Hugh Harmwell dashed blindly into the waiting arms of Karol Ladka, whereupon he collapsed, and would not regain consciousness until he had been shackled and resuscitated in the Prison Ward of nearby St. Charles Hospital.

Banning and Ladka were sitting on either side of the bed when the double agent's eyes fluttered, and he quickly realized what had happened. Harmwell's right wrist was fettered to the bed's frame, as was his left ankle. He was being hydrated intravenously.

"Sorry we didn't bring flowers," said The General. "My partner was afraid you might die of fright when you smelled them."

"I wanted to bring a library book," Carter Banning said apologetically, "…but our friends at Yale said you already have two that are overdue."

"Am I under arrest?" a sullen Hugh Harmwell demanded.

"Naww," Ladka answered. "Why would you ask such a silly question?"

Banning said, "We just figured you'd like a good meal of plum pudding before we turn you over to your pals at ISIS."

"You know ISIS," said Karol Ladka, "…the guys with the big serrated knives…the fellows that make movies of you before they saw off…well…you know what they do."

Hugh Harmwell retched and the watery vomit overflowed the corners of his mouth. Neither Banning nor Ladka moved from the chairs where they sat comfortably with their legs crossed.

When Harmwell had coughed away the mouthful of yellow-green bile he wiped his lips with the arm that held the IV. "I demand an attorney."

"Sure thing," said Carter.

"How about that Cracker Jack, Marcia Clark…the gal that prosecuted OJ?" Karol added. "I understand she's available. Reasonable, too."

"Personally, I suggest you cop a plea," Carter chimed in. "You plead guilty to treason, we let you off with a firing squad—if you go to trial, our guys might have to turn you loose in a pig sty during Ramadan. Whadda you say?"

A nun in white with a stethoscope around her neck entered the room. She disregarded the men flanking the bed and immediately began taking Harmwell's pulse. He watched her with distrust and when she had finished holding his wrist while eyeing her large round watch, he said, "I insist on a lawyer."

"This is a hospital," the nun said opening the door, "...not a courtroom."

"Send your supervisor in here," Harmwell commanded. "I want to see him. What's his name?"

The stout nun turned in the open doorway. "You may speak to my Supervisor whenever you wish. Seeing Him is another matter. His name is Jesus."

Chapter Thirty-five

MEILI SONG WASN'T a 'funeral' person. She hadn't even attended the 'Sky Burial' last year of her favorite uncle in California. The Asian rite had been conducted at the City of Ten Thousand Buddhas north of San Francisco, and even a veteran dermatologist like Doctor Song had considered the chopping of a corpse into fragments easily digested by ravenous indigenous vultures, a bit much to stomach. When the roster was circulated for those VA employees planning to attend even a ritual as inoffensive as Amanda Bragg's military post-cremation ceremony, Meili had promptly checked the 'NO' box.

With the sun setting behind the western hills of Edgewood Links Golf Course, the carillon above the hospital's all-faith chapel tolled a somber version of 'The Naval Hymn.' Meili hadn't heard the moving tribute to *"...all in peril on the sea..."* since attending the fiftieth anniversary memorial of John Kennedy's 1963 assassination. In the intervening three years, she had never forgotten the final-line plea to The Creator for the endangered *"...on land and air and sea..."* and as she was soberly aware on this unhappy day...that included everyone in the military. Or for that matter, the entire human race.

Meili sat in her office...pensive...staring blankly from her second-floor window...wondering if there had been anything she could or should have done to prevent her patient's suicide. How peaceful the lush landscape down there looked in the waning light, she thought. Even the yearling deer that would soon, for the first time, take refuge from winter on the quiet hospital grounds, were resting beside their fattened fathers and newly pregnant mothers.

Strange, Doctor Song mused. *I've never seen them sleeping out in the open like that.*

There was a light knock on the door.

Meili pulled the slats shut on the Venetian blinds. "Come in."

Jean Gustavson the ER Charge Nurse entered, dropped wearily into one of the patient consult chairs, and rubbed her eyes with the knuckles of her index fingers.

"Been busy?" Song asked.

"Just the opposite," Gustavson responded with a yawn. "At least when it's busy you don't have to invent ways to pass the time." She stood and stretched, groaning as she twisted and flexed the trapezius muscles between her shoulder blades. "When do you leave, Millie?"

The Dermatologist looked at her watch. "Any time now. You?"

"I'm outta here. How about coffee at 'Un-Common Grounds'?"

"I was thinking of something a bit stronger...like a vodka martini at the first gin mill I come to."

Jean Gustavson's face broke into a broad grin. "You de man, Doc. In words of one syllable...meet you at 'Mom's.'"

* * * * *

EVERYONE CALLED THE PLACE 'MOM'S,' but the sign over the bar's tastefully decorated front window actually read, *'Magic on Main Street.'* The only thing 'magic' about 'Mom's' (apart from its catchy acronym) was the fact that it was still in business. Of all the booze emporiums in existence, *'Magic'* had to be the only one that limited customers to a single drink! The stipulated maximum dated back to the bar's founding when the Southwick VA Hospital opened in 1933...the year the 21st Amendment ending Prohibition was ratified.

The backstory is that 'Mom's' was, and still is, the closest bar to the Medical Center, and its opening had produced concern among the local populace that doctors, nurses, and patients alike would be overserved in the new era of post-Prohibition overindulgence. The 'Magic's' owner, 'Mom' Murphy, parenthetically a distant relative of Jean Gustavson's, came up with the one-drink solution, and the place has stuck to the rule religiously for eighty-plus years.

Of course, the drinks are a good fifty percent larger by volume than the average cocktail in the State of Massachusetts. Still, the imbiber pays cash for his or her pick-me-up, and may not order, or be served, a second one. It's said that only once was the solitary serving statute violated...apparently by a barkeep attempting to curry favor with a generous tipper. Proprietor 'Mom' Murphy, much to the delight of Southwick teetotalers, had the offending mixologist delivered to the local lock-up by her two strapping brothers. There, naturally, the misguided fellow, having violated no civic decree, was released. But not before his plight had generated more free advertising than a dozen 'Mom's' bars combined could possibly have purchased.

Another residual benefit is that virtually no stigma is associated with visiting *'Magic on Main Street'* for a cocktail. After all, if it's one's intention to get wasted, 'Mom's' is hardly the place to do it. Accordingly, patrons there are considered temperate, level-headed individuals by virtue of their attendance...surely making the place unique among all the world's saloons. The only bad apples falling through the cracks are those rare connivers who bring non-drinkers along and proceed to down their companion's allotment. Most such schemers, however, can be spotted by 'Mom' Murphy faster than you can say, "My friend will have the same."

As usual, 'Mom's' was doing a brisk business with the five o'clock VAMC crowd…even though it was Sunday. The New England 'Blue Laws' had long since been repealed, and strictures that had forbidden a mother's kissing her child on the Sabbath… or forbade an adult male from shaving on Sunday…or prohibited the making of minced pies on Christmas…these and other offensive activities had long since been winked at. Even the sin of running on the Lord's Day was now considered permissible!

When Jean Gustavson showed up, Meili Song had already bought and paid for her vodka martini on ice…with three olives. There was no such thing as running a tab at 'Mom's.' Jean pointed to her friend's hefty 'rocks' glass and laid seven dollars on the bar.

"Vodka?" said Mitch, the bartender. "Olives?"

"You guessed it," the Charge Nurse moaned. "And please, please hurry."

"Sounds serious," Meili said.

"I just feel better when I complain," said Jean, lifting the skewered olives from Meili's drink and stealing one. "Saw you perambulating that size four frame of yours on the golf course today. What's with all the birds circling on the west side of the main building?"

"Beats me," said the dermatologist. "And the size four is a size six, I'm sorry to say." She pushed the two remaining olives from her decorative toothpick into the icy vodka and vermouth mixture. "I did notice a number of our white tailed friends taking a siesta by the maintenance building this afternoon. Maybe that's what attracted them."

"Deer? Sleeping in the open? In the middle of the afternoon?" Jean Gustavson shook her head. "No way, José."

"Hope to die," Meili said, raising her right hand.

"You sure this is your first concoction of the day?"

"Maybe they're celebrating the end of the golfing season. No more scary guys with long sticks and spiked shoes chasing them."

The bartender brought Gustavson's martini, set it on a coaster, and swept the seven dollars from the bar. Jean closed her eyes and took a long, grateful sip.

"Well, I've got the day shift tomorrow. Maybe I'll walk over by the golf course during lunch." The Charge Nurse offered Meili one of her three olives in repayment. "But I'll be one veeerry surprised size ten if there are any white tailed deer dozing on Edgewood Links, m'dear. Golfers or no golfers!"

Chapter Thirty-six

KAROL LADKA FOLLOWED Sister Mary Antoine out of the private Secure Ward where Hugh Harmwell was detained. He waited by the Nurses' Station until the no-nonsense Franciscan nun had filled out her hourly chart, and when she looked up from her chair, he asked. "How does he seem?"

"You'll have to ask the doctor," said an unsmiling Sister Antoine. "The night Resident will be here in half-an-hour." She hung her clipboard on a hook to her right, and added, "You and your partner may wait in the lobby."

The General eyed the stocky woman in the pristine habit and spoke guardedly. "We have reason to believe the patient might pose a danger to others in the hospital," he offered in a low, confidential tone. "We'd rather keep an eye on him, if it's alright. I promise we'll be quiet."

The nun looked at her watch. "Dinner is delivered to the Security Ward at six…after the other patients are served…you'll have to leave by then."

Ladka examined his own watch. *That's twenty five minutes,* he calculated. "As you wish, Sister." He returned to the secure room and let himself in.

"What's up?" Carter Banning asked, as the manacled Harmwell looked daggers at the two men who had restrained him.

"We've got twenty-five minutes," said Ladka.

He swiftly wadded a terry wash cloth from beside the room's small sink, and before Harmwell could utter a sound, Karol jammed the makeshift gag into the prisoner's gaping mouth. As if they'd rehearsed the procedure a hundred times, Carter yanked the pillow from beneath the groaning man's neck and stripped off the pillow case. He knelt on the bed astride the squirming captive and pulled the cover over the frantic man's head.

"Now we're going to kill you," said Ladka seizing the jihadist's free arm in a viselike grip "...unless you do exactly what we ask. Do you understand? Nod your head."

Harmwell's white-shrouded head bobbed rapidly.

"Excellent," said The General. He removed a ballpoint pen from his shirt pocket and signaled for Carter to say something.

Banning recognized the routine. "But you promised me," he improvised. "I want to break his goddam fingers...you promised."

Immediately Hugh Harmwell's head began to thrash from side to side, and Ladka took a firmer grip on the man's sweaty wrist.

"No!" said Ladka. "I think he wants to write something." And The General placed his pen in the prisoner's eager, receptive palm.

"But you assured me I'd be permitted to break his bones... beginning with his fingers..." Banning's pleading words produced more, wilder gyrations in the man fettered to the bed.

Karol Ladka continued, smoothly assuming the role of 'good cop.' "But don't you see? Mister Harmwell wishes to cooperate with us. Don't you, Hugh?"

There was an insistent bobbing of the pillow case.

"There. You see?"

Ladka pointed to an aluminum clipboard at the foot of the bed and snapped his fingers, the signal for Banning to hand it to him. Harmwell moaned and his back arched at the snapping sound. Carter handed the chart to Ladka and Karol placed it under Hugh Harmwell's free hand...the one that held the pen. "Now, my friend, you are going to write the answers to my two questions...promptly and accurately...are you ready? What is Peter Wilkinson's target?"

Soaked with perspiration, his head still enclosed in the pillow case, Hugh Harmwell immediately scratched three words onto the chart.

General Ladka looked at the slanted script of the inscription... and nodded.

"And when is the university to be attacked?"

Two more words were irregularly scribbled.

Ladka read the terrified man's answer, and looked up at Carter.

"Now you can go ahead and break his fingers...all of them," The General said. "But hurry. We don't have much time."

* * * * *

THE THREE-MAN SECURITY DETAIL, the men impersonating fishermen and assigned to protect Elizabeth Banning from Wilkinson, had been alerted...and two of the men promptly arrested young Peter under a waning crescent moon, as he jogged along the seventh fairway of Edgewood Links. Without explanation, the SEALS, who were not particularly inclined to converse with traitors, hauled the suspected jihadist to their camper at the Stony Path *cul-de-sac*. There they handcuffed, gagged, and blindfolded him. And as instructed, they waited.

It was ten o'clock on Sunday night when Ladka and Banning arrived from Port Jefferson and interrogated the recalcitrant would-be terrorist...a process that was suspended after three fruitless hours.

From then on however, whether Wilkinson knew it or not, the bitter smart-aleck from Yale, would not be allowed to venture from his prison cell unescorted...the obdurate youth would never be permitted a private conference with family or associates...and his existence would henceforth be utterly devoid of the barest amenities.

In short, the life of Peter Owens Wilkinson, 793256-16, was essentially over. He would die in Leavenworth Federal Prison...a turncoat stripped of his citizenship...a man without a country.

But say what you may about the vile Mujab Baghdadi, Hugh Harmwell, and Peter Wilkinson, they had all cast their lot irrevocably with the same rigid ideologies associated with Islamic Terrorism, and they would stay true to their nefarious pledge.

As with most zealots, certain of the three were more fanatical in different veins than others. Baghdadi feared disgrace, and he had died...by his own hand...rather than live in what he perceived as dishonor to Islam.

Harmwell openly feared death...and pain...but when confronted by Ladka, he had chosen to lie about the target and time of Wilkinson's attack, rather than undermine the Jihad.

And for whatever reason, Wilkinson had become so embittered...toward his family, his neighbors, his country...that he saw imprisonment as a thing too small to fear when compared with the thrill of executing the chaotic madness he had helped orchestrate.

But Karol Ladka, too, was a determined man, and just as devious. As he ordered the gag re-taped across Peter Wilkinson's sneering lips, he turned to the Lieutenant Commander in charge of the SEAL contingent. "Keep him here. It's obvious he's working with someone on the inside...probably another academic. We'll know by this time tomorrow."

It was Ladka's first mistake...and no one could tell that beneath the duct tape tearing at his mouth, Peter Wilkinson was smiling.

Chapter Thirty-seven

IN A RACE WITH THE SUN, Omar Inbula's Air Canada flight landed at Pearson International in Toronto at 6:30 AM. It was three in the afternoon Teheran time, and the 82-year-old Inbula had been aloft for an exhausting eight hours non-stop from *Imam Khomeini* Airport in the Iranian capital.

Jahan al Shaheetz had arranged for a wheelchair to be waiting for Inbula at his Canadian destination, but that was merely part of the scam. The Iranian octogenarian was nothing if not dexterous on his feet…even nimble…at least for a man of his advanced years.

Using Toronto as Inbula's destination was merely a safeguard against the possibility of some US-Iranian conflict arising literally overnight…a likelihood that was not unheard of. True, the American president had smoothed matters with Teheran considerably eleven months prior, when through Executive Order, he had directed the Secretary of State to lift all US sanctions on Iranian civil aviation. But still…

On the face of it, international travel between Iran and the West could now be freely and openly conducted, but Toronto was nonetheless a wise choice as Inbula's initial arrival point, al Shaheetz had decided. Unlike the touchy Republican-led US Congress, the Canadians would likely take weeks to react diplomatically should any East-West friction develop... if, indeed, passive Canada encountered any such instability whatever. Thus Inbula's mission was virtually guaranteed to continue uninterrupted, no matter the international climate, when he proceeded to Boston's Logan Airport with his false Canadian passport.

And there was another reason for the diversion to Pearson International.

Hardly as meticulous as Americans in applying detection techniques, Canadian Transportation Safety personnel inscribed their findings on the traveler's boarding pass, and that approval followed handicapped passengers wherever continuing flights took them. Thus the 'disabled' Omar Inbula's priority clearance from the Toronto hub would be winked at in Boston...and not examined at all at tiny MacArthur Regional Airport...his final landing destination on Long Island.

Omar Inbula's convoluted route had been calculated with ingenuity. Even the entry on his Canadian passport was inventive... *Felix Ruecuodal, LaSallette, Quebec*...a direct descendant of the first Canadian gold prospector to stake a claim in the Yukon. Any government official would recognize the family name of the legendary mining pioneer. No Canadian agent would dream of detaining a member of such a distinguished clan.

The faux Frenchman was carefully assisted down the steps of the big Airbus and pushed to Canadian Customs in his wheelchair by a pair of fawning attendants. There, Inbula patiently submitted to the security X-ray. It revealed three foot-long metal shafts that appeared to pinion a shattered right femur. A smiling Omar Inbula pointed to the image on the inspection station's monitor.

"Une vilaine fracture!" he said in perfect French. Then he knocked on the cast that encased his thigh. *"Mais je suis bien... merci!"* But the plaster cast enclosed no broken femur...and the twelve-inch rods were in reality hollow aluminum shanks. Each

of them pointed, and containing enough liquid Sarin to kill a dozen swarthy men…in sixty seconds.

"Vous assoirez-vous sur mes genoux?" the false Quebecois said slyly.

The attendants giggled at the cute old man's invitation to sit on his lap. *"Non,"* one of the bi-lingual stewardesses responded, *"…il est contraire aux regles j'ai peur."*

"Quel dommage!" said 'Monsieur Ruecuodal.'

His flights from Teheran, Toronto, and Boston had been smooth and without incident. Upon arrival at Long Island-MacArthur airport, the Iraqi operative proceeded by taxi directly to The Hampton Inn, a few miles north on Veterans Memorial Highway.

Omar Inbula was disappointed to find that the cheaply constructed four-story motel was located at a hectic intersection of two major automotive arteries, whose busy access roads served both the thunderous Long Island Expressway, and the always active Vets Highway. Omar had heard of Long Island's celebrity-laden 'Hamptons' area and he'd anticipated that scantily-clad motion picture starlets and their billionaire escorts would surely be pacing the gilded halls of this 'Hampton Inn'. What greeted him instead was a bare-bones collection of minimally equipped rooms joined by dull corridors with worn carpet and occasionally peeling wallpaper.

Where the faux 'Ruecuodal' had expected to find theater moguls sipping imported champagne, and leisurely sampling Russian caviar, he encountered in the chaotic lobby only denim-outfitted, middle-aged women whose perpetually glum husbands sat watching televised sports reports, while innumerable children whined stridently to their thirtysomething mothers that the vending machines were out of something called 'M & M's'… and the signal on their smart phones often failed in the elevators.

"Speak to your father," was the standard admonition.

This rebuke was invariably acknowledged with the strange rejoinder, "Yeah, right!"

According to the agenda provided by Jahan al Shaheetz...two hours after arriving at the Hampton Inn, Inbula was to call the air shuttle office of Mohegan Sun. He was to make a reservation for tomorrow morning's flight from Republic Airport to the elaborate Indian-owned casino in Uncasville, Connecticut.

It was a mere hour's drive from Uncasville to Southwick.

Having already been booked at the casino's hotel under the name F. Ruecuodal, of LaSallette, Quebec, Omar was to call 860-862-8125 and ask the Casino Cage representative if visitors might use $100,000 in Canadian currency to 'buy in' at the craps tables.

Jahan al Shaheetz had already known the answer, of course, as had Inbula. The query on old Omar's part was intended merely to assure that the plane from Republic Airport in Farmingdale would be waiting for him in the event his cab should be somewhat delayed. Granted, the hundred thousand, Canadian equaled only seventy thousand in American dollars, still the accommodating folks at Mohegan Sun would be more than happy to oblige the apparent high roller, Monsieur Ruecuodal..."...and perhaps you would like a limousine to pick you up, Sir?"

"Why, that would be very considerate," said Omar Inbula. "The name is Felix...Felix Ruecuodal. Also, I will require a late dinner at nine."

"By all means, Felix. Will a table for two be in order?"

"Perfect," said Inbula.

"It will be a pleasure to serve you at our Maurice Richard Steakhouse, Sir."

"Ah, yes," Inbula said, "...the baseball player."

"I beg your pardon?"

"A joke," said Inbula, snickering in an attempt to make light of his *faux pas*.

"Of course, Sir. A joke. Silly of me."

Chapter Thirty-eight

A SUB-BASEMENT composed of wide, white-painted tunnels threads its way deep beneath the workaday levels of the Southwick VA hospital. The main purpose of the underground labyrinth is to provide emergency access to the three large medical buildings under which the connecting tunnels meander. Only the occasional, high window is seen where the undulating exterior grounds descend to their lowest point on the complex. These small windows are made of so-called 'bulletproof' glass, and date back to a time in the mid-twentieth century…long before easily penetrating rounds from weapons like the .50 caliber Smith & Wesson Magnum pistol were even envisioned.

All of the hospital buildings consist of four floors and a basement. Each tunnel in the maze under these areas contains a pair of fourteen-inch ducts suspended from its ceiling. One of the conduits carries fresh air from the hospital's exterior intake fans…and the twin channel next to it returns the air to large exterior vents built into the low western exposure of Building 200.

It was through these interconnecting passageways that Charge Nurse Jean Gustavson elected to make her way to work in the Emergency Room each morning. The east parking lot was the most convenient for her after accessing the hospital grounds about 7:00 most days…maybe closer to 8:00 if the weather was inclement. She would enter Building 100, the smallest of the three structures comprising the Medical Center's non-housing facilities, take the Main Elevator to the basement, then descend a seldom-used flight of dusty stairs to the network of corridors. It was where the tunnels began, and though most female staff members eschewed the dismal passageways, they constituted far and away the most direct and convenient path to the Emergency room a quarter mile distant.

Forget trying to find a parking space in the west lot. If you didn't arrive at that part of the complex before 7:00, you were, as the vets would say in their salty vernacular, 'SOL…Shit outa' luck!'

Gustavson had walked the corridors so often, she liked to say she could do it in her sleep. And the metaphor wasn't so far-fetched on drab late afternoons in winter, when daylight was at a premium. On such days even the occasional small window along her subterranean route revealed a black and forbidding exterior as, tired and sore, she left the ER for the day, and strode wearily east…the squeak of her white sneakers echoing in the otherwise silent void.

* * * * *

"WHEN YOU THINK you've seen it all," Jean Gustavson said to Meili Song over their icy cocktails, "…along comes another poor guy…usually a substance abuser…and he proves you dead wrong." She held up her decorative toothpick and signaled to aproned Mitch the bartender for another set of skewered olives. Unlike liquor, there was no limit on stuffed olives or cocktail onions at 'Mom's.'

"Had a patient this morning…his wife brought him in… his tongue's swollen twice its normal size and appeared to be burned…blistered."

Mitch dropped the new trio of speared olives in Gustavson's drink and rapped the bar lightly with his knuckles. "There ya' go."

Jean nodded her thanks and turned back to Meili Song. "This guy this morning...whaddya' think his problem is?"

The dermatologist looked cautiously at her friend. "No clue."

"Urinal block," she said, letting her shoulders droop.

"What?"

"Honest to God, Millie, the poor bastard's addicted to licking disinfectant urinal blocks."

Meili Song closed her eyes and sat stark still as if in prayer. Finally, she muttered, "Something in 'em gives him a high, I suppose."

The Charge Nurse bobbed her head silently. "He had one of the things with him this morning. Picked up in a Boston Garden men's room last night. Cried like a baby when Doctor Briley took it away!"

"Oh, he'll find more," a distracted Meili Song said.

"'Course he will...it's not illegal. You can find the damn things for sale everywhere...including Home Depot." Gustavson pulled an olive from its toothpick with her teeth. "What's a cop supposed to tell the judge when some jerk swipes a used $2.95 chunk of deodorant from a public urinal bowl? Ten bucks says he's back in the ER before New Year's."

"Probably destined to choke to death," Meili speculated. "Those things have got to be toxic!"

"Toxic?" Jean Gustavson stared at Meili Song in disbelief. "You should have seen this guy's mouth! His tongue and gums looked like he'd gargled with sulfuric acid."

Doctor Song pushed her drink away. "It takes a lot to turn my stomach," said the dermatologist, "...but for some reason, I seem to have lost my hankering for this cocktail."

Chapter Thirty-nine

"WE'RE GOING TO HAVE TO turn the little prick loose," said Carter Banning to Karol Ladka. "You know that, don't you? I mean, with Harmwell in custody…with this Baghdadi asshole God knows where…and half the Istanbul connection dead or missing in Turkey…who the hell are we supposed to watch?"

General Ladka looked pensively across Slater Lake from the dock in front of the Banning house. "It's not as if we're dealing with a bunch of people who tell us nothing but the truth," he said. "No matter how thoroughly we might have interrogated Harmwell, I was sure he wouldn't level with us. The bottom line is, he's a trained actor, and give the devil his due…a damn good one. By the time we get done chasing his false leads we could lose half the population of Connecticut *and* Massachusetts." Karol shook his head. "I'm not surprised he sent us on a wild goose chase. Our friend Hugh confirmed only facts we already knew."

"Like the Wilkinson kid's involvement."

"Exactly."

"So I say we play the one card we've got left," said Banning. "Release Wilkinson and watch him like a fucking hawk…but let him think we've given up on him." Carter turned up the collar of his jacket. The weather was finally starting to feel a bit like winter. "Maybe it's time for *us* to be the actors for a change."

Ladka maintained his peering toward the lights that were sporadically coming to life on the far side of the lake. "Good cop-bad cop, might work," he said. "The boy's young. I doubt he's gone through much interrogation time. You'd know better than I. Has he had any youthful infractions that wouldn't be included on his record?"

"None as far as I know," said Banning. "Yale's said to assess their student candidates pretty carefully."

"So I see," said Ladka looking askance at Carter.

"I could play the part of the good cop…you know… *'Why give the neighborhood a bad name?…Mary's such a wonderful mother…The boy's always been a credit to the community?'*" he droned. "I think I could make that stick, even though I detest the little shit!"

Ladka smiled. "How about I threaten to break his fingers one at a time?"

"Now there's a novel idea," said Carter…and he added, "I wonder how our friend Harmwell's feeling this evening."

"I'm going for a drink, then pizza," said Karol. "We can discuss this business concerning Wilkinson later tonight if you'd like."

"Wait here," said Banning. "I'll go tell Elizabeth, then I'll go with you." He stood and stretched. "There's a place in town called 'Mom's'"

"I'll wait in the rental," Ladka said. "Better wear a warm coat, old man."

* * * * *

"ISN'T THAT YOUR NEW PATIENT?" Jean Gustavson said nudging Doctor Song.

"Where?"

"Table in the far corner. Just came in with another man. Certainly looks like Carter Banning."

Meili craned her neck, then broke into a broad grin. "That's my boy," she crowed. "Did he see us? Who's the big one?"

"I dunno," said Gustavson, "...but whoever he is, I think he just spotted us. Here comes Carter now."

"Ladies!" Banning called enthusiastically as he neared the bar. He gave each of the women a platonic hug. Waving Karol to join them he said, "You have to meet my cousin Karl."

Ladka shook hands with the doctor, who was nearest him. "Meili," she smiled, and motioning toward her companion, said, "My friend Jean...Jean Gustavson."

"Pleasure," said Karol, nodding, taking her hand, identifying himself no further.

"Karl's visiting for Christmas," said Carter. "He just came in from Long Island." He acknowledged the waiting bartender. "I'll have a Chivas on ice, Mitch. What'll it be Karl?"

"Same," Ladka said, following his 'cousin's' lead.

When the drinks were served and the pleasantries completed, the conversation turned to the recent mild weather. The General noted with interest that neither woman had mentioned Carter's recent minor surgery. *They're professionals, that's for sure*, he said inwardly...and saluted them with *'Sante'* as they raised their own glasses in response. "Carter says it's possible to find real New York pizza in Southwick...is that so?"

"You must mean Jimmy's Pizza over on Point Grove Road," said Jean. She looked at Meili and frowned. "Jimmy's is better than Roma for pizza, wouldn't you say, Millie?"

The doctor responded, "If they're going all the way over to Point Grove, I'd suggest Lakeside Pizza. Depends whether you like Sicilian or Neapolitan," she said to Karol.

Ladka shrugged, "I prefer those triangles, whatever they are... the ones you pick up in your hand...thin crust...well done...lots of cheese."

"That would be Neapolitan," Jean said definitively. "Me too! God, I'm getting hungry just thinking about it."

"Why don't you two join us?" Banning suggested. "When it comes to Pizza, four can dine as cheaply as two, right?"

"Great idea," Ladka said...primarily because he had little choice.

Jean looked at Meili inquiringly. "Whaddya' think, Millie. You got plans?"

The dermatologist glanced at Carter and shrugged. "I *had* planned on my normal Sunday night banquet...you know... evening gown, candles, roving violinist, champagne...but what the hell."

Carter gave Karol a sidelong look. "Millie's what we term one of our more imaginative bachelorettes, Karl. She's kidding about the candles and violin."

Karol Ladka sipped his scotch and regarded Meili Song over the rim of the heavy rocks glass. "I know all too well how singles spend their Sunday nights," he said. He continued to clutch the glass at the level of his lips...gripping it with his left hand... plainly, he wore no wedding ring.

Meili smiled and slowly raised her martini...lifting it suggestively...with her left hand, of course.

"Well, then, that settles it," said Carter. "Lakeside, it is. Great view of the water."

* * * * *

AS THINGS EVOLVED, 'Pizza' turned into Chianti... Antipasto...and Linguine...with the Pizza more a 'take home' afterthought than the primary reason for the visit to Villa Lakeside.

Carter had been around the international block with Karol in cities as far flung as Washington, Cairo, Rome, and of course Istanbul. When it came to Continental and Middle Eastern food, both men's tastes were nearly identical—Linguine and clam sauce when in Italy, or the iconic Couscous...small steamed balls of Semolina served with a spicy stew spooned on top...that was available from Marrakesh to New Delhi. As for women, in that department too, Banning could read his bachelor friend like an open book.

Carter wasn't surprised that handsome Karol Ladka, now nearing seventy, though he looked fifteen years younger, had taken a shine to the attractively youthful Meili Song. Indeed Banning would have been stunned had the hormonal chemistry failed to percolate there on the western shore of Slater Lake... despite Millie's being half Karol's age.

They'd decided hours ago to abandon the 'Karl' business. Deception seemed entirely out of place the way things were developing. Carter had even taken the liberty to divulge the fact that his good friend from Virginia held the impressive rank of Brigadier General in the Army.

"Im fascinated," Meili said.

"Don't be," Karol had answered. "I'm the one who should be impressed. There are a lot more Generals floating around than there are expert dermatologists."

Carter looked sideways at Ladka, who was pouring more wine for Jean Gustavson. *You didn't earn that star for being tongue-tied*, he thought. *If Elizabeth were here, she'd be absolutely mesmerized.*

"Then Carter told you about our professional relationship," said Doctor Song.

"Absolutely," said Karol. "Says you're the best in the business. Didn't feel a thing with the basal cell procedure."

"Isn't that nice," Meili smiled. "Did he also tell you that he assaulted me on my waiting room couch?"

"Hey, now," Gustavson squealed. "I didn't hear *that* part! Right on your couch, you say? By all means," the Charge Nurse purred, "...do tell us more."

"Maybe we should conduct a Summary Court-Martial over espresso," said Karol. He smiled at the dermatologist and lifted the thick menu as Carter glowered. "You'll be the first and only witness. Please raise your right hand."

An out-of-town couple at the adjoining table seemed to be taking an inordinate interest in the banter, and a mortified Carter covered the lower part of his face with his hand. "Knock it off, Millie," he muttered through splayed fingers.

Gustavson pulled her chair in closer to the table. She leaned forward eagerly on her elbows. "Take the pledge, Millie girl."

Karol held the menu extended toward Meili and intoned, "Do you swear that what you have said does not remotely resemble the truth, a half-truth, and nothing like the truth, so help you?"

"You betcha."

Carter rolled his eyes.

"Throw the book at him, General," Jean Gustavson urged.

"Did the defendant inflict pain upon your person?"

"Wanna see the bruises?"

"Not just now," said Karol. "Maybe later."

"Promise?"

The young couple at the next table put down their forks and edged closer.

Nurse Gustavson fanned herself with her napkin.

"Hear ye!…Hear ye! It is the verdict of this court that the guilty as hell defendant shall proceed to his domicile unaccompanied by the Judge. He will report to the aforementioned Judge tomorrow morning at the American Inn on College Highway." Karol leaned toward Meili and said, "Got that, Doc?"

"Got it, General."

"Then perhaps the complainant can transport the Judge to his temporary quarters."

"By all means," said Meili, getting up and jingling her car keys. "After you, General…er…Your Honor."

Gustavson stood and blew out a mighty puff of air, "Whew… that was fast!"

Chapter Forty

AT SEVEN IN THE MORNING, Meili Song and Karol Ladka arrived in the doctor's car at the east gate of the Medical Center. Both wore well-traveled flannel sweat suits, his emblazoned with a large white star outlined in gold on a black background. Beneath the star, block letters spelled out U.S. ARMY. Song's outfit was a simple gray affair inscribed with a red rectangle containing white lettering and the image of a fierce-looking canine. The wording explained the animal…'Stony Brook Seawolves' the silk-screened imprint said.

Meili flashed her ID and one of the blue-uniformed police Sergeants inside the gatehouse winked and waved the black car through. The east parking lot had not yet filled and Meili took the Mercedes to a slot nearest the Edgewood Links sixth fairway. From there the two planned to take a one-mile brisk morning jog around the par five sixth and seventh holes, then they would share breakfast in the 'Countrymen's Café.' Ladka was meeting Carter in Meili's office at nine.

"You sure you're up to this?" the dermatologist teased. She flashed the General a saccharin-sweet smile across the roof of the car and checked to be sure the Mercedes was locked.

Karol arched his eyebrows indignantly. "Wanna race?"

"On Monday morning? Heavens no!" She slid the car keys into one pocket and withdrew a pair of wool gloves from another.

"Okay. Shut up and run."

"Yes, sir!" Meili made a cockeyed salute attempt, and the quibblers jogged off on a southern route toward the seventh fairway maintenance shed.

At sixty-eight, Karol was admittedly no match for his jogging partner, but the doctor was impressed by his tempo and endurance nonetheless. Of course, the plain fact was Meili'd gotten good evidence of that stamina last night. He had proven both a strong, and considerate lover. Still, she made it a point not to outpace the man as they followed the sloping contours of the golf course, the chill breeze stimulating them, the sweet fragrance of grass damp with dew refreshing them.

Ten minutes into the run, at the sixth green, the pair turned the corner of their self-appointed course and loped north along the seventh fairway. "How ya' doin'?" Karol huffed, his breath producing puffs of steam.

"Great," Meili answered breathing heavily, and she pointed a gloved finger to the brightening sky above the maintenance shed. "More birds," she panted.

Karol looked but took little notice. The morning sky over the Potomac where he customarily ran was home to several species of birds, primarily gulls that sought bait fish year-round in the tidal estuaries of the river. Had he considered the presence of the black starlings and squawking jays more carefully, however, he might have understood Meili Song's surprise at their swarming... especially so early in the day.

"Let's circle over to that side," the small woman said, and she jerked her head toward the west side of the long, low shed. Ladka nodded without comment and he followed as she veered to the right. "That's my window up there," said Meili as they reached the seventh fairway where it abutted the maintenance building. "Don't I have a wonderful view?"

The General was looking up toward the second floor windows of Building 200, when he heard Meili Song gasp, "Oh my God, Karol...look at this!"

* * * * *

THE TWIN-ENGINE PIPER 'AZTEC' was waiting for Omar Inbula, a.k.a. Felix Ruecuodal, when his limousine pulled onto the ramp at Long Island's Republic Airport. It was 8:00 AM on Monday and the jihadist had spent most of the previous evening familiarizing himself with the New York Metropolitan area, and consulting by cell phone with al Shaheetz in Teheran. The tête-à-tête had been monitored, of course, and both insurrectionists knew it. But the cagey old terrorist, like most covert agents, was well-versed in disguising the true nature of a mission.

There was little doubt that the 'disabled' Ruecuodal was merely a wealthy foreign national, probably not long for this world, who was determined to part with some of his considerable cash at the Mohegan Sun's frenetic gaming tables before meeting his Maker. The possibility of breaking the bank at an American casino was tops on Inbula's (Ruecuodal's) bucket list, at least if the tapped phone conversation was to be believed, and the monitoring agencies in Istanbul, London, and Arlington had no reason to assume otherwise.

Gaming operations in the United States pride themselves in honoring the anonymity of their international patrons. Only the violating of a casino's rules is cause for a high-roller's banishment from the premises. And 'Felix Ruecuodal's' declared intention to buy in at the Mohegan's craps tables for a hundred grand was reason enough to assure that he would remain both faceless and nameless. All he had to do was play nice...basically behave himself with the cocktail waitresses...and drop that hundred thousand Canadian when all was said and done. Was that too much to ask in return for a tender steak, a magnum of champagne, and a few dozen Little Neck clams?

Of course, every 'tables' gambler had his own style of play... his own system...and casinos worldwide recognize and accept the fact. Indeed, the conventional wisdom is that while a gaming host will send a limousine to transport an ordinary compulsive craps shooter to the tables, they'll supply a *private helicopter*, if necessary, to deliver a 'systems' bettor! In other words, there has never been a 'system' known to man that can possible beat the house in the long term, and anybody who thinks he has discovered such a winning method, is red meat for the casino.

Accordingly, once 'Ruecuodal' arrived at Mohegan Sun, ostentatiously tipped the limo driver, doorman, coat check girl, and men's room attendant...all with ten-dollar bills precisely folded in his own lucky configuration...and when 'Felix's' routine was thus recorded by innumerable concealed overhead cameras...the word was quickly passed from the casino's cadre of observers, to the Pit Bosses, and ultimately the craps table Stick Men. *We've got a 'system' player buying in, folks—heads up—do whatever he says!*

But there was a method to Inbula's madness.

Part of old Omar's superstitious routine included the feigned self-imposed rule that he never touched dice between the 'unlucky' hours of 9:00 PM and 1:00 AM...and he was quick to announce the fact.

"Never mind," whispered the Shift Boss to the Pit Boss. "We're jammed at those hours, anyway. Let him go get some air."

Four hours-worth of air to be exact. With Southwick maybe seventy minutes distant to the north. Omar Inbula would have plenty of time to drive to Massachusetts, murder the despicable Carter Banning, and get back to his lucky table by one.

Just part of his lucky system.

* * * * *

THERE IS NO LEGITIMATE WAY for a casino to restrain an RFB-comped (free room, food, and beverage) player who wants to stray to another gambling establishment...or any other venue, for that matter. These wanderers are known in the gaming trade as 'walkers,' and 'walkers' are allowed only one such foray before being confronted and scolded. If a comped player 'walks' a second time, he finds himself denied the right to purchase chips anywhere on the gambling floor until such time as the Casino Host...a house executive empowered with considerable purse discretion...has politely, but firmly, read him the riot act. The conversation usually ends with, "We are not your personal travel agency...nor are we your private bank!"

But upon receiving Omar's request that he be provided with a Mohegan Sun limo and driver for the next four hours, Inbula's hosts were only too happy to comply with his wish. What better way to keep the hobbled old man and his $75,000 under surveillance? For heaven's sake 'Felix Ruecuodal' wasn't planning to jump ship. He only wanted to take a quick trip up to the tiny southern panhandle of Massachusetts—where his former Canadian relatives lived, he'd said—in the little town of Southwick. He'd be back at the fifty-dollar table shortly after midnight, at which time the serious betting would get underway. As for the exact nature of the guest's activity while on his brief sortie, whose business was it but his own? The driver had been instructed only to have him back in Uncasville by twelve-thirty. After that, the driver was to inform 'Ruecuodal' that the limo would be otherwise committed.

After speeding west on County Route 2 to Hartford, the big white Lincoln turned north at Manchester and raced through virtually no traffic along the Connecticut River Valley to Longmeadow, south of Springfield. From there the plush vehicle made an unobstructed run to tiny Feeding Hills...then to Southwick proper.

Elapsed travel time to the Slater Lake Dock on dimly lit Stony Path, exactly eighty minutes.

The following morning Lieutenant Frank Brogan would find the partially stripped body of the limousine driver lying face-down on the rocky Slater Lake shore. Almost immediately thereafter, he would discover the corpse of Carter Banning in the foyer of his colonial-style home. Elizabeth Banning would be found dead on the kitchen floor not far from her husband. Like the uniformed chauffeur, they would have succumbed to massive injections of swift-acting Sarin toxin.

A man who identified himself only as "…Karol Ladka, a friend…" having arrived at the discovery scene minutes after Brogan had secured the Banning home…was otherwise strangely reticent…and he had some explaining to do.

Chapter Forty-one

GENERAL LADKA MIGHT HAVE saved himself a lot of serious trouble if he'd reported the dead deer on the Edgewood Links as soon as he and Meili Song discovered them the previous morning. As it was, determining accurately that there was nothing to be done for the dead animals, he'd suggested to the dermatologist that they keep mum, at least until the following day, to see if anyone who might have been somehow responsible for the bizarre situation would show up. Cruelty to animals, he knew, was one of the telltale indicators of deep-seated antisocial behavior.

With that in mind, Karol had convinced a shaken Meili Song to permit him to keep watch from the vantage point provided by her office window. There he could stay, and observe the gruesome scene for the remainder of the day and night. Carter had expected to meet him and Meili at the 'Countrymen's Café' for breakfast, but Ladka phoned from Song's office at 8:30 Monday morning outlining the proposed change of plan, but without explaining it in detail.

"Let Wilkinson out from under the SEALS' watch," he'd said. "My gut keeps telling me we're due to turn up an accomplice.

Unless we spring the kid now, we might spook any collaborator. That's not a good prospect!"

Carter Banning hadn't made it a habit to second-guess Brigadier Generals...and he wasn't going to start now. As things turned out, however, Ladka's strangely clouded analysis of goings on at the Medical Center proved unfortunate in two ways.

First: Had he and Song met with Banning as planned Monday morning, it's likely they'd have decided to arrange for the SEALS to free Wilkinson and merely keep an eye on him...while Carter would join Ladka in watch over the mysterious golf course scene. This would have had the effect of saving the unfortunate Bannings' lives.

Second: By extension, if free to concentrate on the Stony Path houses by the lake, the SEALS probably would have nabbed the 82-year-old Inbula. This was the sort of fortuitous outcome the normally alert Karol Ladka would have hoped for, even if he had no way of actually anticipating such a turn of events precisely. With the old man in custody, enhanced interrogation could have brought the entire Southwick incident to a prompt and auspicious conclusion.

But alas, the best laid plans...even of veteran sleuths like General Karol Ladka...often take inauspicious turns. And this twist of fortune left even Karol himself in jeopardy.

Because the man who murdered the Bannings...and his own hired driver...was obviously at large. Probably nearby, Karol estimated.

And Hugh Harmwell would also be released from his Port Jefferson hospital room in a day or two...or as soon as someone in his immediate family came to sign his release form.

But most significantly, Karol Ladka had just been informed by digital technician, Albert Tremaine, that there was news... important news! The computer whiz had spotted a person of interest whom Ladka had formerly alerted him to. It was the radicalized Islamic terrorist, Peter Wilkinson, and he was on the ferry, *Grand Republic*. The boat would be docking at Port

Jefferson in ten minutes or so…and Wilkinson was accompanied by a well-dressed older man. "He appears to be well-off," said Tremaine. "In his mid-eighties, I'd estimate."

This was not turning out to be the General's best day, by any means.

Though for Carter and Elizabeth Banning, it had been infinitely worse.

*****

MEILI SONG HAD BEEN DEVASTATED beyond description upon hearing of the Bannings' murder. Carter was such a nice man…an all-around good guy who had served his country with distinction…and though few including Meili, were aware of the fact, in the final analysis he had died at the hands of the enemy.

It was Jean Gustavson who broke the news to the pert dermatologist. Word of such sudden deaths spreads like wildfire in any medical community, but especially in one as tight-knit as the VA Medical Center, where practitioners in a dozen different disciplines interact on a daily basis. Doctor Jim Briley had told the ER nurse Ryan of the double homicide, and Ryan had passed the word along to his Charge Nurse. An astonished Jean Gustavson had made her way up to Song's office and tearfully informed her in person of the horrific crime.

"But we were with him thirty-six hours ago!" the stunned dermatologist had murmured.

The nurse embraced her friend. "Do you want me to cancel your afternoon appointments?"

"No," sniffed Meili, drying her eyes and trying to compose herself. "I have two post-op consults. I'll be okay." She shook her head slowly. "But, God, I wish I didn't have to process this information."

The phone on her desk rang and the Charge Nurse turned to leave. "Stay," said Meili. "Maybe that's Karol." She lifted the receiver. "Doctor Song...Yes...Yes...Not at all, what is it?...Of course." Meili looked at her watch. "Yes...Yes, I'll be ready."

Meili Song replaced the receiver. She looked blankly at her friend. "That was the Southwick Police Department. A Lieutenant Brogan wants to talk with me." She dialed the four-digit extension of her Scheduling Clerk while murmuring to Jean. "I have to cancel my appointments after all. He's picking me up in twenty minutes."

Gustavson's hand went to her mouth...and at that moment the cell phone in her pocket sounded. The ring tone was the first seven notes of 'Jailhouse Rock.' Frank Brogan was calling, and he wanted to talk with Nurse Gustavson, too...at headquarters.

"I can be in Doctor Song's office when you..." She stiffened at Brogan's obvious interruption. "I see. Very well." Jean tapped the 'End Call' icon and the phone's display screen went dark. "Lieutenant Brogan is sending a Sergeant Beamish for me. He suggested that we refrain from discussing the matter with anyone...including each other."

"Why?" cried Meili.

"He reminded me that this is a criminal case," said Gustavson.

"So?"

"I'm no lawyer, Millie," Jean shrugged, "...but maybe we better do as he says."

* * * * *

IN THE FOYER of the Banning house, Karol Ladka had produced his government ID and voluntarily turned over the weapon that he wore in an ankle holster. Frank Brogan had extended the usual courtesies that all peace officers proffered to one another in such circumstances, and he reminded the Army official that Southwick in general, and the Stony Path crime scene in particular, fell within his (Brogan's) jurisdiction. Ladka understood.

"A few questions, General. First, do you require a lawyer?"

"Am I under arrest?"

"No."

"Then I don't need a lawyer."

"What's your relationship to Carter and Elizabeth Banning, Sir?"

"Carter's a former Army associate," Karol said simply. "Elizabeth's his wife."

"When's the last time you saw them alive, General?"

"I had dinner with Carter the night before last. I haven't seen Elizabeth since I've been in town."

"You dined alone with Carter night before last?"

"I didn't say that."

"Where did you dine?"

"Lakeside. Italian place."

"Who was with you?"

"That should be easy for you to find out, Lieutenant."

"How many people were with you and Carter Banning at Lakeside?"

"As I said, your people can undoubtedly…"

Frank Brogan had a fairly good idea of what was going on. And he also knew it wouldn't be necessary for the General to state the intimate details of the liaison for the record. Not just yet, at any rate. But while he had Ladka sitting across the table, Frank Brogan figured it couldn't hurt to ask one last question… one that bore directly on Elizabeth and Carter Banning's bizarre killings.

"General, you are familiar with the toxicity levels of certain particularly volatile poisons, are you not?"

Karol paused for several seconds and looked, unblinking, into Frank Brogan's equally fixed gaze. "Now I think we'll wait for that lawyer, Lieutenant."

"Your call," said Brogan. Both men stood. "You have a right to legal counsel. And you are now under arrest in the matter of the murders of Carter and Elizabeth Banning. You have the right to remain silent…anything you say may be used against you." The police chief activated his mobile radio and handed it to Ladka. "Make your phone call, General."

"I prefer to do that in private," Karol said.

"Sorry," said Brogan. "Under the circumstances, privacy is not one of your constitutional rights," He removed a set of handcuffs from his wide leather belt.

Karol Ladka dialed a number in Arlington, and handed the radio back to Brogan. The Lieutenant pressed a button activating the Walkie-Talkie's 'speaker' option. He twirled his finger for Ladka to turn around. With his hands cuffed behind his back, Karol heard the phone ring twice in The Pentagon. A clear female voice emanated from the radio on the Bannings' kitchen table. "Judge Advocate's Office."

The General knew that the call was being recorded. He turned halfway and spoke over his shoulder. "Karol V. Ladka, USA 12388765. Request assignment of representation forthwith. Confirm."

There was a brief pause…then…"Request noted. Representation assigned. File number 765-12-16. GPS has you Stony Path, Southwick, Massachusetts 01077. Confirm?"

"Roger, that."

"Counsel en route twelve hundred hours. ETA 1345 hours. Good luck, Sir!"

Frank Brogan draped Karol Ladka's windbreaker over the tall man's shoulders and motioned for Patrolman Steven Volker to escort the prisoner to a holding cell at headquarters. Outside the Stony Path murder scene a small group of neighbors in jacket-covered sleepwear had gathered at a discreet distance. As Ladka and Volker exited the colonial home through its red front door, the General heard Brogan's radio squawk, "Song and Gustavson are here, Lieutenant."

Frank Brogan picked up the mobile unit and fingered the microphone's 'send' button. "Bring them to the Turbish residence" he instructed. "Meet me there in ten minutes. And send Carrick and Dunkhase to secure the Banning house."

Chapter Forty-two

SAINT CHARLES HOSPITAL sits grandly atop a high promontory that overlooks Long Island Sound from Port Jefferson. The town's two harbor landmarks…the Cross-Sound Ferry to ramshackle Bridgeport in Connecticut…and renowned old Theatre Three a few blocks south of the ferry dock…are both clearly visible from most rooms on the institution's west side.

At a quarter to twelve, Hugh Harmwell sat on a long second-story veranda, tightly wrapped in blue woolen blankets against the chill breeze that blew in from the water. He was lightly sedated though frankly surprised he was still alive. His hands, all of whose broken fingers had been set and were immobilized in two separate casts, were virtually useless on his lap.

No one had come to visit him…because not even the medical staff members who had ministered to the surly man recognized him. Who would have dreamed that the odd-looking fellow in the St. Charles Prison Ward was, in fact, one of Long Island's most heralded theater artists?

Indeed, understudy, Brett Chizever, cast in 'A Christmas Carol' as 'The Ghost of Christmas Present,' had stepped into the 'Scrooge' role with such élan that it was widely assumed Hugh

Harmwell had abdicated his part in favor of the Encore Award-winning prodigy.

But though the acting impresario and double agent might be manually incapacitated, there was nothing wrong with his eyesight. Harmwell hadn't seen Omar Inbula in years, but old men don't change greatly once in their eighties, he'd learned, and Hugh Harmwell was certain that it was the jihadist from Teheran who had just disembarked from the *Grand Republic*.

The faux Frenchman from Canada had long since discarded his limp along with the hinged plaster cast that once concealed the Sarin darts used to kill his chauffeur and The Bannings. Now, he was the picture of good-natured agility, as he strode across the *Grand Republic's* wide gangplank…his arm draped affectionately across the shoulders of Peter Wilkinson.

Omar Inbula had enlisted the aid of the radicalized student for one reason only—to assist in carrying out the murder of Hugh Harmwell.

Watching from his vantage point on the hospital balcony, Harmwell carefully followed the course of the two jihadists as they walked arm in arm from the ferry dock…south on East Main…then east on Thompson Street…trudging up the Thompson Street hill almost directly toward him.

The disabled double agent panicked and he cried out for the nurse's aide who had been replenishing his restorative juice drink. The teen, a pretty girl in a candy-striped dress that was gathered at the waist, had been sitting opposite Harmwell, reading an assigned novel for a high school class.

Suddenly she leaped from her large rocker and rushed to his assistance, only to find him wide-eyed and babbling incoherently, as he pointed a trembling bandaged hand in the direction of the steep road that rose more than a hundred feet above sea level as it curled up Hospital Hill.

The frightened aide swung her gaze toward the narrow street. She could see nothing that should have alarmed her patient. On this sunny morning, only a mild breeze scattered the fallen leaves on Thompson Street, as two congenial men paced leisurely along… one young and smartly dressed…the other old…probably his grandfather.

By now, Harmwell was sobbing, his face partially buried in the crook of one arm, dark eyes peering over his elbow, while what he recognized as certain death approached, step by inevitable step.

"Look, that's him," Peter called pointing to the famed Theatre Three director, as he and Omar Inbula reached the Belle Terre Road hospital entrance.

"Ah," said Inbula, "…so it is." And he waved up at the balcony cheerily. "*Salaam*, old friend. We've come to bring you home."

Hugh Harmwell gagged on his own utterances as he attempted to alert the young volunteer to his impending fate. But he could not string together even three or four of the evocative words that he had once commanded so eloquently on stage. It was as if the language had become his enemy…fashioning a dire threat that doomed him with each incriminating syllable…sealing his fate with every turn of phrase…converting even innocent idioms into deadly pejoratives.

"Help me," he tried to implore the girl in red and white.

With a tongue that had turned to dust…and a gown now soaked with perspiration, he attempted to clutch her sleeve with useless, awkward hands the size of swabbed footballs.

"But it's your family," the aide smiled reassuringly. "Won't you be glad to see them?" She smoothed the blanket that covered Hugh Harmwell's quivering knees before, with one, final, superhuman thrust, he propelled his wheelchair forward, flinging it over the balcony's low railing…and impaling himself scant yards from his intended murderers…ironically on the spiked fence designed to protect him.

With the wheels of the chair still spinning at the base of the fence, and the speechless girl staring down in horror from the veranda, Omar Inbula ambled over to Harmwell's rapidly bleeding-out corpse. Wilkinson followed him at a ten-foot distance. Even the youthful radicalized terrorist was too shocked to speak, and he stopped his approach when the old man reached the gory scene. Harmwell's torso had been pierced in three places as if a massive, wrought-iron pitchfork had been thrust upward through his body. In the midday sun, the bloody skyward-pointing tines glistened scarlet in contrast to the bulbous, snow-white dressings that enclosed his lifeless hands and hung, like his head, straight down from the folds of his hospital gown.

Methodically, Inbula reached upward, lifted one of the dead man's eyelids, and with his thumbnail he scratched Hugh Harmwell's protruding cornea. When the dangling man neither flinched nor groaned, old Omar turned to Peter and said in Arabic, *Alahu Akbar*.

"Yes...God is Great!" Wilkinson seconded weakly.

"No," said Inbula in a loud voice. "I have said, *Alahu Akbar*. It means 'God is *Greater*.' And wise men know that the words are to be shouted, my boy...not whispered!"

With that, Inbula placed an arm across Peter's shoulders once again, and as an alarm sounded throughout the corridors of the building behind them, they meandered down Thompson Street. When they reached the ferry dock, the old jihadist tossed $75,000 in Mohegan Sun casino chips into the oily water of the harbor... and they doubled back to The Steamroom Restaurant for a late lunch.

Chapter Forty-three

THE PILOT OF THE Dolphin helicopter had been through many covert missions with Karol Ladka; he knew better than to question the General's strategy. He hadn't heard from the boss since securing the MH-65 back at Tweed-New Haven the day before yesterday, and three days of hiding a brand new whirlybird were one too many. So the Lieutenant Colonel used his discretion and moved the big aircraft west to Danbury Airport.

Tucked between two long, rolling hills and flanked by a federal prison, Danbury Municipal was about as good a spot to hide a $20 million-dollar chopper on the lam as any place you were likely to find in New England. With the possible exception of northern Maine…and there wasn't any Avgas up there…only maple syrup and a hotshot writer named Stephen King.

Speaking of which…

Ladka's pilot, Pedro Avila, was a newly minted Light Colonel who, when he wasn't flying the often unfriendly skies dodging or pursuing CIA adversaries, could usually be found with his nose in one of Stephen King's fifty-four novels. Avila had read the entire King *oeuvre*…all, that is, except for the one book that had turned into arguably one of the most renowned motion pictures of all time: 'The Shawshank Redemption.' That novel, he hadn't yet read.

Confined, as he now was 24/7, to either the cabin of the thoroughly equipped Sikorsky Dolphin, or the meager second-floor restaurant above the office of Danbury airport's Fixed Base Operator, Avila was looking forward to starting King's story of a man wrongly convicted of murder. *What better place to catch the local color of a maximum security lockup,* he'd speculated in gleeful anticipation, *than in the shadow of a federal detention center?* For all Colonel Pedro Avila knew, the prolific author from Maine might have patterned Shawshank Prison on the selfsame Danbury Penitentiary that loomed in the valley just south of runway 8, and was clearly visible from the restaurant.

Avila sat washing down a cheeseburger and a double order of fries with a diet Coke, while simultaneously studying Danbury Municipal's most recent 'Noise Sensitive Area Chart.'

This was a difficult place to fly in and out of...even in a helicopter. It wasn't just the tricky topography, though God knows that was enough to test the airmanship of even the most experienced aviators, but it seemed that the residents of Danbury and environs would never be satisfied with anything short of total silence in the skies over their town.

It had all started ten years ago.

Some politician from New Jersey had decided to make a name for himself (as if his Child Molestation rap hadn't assured that already) by complaining to the Newark Star Ledger that he and Danbury's other inmates were sleep-deprived due to noise from aircraft flying a traffic pattern that brought planes within a mile of the slammer.

When airport administrators shifted the landing and takeoff routes to accommodate the jailbirds, overseers of a nearby hospital demanded similar treatment. Soon, half a dozen small residential communities caught the fever and bitched to their 'all-ears' freshman congressman. Almost spontaneously, Senator Chuck Schumer from New York threatened a class-action suit on behalf of his constituents institutionalized in Danbury… and the floodgates opened wide. Within weeks, every mayor, councilperson, alderperson, and committeeperson was on the warpath…and just about the only place a pilot was allowed to fly over Danbury was straight up!

The whole fiasco came to a head when Schumer, sensing that perhaps there was more publicity to be harvested from this unlikely crop ('CRAP' the New York Post had called it) threatened still another suit. "Danbury inmates," he griped, "…are being unfairly deprived of what every man, woman, and child in America is entitled to…the right to view American commerce as it's plied in the free and open air." Incredibly, the indefatigable Schumer had shifted gears and summoned the temerity to proclaim that diverting air traffic from the vicinity of Danbury Penitentiary was, in fact, an insidious form of Solitary Confinement, "…matched only by the isolation found in that Fascist bastion, Guantanamo Bay."

'CRAP' indeed!

Colonel Avila finished his dinner, jammed the 'Shawshank' paperback in his pants pocket, and deciding that a modest brandy would not be out of the question at this hour, ordered a Cognac. When he paid the total twenty-dollar tab with his credit card, it was one of the very rare instances in which Pedro committed two *faux pas* in a single transaction: drinking on the job…and recording the indiscretion on American Express.

* * * * *

ALBERT TREMAINE WAS LEAVING his counter seat at The Steamroom just as Peter Wilkinson and Omar Inbula entered the popular eatery. Though taken somewhat by surprise at the sight of the men he'd assumed had left the area, Tremaine had the presence of mind to fire off two quick photos of the pair with his smart phone…one showed them standing…the other, seated… and once outside, he promptly mailed copies to Karol Ladka.

The coded acknowledgment that was usually forthcoming from The General...the prompt response that approved Tremaine's standard five-hundred-dollar fee...for some reason didn't appear. So Albert sent the email attachment a second time. The duplicated transmission automatically triggered a unique default alert in Ladka's Samsung Galaxy...and the device now sat vibrating and sounding insistently on Frank Brogan's desk.

From his bench in the headquarters holding cell, Ladka heard the distinctive notification clearly. He knew that Albert Tremaine was calling again...and he was also certain that the Lieutenant would answer. "If it's my wife," he called from down the hall, "...tell her I'm tied up."

"What if it's your girlfriend?" said Brogan, tapping and opening the text file.

"Same message," Karol said. "I'm not married."

There was no text inscription...only two grainy, side-by-side photo attachments. The dim pictures were obviously taken without benefit of a flash. They showed two men in a restaurant. One photo...the one on the left...had apparently been taken first, and it showed the subjects approaching the camera head-on. In the other picture, the men...one young and somewhat nervous, the other old and nonchalant...were seated. The youth was shown in profile.

Lieutenant Brogan recognized Peter Wilkinson immediately, but he was sure he'd never in his life seen the old man. He was also nearly positive that the small pin in the well-dressed stranger's lapel was the colorful logo of the Mohegan Sun Casino. Only a very few Mohegan Sun guests were issued the expensive enamel and gold token. It was the tiny badge that identified the wearer as a high roller...an individual to be afforded all the amenities the casino had to offer.

Brogan extracted a pair of handcuffs from his center desk drawer and took them to the holding pen. He instructed Ladka to approach the bars and extend his hands. Brogan reached inside the metal rods, cuffed his prisoner, and withdrew his own hands.

He unlocked the slatted cage, and ordered Ladka to precede him to a chair in front of his desk. "Don't do anything that'll get you shot," said the policeman. "Sit down. I've got some questions."

Frank Brogan sat in his rolling wooden chair and picked up Karol Ladka's smart phone. He thrust it toward Ladka at eye level and pressed the Power switch. "You ever seen these men?"

With hands manacled in his lap, Ladka leaned forward from the waist and squinted. "Yes. Both of them, I think."

"Who are they?"

Karol paused for half-a-dozen beats. "The old one's an Iranian…name is Inbula…Omar Inbula."

It was not what Brogan had expected. "An Iranian?"

"It's been a long time. Forty years. It was in Istanbul."

"And the young one?"

Ladka squirmed in an attempt to relieve the pinching of his wrists. "You know him," said The General. "His name's Wilkinson. He lives down the road. What you don't know is that he's a radicalized Islamic terrorist. And that picture was taken in a Long Island restaurant called The Steamroom."

"You've been there?"

Karol Ladka nodded. "It's a popular place." He motioned toward the smart phone. "According to the date/time stamp on those photos, Inbula and his protégé were in the restaurant six minutes ago." He glanced at the round clock on the wall, then at Brogan. "Omar Inbula's a professional killer, Lieutenant. Furthermore, we can assume that he's also a jihadist and a terrorist infiltrator…just like our radicalized friend Wilkinson." The sweep second hand on the round wall clock seemed to be flying as it inexorably spun away precious seconds. "Regardless of what you might think of me, we have no choice but to grab Inbula and Wilkinson while they're together in one place." He gazed at Brogan from under arched eyebrows. "You might not get a second chance, Officer."

Frank Brogan was skeptical. "And just how do you suggest we go about that?"

"There are only two major roads in and out of Port Jefferson," said Ladka, "...one from the southwest...the other from the southeast. If we can have them blocked in the next ten minutes, maybe we can close the net."

Now it was Lieutenant Brogan's turn to check the clock high over the desk...and Karol Ladka knew the policeman would play along. He held out his hands. "Just let me make one more phone call, Lieutenant."

Brogan fished the handcuff key from his shirt pocket. "Okay... one call...thirty seconds...and this better work, my friend." He circled the desk and removed the cuffs from Ladka's stinging wrists. "Who are you calling?"

The General picked up his cell phone and speed-dialed CIA headquarters in Arlington.

* * * * *

AS HE'D PROMISED, Karol Ladka had limited himself to the single, half-minute call...but he'd voice-copied Pedro Avila in Danbury, Albert Tremaine in Port Jefferson, and the three Navy SEALS in the compound at the Stony Path *cul-de-sac*. Within minutes the SEALS were on their way to the Bridgeport ferry dock...Tremaine had taken up a surveillance post outside The Steamroom with his GPS activated...and Colonel Pedro Avila had the Dolphin helicopter in the air, headed for Southwick— and Edgewood Links.

Even before Karol had used his allotted thirty-second phone conversation, The Pentagon had called the Suffolk County Civil Preparedness department in eastern Long Island. They, in turn, ordered municipal road blocks immediately installed on Route 25-A in Port Jefferson's neighboring village of Setauket...and in Port Jeff itself, where Mount Sinai Road meets Main Street.

Though Wilkinson and Inbula had no clue, before the jihadists had even digested their crab cakes the entire harbor hamlet that surrounded them was sealed up tight as a drum.

Chapter Forty-four

THE FLIGHT FROM Danbury to Southwick took Colonel Avila a full twenty minutes, because in traversing that eighty-mile span he'd had to dodge no fewer than eight airports, large and small. The final field in the group was brightly illuminated Bradley International at Windsor Locks. Once there, Avila was just a few miles east of his destination…the sprawling golf course that flanked the several four-story buildings of the VAMC in Southwick.

As specified in General Ladka's cell phone communiqué, he and Police Lieutenant Frank Brogan would be ready for pick-up at 1630 hours. They would be waiting in the middle of Edgewood Links' sixth fairway, their rendezvous point marked by the high beam headlights and flashing blue emergency lights of Brogan's police cruiser. The landing spot had been chosen by Brogan, an avid golfer who knew the Edgewood Links topography well. His familiarity with the layout proved essential because Edgewood was known to be one of the hilliest golf courses in all of Massachusetts—and only the long sixth fairway provided what could be called an acceptably wide, flat landing area for the sleek Dolphin chopper.

Still, as he approached the long darts of white from the headlights, and the alternating strobe flashes on the car's roof, Pedro Avila wanted to inspect the wheels-down site for himself. The fact that the grassy strip of turf sustained the weight of the dark police sedan illuminating the area was no guarantee the ground was solid enough to support the big MH-65. Despite being empty, the helicopter weighed three times as much as Brogan's cruiser—with the addition of Ladka and Brogan when they came aboard, Pedro would have to factor in another four hundred pounds to the payload. Should he take on both men?

The veteran pilot decided not to chance it. He would load only Ladka from a three-foot hover position. Even if that extra weight brought the helicopter down to ground level as Karol climbed the rope ladder, the lift provided by the spinning main rotor would keep the tricycle gear from sinking significantly into the damp turf. Colonel Avila lowered the Dolphin to three hundred feet… one hundred…fifty…

* * * * *

ALBERT TREMAINE SAT in semi-darkness on a slatted bench in front of The Steamroom. The restaurant's tall, wide windows made it much easier for him to see Wilkinson and the old guy than vice versa. They were apparently having an early dinner of either crab cakes or sea scallops…he couldn't tell…and they drank some sort of white wine. Had Albert known the pair was enjoying a bottle of Pouilly-Fuisse 2013 Domaine Ferret, he would have been envious in the extreme. Anyway…he took another picture when he saw Wilkinson lift the bottle from an ice bucket and pour a second glass for each of them. Maybe Albert could enhance the label's image back home on his desktop computer. Wine lovers are a nosey bunch by definition.

Tremaine still hadn't heard from Ladka, except for the mysterious copy of the voicemail message whose recipient had to be somebody important. The address was scrambled at the receiving end, as were every fourth word of the message, and only top-secret recipients had the capacity to muddle their addresses that way. It was obvious, though, that Ladka had wanted Albert to continue surveillance of Wilkinson and his companion (whose name had been jumbled in the encryption process). Why else would The General have sent him a voicemail copy of the communiqué?

As he sat fiddling with his smart phone—the way billions of other users were idly doing worldwide at this very minute—Albert Tremaine wondered why all those red emergency lights continued to flash high up on Hospital Hill. Usually they stopped after a patient had been delivered to the St. Charles Emergency Room...but these strobes had been flaring for a good half-hour. *I'll try the PJPD website,* Tremaine said inwardly. *Maybe they've posted a bulletin...*

* * * * *

THE THREE NAVY SEALS wheeled their Humvee to a squealing halt on the Bridgeport Ferry dock...they burst from the distinctive vehicle...and ran up the gangway ramp that the *Grand Republic* was preparing to withdraw into its bow. In one hand, each of the men held a modified AK-47 machine-pistol hidden beneath his woolen civilian shirt...and with their free arm they waved the astonished passengers to the enclosed second deck, where two of the men promptly blocked the passageway doors behind them.

The third SEAL ran to the bridge where the big boat's captain and his First Mate were preparing to get their early evening cross-sound departure under way. As the SEAL rushed into the glass-enclosed tower—the highest vantage point on the *Grand Republic*—the startled Mate reached for a narrow drawer that could only have contained a radio...or a gun. The Special Forces man had no choice but to fire a silenced round into the uniformed assistant's hand, and the .39 millimeter slug pierced the flesh between the young man's thumb and index finger, ultimately lodging itself in the splintered wooden compartment.

The Mate groaned and dropped to a kneeling position, whereupon the Captain leaped between him and the shooter, desperately shielding his fallen officer from the burly, civilian-clad man he had never seen before. "Don't shoot him," he begged, turning in a squatting posture to cradle the Mate's limp arm.

The SEAL reached for a small, white First-Aid kit spring-loaded in a clamp on the wall. He yanked it from the fixture and threw it to the Captain. "Bandage him," was all he said as he brushed by the two men. With the muzzle of his gun he prodded the shattered face of the small drawer on the bridge desk, and pried it full open. Inside, was indeed a .45 caliber Glock pistol. And inserted in its handle was a magazine fully loaded with ten deadly hollow-point rounds.

The Navy man seized the weapon, slid open the starboard window nearest him, and flung the Glock into the oily water of Bridgeport Harbor. He turned to the Captain whose hands and shirt were now smeared with blood. "Drag your Officer into that corner and sit there," he said with a jerk of the AK-47. "Stay with him. If either of you moves I'll shoot you both." There was no question that the man with the machine-pistol meant exactly what he said. With a calm that was both confident and chilling, he added, "Don't test me. My friends and I are accustomed to this sort of thing."

Chapter Forty-five

JAHAN AL SHAHEETZ HAD a lot to lose should Omar Inbula be taken into custody and subjected to what the Central Intelligence Agency euphemistically called Enhanced Interrogation. The more descriptively accurate, if politically incorrect term, was *waterboarding*…and the simulated drowning process invariably loosened even the most recalcitrant tongues of those subjected to its terrors. There was no known way, it seemed, for a human being blithely to disregard the combined sensations of suffocation and strangulation. Or if there was, the CIA had not encountered it.

Unlike 82-year-old loner Inbula, the jihadist ringleader al Shaheetz was in the relative prime of life, and the husband of three wives. Three of his fourteen children were males and it was these prized specimens who would, along with the octogenarian Omar, surely be subjected to unspeakable torture, should the old terrorist's identity be revealed during his murderous American mission.

Within minutes of Hugh Harmwell's spectacular death, news of the incident flashed throughout the digitally sensitive world. In a cyber-universe where information is transmitted at the speed of light, the distances that separate Earthly nations, oceans, and continents mean little or nothing. Communication with even our celestial space neighbors is being conducted on a near-daily basis as the planet's warring combatants go about planning the colonization of the Universe. In point of fact, Harmwell's obituary could have been sent to a listening post on The Moon... and received there well before his body had fully assumed room temperature in Port Jefferson, Long Island.

No one was more acutely aware of twenty-first century technology than Albert Tremaine. He was a bright young man who, like most tech-savvy innovators, found it difficult to spend time in unproductive indolence when he could be expanding the horizons of his art. As he peered over the top of his customized smart phone, the glow from its generous six-by-three-inch screen illuminating his lightly bearded face, the cyber-visionary wondered if either of the two men he was watching might be carrying a device that was subject to hacking.

Every microelectronic contrivance emitted a unique footprint when activated by its user, Albert knew, and once that device had been triggered, the rest of the hacking process became a simple matter...at least for geeks like Tremaine. The trick was to have the user actuate the machine...something easier said than done when neither the device's password, nor the owner's name was a known factor.

But perhaps he knew enough to compromise the objects of his surveillance, Albert Tremaine thought...and he Googled The Steamroom's phone number. It was (631) 928-6690, and he dialed it. Tremaine watched through the floor-to-ceiling windows as the always-busy bartender picked up the receiver and tucked it solidly between his ear and shoulder. "Steamroom."

"My friends...the men seated in the corner beneath the boat models...have them call home." And Albert broke the connection.

The bartender impatiently jammed the handset back onto the wall bracket. He finished stirring a vodka martini, and summoned the waiter for Station Three as he poured the cocktail into a delicate, long-stemmed glass. "Extra dry with a twist," he said, and the waiter lifted the small tray. "And those guys at Table Six...tell 'em to call home."

The young waiter frowned. "Did they leave a number?"

The bartender set three highball glasses in front of him and filled them with ice. "I'm not a telephone operator, Tommy." He poured three ounces of scotch into each of the abutting glasses in one uninterrupted, left-to-right flow of whiskey. The white-shirted waiter shrugged, delivered the straight-up martini to Table Five, then approached the party of two in the corner.

From his bench seat outside, Albert Tremaine followed the movements in the restaurant. Both Wilkinson and his elderly companion seemed stunned by the waiter's message, and the old man looked around the room suspiciously. Young Wilkinson leaned and appeared to whisper something to him.

Certain that one of them was going to initiate a phone call, Tremaine quickly activated an application of his own creation. It would detect the triggering of any new electronic impulse within one hundred yards...and lock onto it. Thus, when Inbula dialed the private number of Jahan al Shaheetz, neither he nor the jihadist in Teheran would know it, but they'd unwittingly be talking to a third party.

The 'secure' apparatus that Omar Inbula trusted so implicitly... had been hacked!

When Inbula had transmitted the call to al Shaheetz, it was nearly 1:00 AM Teheran time and the former *Imam* was busy planning a strategy meeting in Mosul. Noting that his unexpected caller was utilizing a disposable phone, and that the message originated in the US, al Shaheetz answered in near-perfect English.

"I have good news, My Brother," the elderly Inbula fairly chirped.

There was a four-second pause. "Speak," al Shaheetz said in a dull monotone.

"The target is down," Inbula said cryptically...and he waited for another three beats.

"I know that, idiot."

Omar Inbula's scarred and wrinkled face took on a puzzled look. He paused again. "Then what is the purpose of your question to me?"

"What question?...you goat!"

"I...I do not understand."

"Of course not," said al Shaheetz sharply. "...what else is to be expected from a despised and ignorant goat?"

"Why, then, have you instructed me to contact you, worthy partner?"

Al Shaheetz's response came in a growl that chilled even the veteran terrorist. "I am not accustomed to being questioned by asses, Omar Inbula. Do you hear?" He dropped his voice an octave, "And I am your master, not your partner.

"But..."

"Silence! Not another word. You will call me in precisely eighteen hours. At eleven PM East Coast US time you will report to me that, like Harmwell, Wilkinson is dead."

"At your comm..."

"Silence! But first our American friend will have dispensed the Phosgene. If this is not accomplished effectively...and on time...be assured you will have written a most damnable legacy of failure."

The old jihadist choked back a sob at the thought of such disgrace.

"And Omar...should you miscarry, do not even contemplate the taking of your own miserable life. I will not be deprived the personal execution of Allah's vicious wrath." The line went dead.

Albert Tremaine tapped the 'Phone' icon and the Galaxy's screen went dark. He moved to a different bench...one nearer the ferry slip...and he re-dialed Ladka's cell number.

Phosgene, Tremaine pondered. *The General will want to know about this.*

* * * * *

INSTINCTIVELY, Omar Inbula tossed three twenties on the table, grabbed his suit coat from the back of his chair, and jumped to his feet. Peter Wilkinson seized a windbreaker from the empty chair next to him and leaped up also. Both men charged toward the door and out into the chill wind blowing from Long Island Sound. Police cruisers, their red and blue lights piercing the early evening twilight, had taken up positions at Route 25-A West, and Main Street South. Traffic in town had come to a virtual stop as officers with long black flashlights methodically inspected the interiors, and particularly the occupants, of every vehicle entering or leaving the village.

A strident horn sounded in the ferry slip two city blocks away from The Steamroom. The *Grand Republic's* sister vessel, *P.T. Barnum*, a stout chain stretched across its stern, was preparing to get underway. The scenario of latecomers rushing to board the departing boats was a familiar one in Port Jefferson. Accordingly, no one except Albert Tremaine paid the slightest attention to the scurrying Wilkinson and Inbula. As they clambered aboard the *Barnum*, Tremaine sent a terse message to Karol Ladka, who received it in the Dolphin helicopter that was now skimming low over mid-Sound.

Subjects are aboard the departing ferry Barnum.

Ladka ordered the pilot to hold the chopper in hover mode at fifty feet.

The *Grand Republic* had cleared the mouth of Bridgeport harbor and was steaming south toward Port Jefferson at full throttle. She would come abeam of the *P.T. Barnum's* port side as the boats passed each other twenty minutes later in the deepest part of the choppy tidal estuary. Thirty seconds after receiving Tremaine's message, the three SEALS aboard the *Grand Republic* had gotten their orders from Ladka.

Intercept and board the Barnum.

The big Sikorsky would be suspended over the rendezvous point to assist in the boarding, should the procedure go awry.

Panic was a distinct possibility; the passengers on neither the *Grand Republic*, nor the *P.T. Barnum* were aware that they were to be involved in a perilous activity on an increasingly fitful sea.

The MH-65 Dolphin was a mere spot in the sky when viewed from the unusually choppy Port Jefferson Harbor and the fairly calm Connecticut coast that lay in the lea of a rapidly developing nor'easter. In the fickle weather corridor from Philadelphia to Boston, such perilous conditions are notoriously difficult to predict in winter, forming, as they usually do, amid deceivingly fair-weather conditions. The moisture-gathering breezes typically sweep landward from the still-warm Atlantic and follow a twisting counter-clockwise pattern until the hundred mile trench that is The Sound becomes a convenient east-to-west conduit for cyclonic, near-hurricane winds.

Tonight's big blow had developed in less than an hour, and both the NOAA National Weather Service and the Cross-Sound Ferry Company were caught totally off guard.

Had the *P.T. Barnum* and *Grand Republic* been ocean-going vessels, their respective captains might have decided to weigh anchor and ride out the storm in the 200-foot-deep waters between central Connecticut and mid-Long Island. But these boats were not made to withstand that kind of heavy buffeting. They were virtual corks bobbing crazily in an unforgiving tempest. What's more…the cargo they carried could neither be stored nor jettisoned. These were human beings…frail souls whose well-being trumped every other consideration, including the very integrity of the ships themselves.

Navy SEALS, arguably the best-trained members of America's elite Sea, Air & Land warriors, know when weather has become their enemy, and as the *Grand Republic* began to emerge from the lea provided by the Connecticut coast, they could see the telltale whitecaps to the south that foretold angry sailing conditions.

"Nasty ahead," the team leader noted.

The Captain of the *Barnum* sensed that he might soon have to call upon his crew, and the most able-bodied of his travelers, to tend to any passengers who might need attention. He ordered his First Mate to dispense dozens of first-aid kits…initially to the parents of small children…and secondly, to those escorting the elderly.

Ironically, one of the first such precautionary distributions was made to Peter Wilkinson…the young fellow accompanying the tawny old man in the brown suit.

Chapter Forty-six

MEILI SONG SAT in front of her computer reviewing the updates on the electronic charts for each of today's patients. It was nearly six o'clock and she had expected to hear from Karol Ladka by now…but the night was young. There was always some refinement to be made on the computer entries that she characteristically reviewed daily before signing off on them. Actually, the petite dermatologist, admittedly distracted this afternoon, appreciated the extra time to check her records. Besides, she was confident Karol would be calling any minute.

There were two gentle taps at the Consultation Room door.

She brightened. "Yes."

The door opened ten inches and Jean Gustavson thrust her head inside. "Busy?"

Meili looked up and pointed to one of two green institutional chairs. "Just finishing up. Be right with you." She scrolled down the length of the Patient Record file that filled the monitor, stopping briefly here and there to make minor adjustments to the notations. Finally, she clicked the 'Save' icon and the screen went dark.

Meili peeled off her white lab coat and hung it behind the door Gustavson had entered. Then she scrubbed her hands at the small sink that each examining/consult room contained.

"Not to be inquisitive or anything," said the Charge Nurse, but how'd the, uh, Scrabble game go the other night?"

Meili Song gave her friend a Cheshire cat smile and said nothing as she dried her hands on a paper towel.

Jean discreetly changed the subject. "By the way, I didn't get a chance to go look for those deer you mentioned," she said. "Three Springfield boys home on break decided to wrap their car around a pole on College Highway this morning. They'll be in traction for a while…nothing critical. But I've been in the ER with the cowboys non-stop since nine…haven't even had lunch."

"Well, you spared yourself a helluva sight, lady." Meili went to the window and looked through the slats of the Venetian blind. The sprawled animals were invisible where they lay under the moonless sky. "Karol and I ran a mile near fairway seven yesterday morning." She closed the blind and flicked a thumb over her shoulder "Those deer aren't *sleeping,* Jeannie…they're dead!"

"What?"

"Dead…all of them."

"Poachers?"

"Don't know. Karol thinks they were poisoned. 'Veterinary Forensic Sciences' is sending a Toxicology team from Amherst in the morning."

"Where's The General now? You two got plans?"

"I really don't know. He's making arrangements for Carter as we speak. C'mon," Meili sighed, "I'll buy you a cocktail at 'Mom's'"

"Good deal," said Gustavson. She idly fingered the window blind on the way to the door and took a cursory peek out toward the jet black golf course. "Sometimes this place gives me the creeps."

"Me too," said Meili Song. "An hour ago I could have sworn I heard a helicopter floating around in the dark half a mile from here. I looked out and all I could see was a car parked on the grass...with its lights on."

"Maybe we both need a vacation," Jean Gustavson said. "Someplace nearby...y'know...someplace convenient."

"Yeah," said Meili, "...like Australia!"

"Great honeymoon spot, they tell me," Gustavson quipped.

The dermatologist gave her friend a sidelong look. "Let's get you that cocktail."

"Get *me* that cocktail?"

"I'm on call again. You drink your martini...I'll watch with my Diet Coke...enviously!"

* * * * *

MEILI SONG AND KAROL LADKA weren't the only ones who'd seen the dead deer. The Korean-born Freddie Young, a resident *Post Traumatic Stress Disorder* patient living in the dormitory section of Building Three, had actually been the first to spot them...and the sight virtually broke his heart. An Army Corporal medically-discharged ten years prior, and now assigned a part time job as one of four Edgewood Links golf course greens keepers, Freddie had considered the herd of deer that roamed the Links, his adopted family...and the shocking discovery had undone in an instant, a decade of Freddie's progress with the Southwick VAMC's psychiatric team.

Poor Freddie Young had been sobbing in his cot since six o'clock yesterday morning. Had he been able to voice his grief, the two doctors who attended him might have been able to detect and reverse the trauma, but the sinewy 32-year-old simply could not express emotion verbally. Accordingly, nobody knew the reason for the sudden relapse. Freddie wouldn't eat or speak. It seemed he was able only to repeat the word, *Dongsaeng... Dongsaeng*. It meant *Little Brother* in Korean.

Everyone at Southwick knew and loved Freddie Young. An honors graduate of UConn who had opted to enlist in the Infantry, he'd distinguished himself during three years of honorable military service. It was on his final deployment in Iraq that he'd earned a Silver Star...and with it, two severely fractured legs. But the PTSD associated with his injuries would prove even more devastating, and its effects longer lasting than the physical wounds themselves.

Most of Freddie's early psychiatric symptoms, though they had taken years to resolve themselves, had finally disappeared months ago: The outbursts and irritable behavior were essentially things of the past...the sense of guilt was fading...and self-destructive inclinations had mercifully waned. Such significant improvements in these three telling categories had qualified Freddie for Trustee status...thus, despite his being rather easily frightened, Freddie Young had been assigned the custodial job he'd loved so much.

Upon inspecting their star patient relative to the crying episode, Doctors Rupert and Shaefer attributed the sobbing phenomenon to what they termed, 'Lonely Interlude Syndrome,' "No doubt occasioned by spending the Christmas holiday away from family and friends," Rupert had pronounced, before signing off on the examination and leaving for a week in California.

But perhaps the key symptom that had gone unnoticed in the analysis was Freddie's unwillingness to look for more than a fleeting moment at animal silhouettes during his Rorschalk test. When asked what he had seen in these instances where ink-blot images were presented to him, Freddie would only say between sobs, *Dongsaeng.*

The psychiatrists never asked him the meaning of the term *Dongsaeng.* They assumed it meant, *dog.* 'Childhood pet,' Doctor Shaefer had written in his barely legible notes, and he released the patient to his room...where, the psychiatrist was confident, Freddie Young would soon regain his self-assurance. All he needed was a good meal coupled with a long walk in the fresh air and familiar surroundings of Edgewood Links. No prognosis, of course, could have been more misguided.

* * * * *

WHEN MEILI SONG AND JEAN GUSTAVSON left the Medical Center's parking lot on the way to 'Mom's' Bar, they didn't see the slender figure of Freddie Young watching them from the slight depression on Edgewood Links' seventh fairway. He had not obeyed Doctor Shaefer's order to return immediately to the Psych Ward to rest. Instead, he'd rejoined his little family, his *Dongsaeng*, where they lay sprawled in death. Freddie was sure that it was the Asian Dermatologist and her new male friend who were responsible for the collective deaths of his *little brothers and sisters*, but he would give her every opportunity to deny her involvement.

He noted that Song took a long lingering glance in his direction as her black Mercedes eased past the guardhouse that led to Middleville Road. For Freddie Young, that one extended gaze was enough to feed his paranoia-fueled suspicion. He would permit her to refute his skepticism, however…later.

But if she failed to do so, Meili Song would be one sorry woman.

Chapter Forty-seven

AT ONE THAT MORNING, after Jean Gustavson had left 'Mom's' Bar for home, and Meili Song had finished a large diet Coke and returned to the hospital to fill her solitary on-call midnight shift…the lights in Building 200 suddenly went out.

Meili had been alone in her private lavatory when it happened, and she assumed that as usual in such rare instances there would be a two-minute delay before the emergency generators feeding the second floor Dermatology Clinic kicked-in.

The doctor cursed in the dark and felt for the handle on the toilet behind her. She adjusted her clothing amid the sound of the flushing that seemed artificially loud, and pushed open the door to her pitch-black Examination Suite. Only one dim Exit sign shone red over the door to the clinic's waiting room…where the long metal security grate had been automatically lowered at this early morning hour. Song groped for the cold-water handle on the sink immediately outside the small lav, rinsed her hands, and made a blind pass with one open palm in front of the paper towel dispenser.

These randomly placed machines required little electric current and were battery operated…and Meili heard the scratching whine of the paper-feed as twelve inches of brown toweling was automatically ejected from the wall unit. She fumbled for the sheet of paper, tore it free, and dried her hands. Doctor Song then felt her way along the familiar few steps that led from the washroom to her desk.

On her computer monitor, a faint, multi-colored screensaver faded in and out of view, and the doctor sat waiting for the appearing and vanishing impression to coalesce into its normal, steady image.

Freddie Young emerged from the coat closet where he had hidden when Meili entered the lavatory. He was accustomed to the dark. Indeed, Freddie preferred it, if the truth be known. Darkness, like the gloom that spread through the Edgewood Links after sundown, was his reliable friend, the trustee thought, and after making his way along the hospital's sub-basement corridor…up the broad stairway leading from the cafeteria level…and into Doctor Song's waiting room through a side entrance…the painfully thin Psych patient could virtually see with his probing hands.

The indistinct glow from Meili's muted computer screen permitted Freddie to detect only the outline of the petite doctor's head, neck, and narrow shoulders from behind. Everything else on either side of the pair was lost in shadow. As the thinly clad man advanced toward Meili Song's vague silhouette, he guided himself with only one flattened palm that he brushed gingerly and carefully along the wall of the Examination Room.

In the process, Freddie accidentally stroked the front of the automatic towel dispenser…instantly activating it in the otherwise silent room.

Freddie Young took a deep, involuntary breath…a gasp…and Meili stiffened when she heard it.

Behind her, the familiar, rasping buzz of the paper toweling being fed from its dispenser could have been caused by only one thing—the machine's motion sensor. Someone, or something, had actuated the device, but the startled woman dare not turn to determine what…or who.

Slowly, silently, Meili Song eased open the shallow desk drawer beneath her keyboard. There, she placed one moist hand on the cold handle of a .38 caliber pistol. It was her ultimate defense against assault.

The droning noise stopped...replaced only by the imprecise sound of Freddie Young's deep breathing. The Dermatologist closed her trembling right fist around the handle of the Smith & Wesson automatic, and she brought the gun to her left armpit. Without turning, Doctor Song pointed the stubby muzzle straight to the rear...directly at the steady, panting, sound of the advancing man behind her. Simultaneously, Meili cinched her eyes...gritted her teeth...and squeezed her fingers tight...pulling the trigger and firing the gun.

The flash accompanying the automatic's explosion was largely shrouded by the bunched sleeve of Meili Song's white lab coat; still, she could clearly see Freddie Young's astonished features reflected in the computer monitor...as the hollow-point .38 slug ripped into the doomed man's face. The impact pulverized Young's lower left jaw creating an airborne spray of blood and splintered bone.

With her eyes once again pinched shut, the small woman fainted...as the hospital's emergency generators that fueled the computers groaned to life...and the approaching sound of running feet echoed along the wide western corridor of Building 200.

Chapter Forty-eight

HELICOPTERS ARE NOT DESIGNED to ride out gale-force winds, though they've been known to do so in the hands of highly experienced chopper pilots. A helicopter's big main rotor makes it susceptible to violent buffeting in such blustery conditions. Accordingly, most helicopter commanders are wary of venturing aloft when winds exceed forty knots or so. The MH-65Dolphin would soon need to withstand nearly twice that pounding.

But that was of little concern to Colonel Avila and General Ladka. They were known as daredevils. In fact, it seemed that when presented with alternative choices, both men, for whatever reason, usually elected to choose the more dangerous option for just about everything. Thus, when others might have disdained any notion of boarding the *P.T. Barnum* in the rough seas that were already building on The Sound, Ladka and Avila actually relished the challenge.

The growing chop on the water's surface was already intense…and the sister vessels approaching headlong were clearly in danger of colliding as they advanced on one another, all the while rocking and swaying to the erratic rhythm of the four-foot swells generated by the sudden gale.

As the ferry *Grand Republic*, heading south from Bridgeport, threatened to sail perilously abeam of the northbound *P.T. Barnum*, the eastern horizon over Block Island and Orient Point had turned nearly black…only the occasional bolt of still-infrequent chain lightning illuminated the string of huge cumulonimbus clouds that seemed to battle one another in a fight for position in the angry evening sky.

Great sheets of sweeping, nearly-horizontal rain rendered the radar of both ferries useless…such was the density of the deluge the dense thunderheads generated. As for unaided visual detection, it was virtually non-existent. Even during split-second flashes of stormy brilliance, when visibility was temporarily enhanced by lightning streaks, the jittery illumination was of such brief duration that there was insufficient time to react effectively.

Amid the forked flares and near-simultaneous thunder explosions overhead, Colonel Pedro Avila somehow held the sturdy MH-65 within an imaginary quarter-mile-diameter cone over the big white boats that were now less than forty yards apart. Karol Ladka, his shoulder harness double-lashed to a pair of stout safety rings anchored in the helicopter's steel floor, flashed a Morse code instruction through his open side door to the undulating bridge of the *Grand Republic*.

Board the Barnum on my command, the flickering message ordered.

Aye-aye, the lead Navy Seal on the *Grand Republic* signaled in response. *Grappling hooks ready.*

General Ladka then turned and focused his device on the *Barnum's* bridge. *Prepare to be boarded.*

There was no response.

Ladka signaled a second time.

Still nothing from the *Barnum*.

Karol Ladka clambered toward Avila in the pilot's seat. He clapped the Colonel on the shoulder, and made two sudden downward thrusts with his index finger. "Put us amidships, Pedro."

Pedro Avila craned his neck and peered down over his left arm.

Ladka crawled back to the aircraft's open side door. He aimed his signal flasher at the thrashing *Grand Republic*. In Morse code, he triggered one word: *dah dah dit, dah dah dah*...and repeated it twice more. *Go...Go...Go.*

Aye-aye. Came the confirmation from the SEALS...and Colonel Avila began to drop the helicopter closer to the wallowing vessel beneath them.

As both iron-clad ferries neared and menaced one another in the raging mid-Sound waters, visibility had become nil and Avila depended on his own downward directed radar to tell him the Dolphin's height above the *P.T. Barnum*. On his eerie, green monitor, the outline of the big boat had grown ever larger, and now it filled the state-of-the-art screen on the helicopter's control panel. The resolute pilot read the white numbers on the corner of the screen and hollered over the roar of his rotors, "...forty feet...thirty, sir...twenty-five..."

"Can you get me within twenty?" Karol Ladka bellowed. That would put the chopper two stories above the crazily pitching boat. Ladka was confident he could successfully jump the rest of the way.

"Negative, General," Avila yelled back...his eyes firmly fixed on the scope. "Can't do twenty. She's tossing too much."

With his civilian clothes now soaked and plastered to his body...his wing-tipped shoes awash in chill, salt-water sprayed upward from the lurching *Barnum*...the big man cursed and extended his sopping head as far as he could through the five-foot opening in the side of the helicopter. The salt spray burned the General's eyes as he peered down into the utter blackness of the water, attempting in vain to locate the exact position of the ferry's amidships deck somewhere beneath him.

He could see nothing.

Ladka's one concern was that he might misjudge the position of the fiercely rolling boat altogether. If he were to miscalculate his leap, he knew, he might land in the wind-whipped swells between the *Barnum* and *Grand Republic*...and be crushed like an egg shell, should the two multi-ton craft pin him in the huge vise formed by their cold, steel hulls.

But the stoic man quickly dismissed the thought of that eventuality.

He reached for the clips that held his harness straps fastened to the chopper's floor.

At the same time, the SEALS...their night vision goggles revealing the lime-green image of the approaching *Barnum*...were preparing to fling their barbed grappling hooks blindly toward where they knew the boat's side rails must be.

* * * * *

THE VAMC POLICE SERGEANT on duty in Building 200 had heard the blast of Meili's .38.

From his post adjacent to the first floor Emergency Room, he'd rushed, flashlight in hand, to the west stairwell and bounded up its two flights, three long steps at a time. With his own weapon drawn, the uniformed officer burst through the second floor doorway, stopped, and immediately detected the distinctive smell of cordite. He wheeled to his left and instinctively sprinted in the direction of the source of the odor...toward the Dermatology Clinic.

With his service flashlight trained ahead along the empty corridor, the Sergeant could see that the security gates of all four clinics were lowered. He fumbled for the large key ring at his waist as he ran, causing the beam from his flashlight to wobble madly over the floor, walls, and ceiling.

Meili Song, weak and emerging from unconsciousness, had only a vague idea where she was. Her small fist was still glued to the automatic pistol...her finger wrapped tightly around the trigger. Her only fear was that she would lose possession of the gun she assumed had saved her life.

From the vestibule outside her Examination Room suite, the sound of the police officer's hastening feet grew louder. With only the dull glow from the computer's automatic screensaver to guide her, the Doctor slowly raised her head from the desk where she still sat. She tentatively dabbed a small cut on her forehead with her free hand, then, twisting around, she attempted to stand.

An incessant ringing in her ears caused a sort of vertigo, and Meili leaned on the back of her swivel stool for support. The free-spinning chair failed her, and she lost her grip. Instantly, the disoriented woman crashed face-down…onto the bloody corpse of the man she had just killed.

The Dermatologist screamed and the automatic pistol discharged…this bullet tearing into the computer screen and plunging the room into a pitch-black void littered with shattered glass.

In the equally dark second floor corridor a mere two dozen yards away, the blue-clad Sergeant thrust the muzzle of his nine millimeter weapon through one of the openings in the heavy brass grate. Simultaneously, he focused his light on the Examination Room door and roared, "Police! Drop the gun! Come out with your hands where I can see them!"

The heady odor of the explosive propellant had intensified with the firing of the second round…and Meili Song coughed twice involuntarily.

The policeman felt he had no choice but to neutralize the uncooperative target in the Examination Suite. He fired three quick shots into the closed door.

"Hands high! Put down the gun and exit slowly!"

There was no further sound from Meili's room.

Chapter Forty-nine

ON HIS HANDS AND KNEES...the Dolphin MH-56 threatening with each plummeting and escalating roll to hurl him into the raging depths...Karol Ladka released his harness from its anchor points, and scrambled unsecured to the helicopter's open hatch. Once in the doorway, he assumed a prone position and thrust his legs and lower body through the gaping void. With the aching fingers of his bare hands clinging to the entranceway's bottom casement, the General let his lower extremities drop into the dual blast created by the storm and the overhead rotary blades.

"Twenty-five feet," the pilot called over his shoulder. "Good luck, Sir."

"Ten-four, Pedro," Ladka hollered...and with his violently swinging legs approximately eighteen feet from the bridge of the *Barnum*, he released his hold on the chopper's superstructure.

Karol Ladka had no way of knowing where on the ferociously pitching boat he would land...or whether he would hit the vessel at all...he only knew he had no choice but to forfeit his tenuous grip come what may. In a few seconds, he had his answer.

General Ladka...or Colonel Avila...or both of them...had miscalculated badly.

The big man struck the turbulent water at a forty-five degree angle. Instantly he was thrown astern of the churning ferry like a sodden rag doll...and he knew intuitively that he'd been slung into the path of the boat's huge, grinding propellers.

By the blinding light of a sustained lightning bolt, one of the Navy SEALS on the *Grand Republic* spied the helpless General, his arms flailing in vain, as he was drawn inexorably closer to what could only be envisioned as a horrible death.

The sailor's reaction was immediate and bold. With complete disregard for the consequences of errant judgement, he heaved his spiked, twenty-pound grappling hook short of the *Barnum's* churning wake, but beyond the struggling Karol Ladka. Hopefully he had launched the potentially deadly device far enough to reach its target...the sucking vortex created by the boat's twin screws.

The four-pronged iron hook sailed through the pelting rain, its trailing length of two-inch rope uncurling behind as it flew against the gale...but accuracy under these conditions was too much to ask for. Too late, Ladka saw the oncoming anchor-like contrivance glittering in the radiance of a second lightning flash. Evasion was impossible. One of the curved arms struck the vulnerable man full on the side of his head...knocking him unconscious...before draping its stout rope across his limp shoulders and dragging him underwater as the heavy hook sank.

The SEAL shouted for help from his companions and the three men hauled mightily on the grappling rope. The barb on one of the large hooks buried itself in a thick fold of Ladka's jacket, and the pulling action fortuitously plucked his upper body above the surface of the raging Sound. The froth thus created washed against the General's face and slowly...miraculously...revived him.

But now the team of SEALS was faced with a new and greater problem: The *Grand Republic*, on whose port side they were poised, was gradually closing on the *Barnum*, and there was little the Navy men could do to forestall the incipient collision.

Karol Ladka, too, could clearly see the perilous fate that threatened him. "Raft," he screamed, gesticulating one-handed toward the *Grand Republic's* stern.

The Lieutenant Commander who had flung the hook that saved Ladka, swiftly dashed, skidding and sliding, to where the nearest cork-reinforced contraption was lashed to the ferry's port rail. With four precise slashes of his Bowie Knife he severed the plastic bonds that secured the eight-foot raft...and it fell awkwardly into The Sound.

The two steel-hulled vessels were now scant yards apart, and the General was growing weaker by the moment. With what he thought might be his last ounce of strength, Karol seized the bobbing safety device with one arm...and with the other, pried the grappling hook free of his coat, and heaved it into the raft's bow. "Slack," he cried. "Gimme slack!"

The leader of the team understood. "Let out the grappling line," he ordered. "Put him well aft. Let him ride the wake."

In seconds the raft...secured by the hook...and with Ladka clinging to its gunwale...was clear of the narrowing space that separated the vessels.

The huge, white boats closed to within two feet of one another.

General Ladka grunted, and with a superhuman effort, rolled into the life raft.

The three Navy SEALS leaped onto the high aft deck of the tossing *P.T. Barnum* where they formed a circle...their automatic pistols trained outward like the points of an equilateral triangle.

* * * * *

JEAN GUSTAVSON had been home only a few minutes when she realized what was nagging at her. During lunch she'd taken her daily, brisk walk with two Long Island friends, Doctors Liz Romano and Barbara Feldman. They'd followed the usual route of their 'constitutional' along the concrete sidewalk flanking the sloping, serpentine road that led from the hospital's main gate, down to the fenced perimeter of Edgewood Links...then they trekked back up the hill.

The golf course through which they strode wasn't technically affiliated with the Medical Center, but it had been there as long as anyone at the VA could remember, and the pretty, green expanse seemed as much a part of the place as the imposing brick buildings themselves. Indeed, the informal affiliation between Edgewood and the government institution was such an amicable one that all VAMC Staffers held complimentary golfing memberships.

At one point on their lunchtime walk, the tall blond Doctor Romano had commented on how pleasant it was to get out of doors on days like today and stroll through Edgewood Links... when the vast fairways had just been cut, as she said...and the aroma of newly-mown grass still permeated the air. "Reminds me of home," she'd proclaimed taking a deep breath.

"Bullshit," said Feldman, "...you're from Staten Island. There's no grass in Staten Island."

"And how would you know?" Romano responded, "...you've never been west of frigging Syosset."

"Girls, girls," Jean Gustavson chimed in, "...let's just be thankful for a mild day in the country, shall we?" And that's the last she'd thought of Romano's offhand observation.

Until now.

Without question, the lunch hour hike along the perimeter of fairway seven had been a pleasant one. True, the delightful aroma that smacked of a freshly mown lawn wafting on the air was invigorating. But it was almost January, and Edgewood Links hadn't been mowed since the end of October...nor would it be for another three months. Something else must have caused the place to smell like new-cut grass...and as she pondered the pungent aroma...and pictured the deer she knew still lay dead beyond the maintenance shed...Jean shuddered.

Phosgene, thought the nurse. *New-mown hay is the characteristic odor...of Phosgene.*

In the dark foyer of her apartment, Gustavson searched the face of her large, nurse's wristwatch. It was after one in the morning. She wondered if Meili Song would still be in her office at this hour.

Turning on the desk lamp where her telephone sat, Jean Gustavson noted the blinking light that indicated she'd received one or more calls. She depressed the 'Play Messages' button, and the automated voice said, *You have...one...new message. First message:*

The call was from a polling organization asking her opinion of something or other...and the nurse impatiently pressed the 'Delete' button. *End of new messages,* sounded on the speakerphone.

Gustavson broke the connection and dialed Meili Song's cell phone.

* * * * *

THE DERMATOLOGIST SAT on the floor hugging her knees and peeking over her extended arms. Her wide eyes were fixed on the three jagged bullet holes in the door to the Examination Suite. She'd crawled to the corner of the darkened room farthest from the corpse of Freddie Young. His grotesque features remained vaguely visible in the red glow of a lone 'Exit' sign above the door. Incredibly Meili still clutched the gun she'd used to kill the man with a single, fortuitous shot.

Hesitant even to breathe, she aimed the automatic at the only portal that the gunman, who called himself a policeman, was likely to enter...and as she sat crouched in utter silence, she vowed to empty the pistol's remaining rounds in the direction of the man...whoever he was...the minute he appeared in the entrance.

Meili hoped her antagonist had concluded he'd killed her with one of the three rounds that smashed through the door. If so, perhaps he would go away. But as she peered at those crude holes, they were suddenly illuminated by the skittering radiance of a flashlight playing on the door from the far side.

The small woman took a firmer grip on her '38. She knew that the gun...and complete silence...were her only allies. With them on her side, maybe she had the advantage.

Then her cell phone trilled its familiar ring tone...and her heart sank.

Chapter Fifty

THE RADICALIZED PETER WILKINSON and the jihadist Omar Inbula were confident that by now they had achieved their wicked goal. They almost certainly had diverted the attention of Karol Ladka and his Special Forces team from the volatile stash of Phosgene long enough for the poison to have eaten its way through the polyethylene bags in which it had been shipped. All that remained was for the crystalized balls to decompose and form a powder. That residue would then leach into the VA Hospital's elaborate ventilation system…and kill everyone who breathed the lethal dust.

The Yale student had done his job well, Inbula thought as the two terrorists clung to the arms of the wildly rocking bench where they sat. And had young Wilkinson not been a despicable Infidel, he might soon be enjoying all the benefits of martyrdom in the company of Baghdadi…al Jamil…Yildiz…and the rest. Because now that *'Wif.en.poof's'* protégé had completed his assignment, it was time for old Omar to dispose of him.

The lurching floor of the *P.T. Barnum's* crowded interior deck was awash in broken glass, scattered personal belongings, and vomit. Remarkably, only Inbula, who had never before today been on a boat of any sort, was the only passenger spared seasickness. Even the ferry's six-member crew was deathly ill, and unable to assist the stricken travelers.

Neither Inbula nor Wilkinson was aware that on the open top deck directly above them the three Navy SEALS had boarded the *Barnum*, and were now dispersed to the aft section of the three-hundred-foot boat's lower compartment At this very moment, one of the black-clad men stood watch by the ferry's vertical gangway, and his mates hauled on the line that secured General Ladka...injured, but alive and conscious...in the trailing life raft.

The leader of the trio jury-rigged a rope harness from the line as Ladka was drawn nearer through the froth of the *Barnum's* wake. When the cork-lined life raft was clear of the turbulence caused by the boat's propellers, the two rescuers lowered the coil and Ladka climbed into its loop. In minutes he was standing... weak but alert...amid the dozens of grinding automobiles and small trucks...that threatened to rip free from the straining chains that held them to the Vehicle Deck.

In the boat's enclosed passenger level, the stench of bile had become too much for Peter Wilkinson to bear. To add to his distress, he had been overcome with a sense of vertigo and extreme weakness. "I can't take any more of this," he moaned to Omar Inbula. "I need air."

"Are you able to walk?" Inbula asked, standing and swaying while extending a supportive hand.

"I think so," said Wilkinson...as he continued to retch.

Inbula seized the gagging man's arm and draped it around his own shoulders. "Come," the Iranian said. "The rail. The sea spray will do you good."

The two disheveled men staggered to the nearest side door leading to the ferry's port walkway. None of the ninety-some panicky passengers paid them any attention. "Hold on to me," said Omar Inbula, and he put his shoulder into the door that was being forced shut by the pelting wind and rain.

After the third thrust, the door to the port gangway gave, and Wilkinson and Inbula burst onto the narrow side aisle.

In agony, the stricken Wilkinson gripped the slippery windward rail, and he opened his mouth wide in an attempt to take in the air and water that lashed the side of the boat...just as Omar Inbula heaved him overboard into the steel-gray waves.

Ma'a as-salaama! said the terrorist...*goodbye!*

He returned to the sheltered deck, wedged himself into a corner seat on the wooden bench he'd just vacated, and promptly fell asleep to the labored growling of the *Barnum's* powerful diesel engines.

Only the peripatetic Albert Tremaine had observed the murder of Peter Wilkinson. Never one to miss any opportunity, the entrepreneur had used his smart phone to videotape the entire violent sequence through the boat's Plexiglas windows. It was too late to help the treasonous Yale man, of course...but at least General Ladka and the SEALS could now identify the Islamist who had killed him.

*Younger man drowned...*Tremaine texted Ladka, unaware that the General was scant yards away on the lower level of the vessel...*partner on amidships deck...appears unarmed...*

Albert Tremaine was wrong in that last assumption...as he was soon to find out.

Chapter Fifty-one

THE OVERNIGHT GUARD at the VAMC's east gatehouse was not surprised to see Jean Gustavson's car approaching from Middleville Road...even at two-thirty in the morning. Of all the world's professions, the two best known for erratic schedules are probably Law Enforcement and Health Care Provider. After all, criminals do not operate on a nine-to-five schedule...nor do balky gall bladders.

The Sergeant stopped her only long enough to point out that Building 200 was experiencing a temporary power outage. "It'll be fixed in a few minutes," he assured the Charge Nurse. "The Cafeteria's back in business already if you want to wait there."... and he waved her into the chill, sparsely occupied parking lot.

Gustavson hadn't gotten a response when she'd called Meili Song's cell phone, and she wondered if the power failure had somehow been responsible. *It can't be because she's home asleep,* the nurse said inwardly...*there's her Mercedes parked where it always is.*

The entire four stories of the imposing main building had been plunged into darkness for nearly an hour, and viewing the brick structure from the outside, Jean Gustavson could see that the only illumination came from the red-canopied entrance to the Medical Center's Emergency Room. It was her home away from home, and she knew that inside…in the Receiving Area itself…there would be no interruption in the normal diagnosis and treatment of critical cases. They dare not be preempted or postponed.

She parked beside Meili's Mercedes, the black sedan with the MD license plate, and locked her Toyota. All the windows on the hospital's second floor were dark. If the backup lighting in the interior corridors had kicked-in, it wasn't apparent from where Gustavson stood.

She pulled up the cowl collar of her woolen jacket until it covered her ears. The weather advisory on the car radio had been explicit, the temperature was about to drop precipitously, and travelers were warned to watch for black ice forming on Northern Connecticut and Massachusetts roadways.

If necessary, she could nap in the staff lounge until her eight-o'clock shift began. *Hell, it's almost time to get up anyway*, she griped as she walked.

She leaned into the stiff coastal gale, and the first snowflakes of what had been a record-breaking warm winter, began to cling to her eyelashes. "Please…PLEASE, Dear Jesus…don't let it ice-up," she implored.

Behind her, Jean heard the rumble of a dump truck approaching. It was loaded with salted sand, its spinning distributor disc scattering the abrasive cargo along the road that led to the ER.

Like it or not, Southwick was in for a bitterly cold nor'easter.

Inside Building 200's vast pavilion a Special Duty policemen stood by the Information Desk unpacking a box. The officer had been brought in to assist during the blackout. He was preparing to distribute small, black flashlights to anyone who might need one during the overnight shift. Jean Gustavson accepted one of the disposable lights with thanks, and unzipping her coat, noted that the temperature in the vestibule was cooler than normal for this hour. She wondered if Meili Song's office suite was as cold, and decided to leave her jacket on as she made her way up the central stairway to Level Two.

Nearing the second floor landing, Jean noticed the slightly acrid odor of what she assumed must be one or more gas-fueled lighting generators.

That can't be, she mused as she climbed the last few stairs… the entire second floor was dark as a tomb…and just as silent. Furthermore, now that she'd arrived at the upper corridor, her intensified suspicion took on a new dimension. What she'd initially thought was the scent of burning gasoline…was more like…the harsh smell of fireworks.

Gustavson frowned, turned left at the top of the staircase, and played her light along the hallway's wall. Immediately, the thin beam focused on the door of a ladies bathroom and instinctively Jean switched off her light. She pushed her way inside and pulled the door closed behind her. When she'd scanned the room, and it was clear that she was alone, the now-nervous woman placed her ear against the inside of the door. Part of her hoped to hear some telltale noise…another part feared to. She knew only that in addition to the power failure…something else was very wrong here.

* * * * *

WITH THE BOARDING PARTY and General Ladka safely on the *Barnum*, the SEALS team leader arm-signaled for the *Grand Republic* to steer clear of her sister vessel, and the delicate maneuver was accomplished with less than twelve inches of separation to spare.

The Special Forces men were plenty warm in their double layers of waterproof gear, but with the temperature falling rapidly, Karol Ladka was freezing. He simply had to get out of his soaked civilian clothes, or hypothermia would paralyze him…and soon! The Lieutenant Commander recognized the

General's dilemma and pointed to an unsecured locker adjacent to the *Barnum's* retractable ramp.

As expected, the metal cubbyhole contained a spare set of foul-weather gear bearing the Captain's name and insignia. Fortunately, the boat's Chief Officer, like Ladka, was a big man. Karol quickly peeled off his clothing, discarded everything in the boat's wake, and climbed into the fleece-lined boots, trousers, and yellow slicker from the cabinet. The oilskin coat bore the word 'CAPTAIN' stenciled across the shoulders in black capital letters. His name was also printed on the front breast.

The team leader handed Ladka a Glock machine pistol and signaled for the General to follow him up the metal stairs that led to the amidships deck. The other two black-clad SEALS followed, their weapons drawn, eyes constantly moving.

When the four men reached the passageway door that opened on the *Barnum's* Passenger Compartment, Ladka tapped the Lieutenant Commander on the shoulder. He motioned for him to stay crouched on the staircase with his men, indicating that he would venture onto the crowded central deck alone. Everyone, including Wilkinson's terrorist partner, would mistake him for the Captain, Karol assumed. Thereafter, Ladka would have to depend on his informant, Albert Tremaine, to identify the Islamist. Once that had been done, the SEALS could seize and neutralize their prisoner...and General Ladka would call in Avila and the hovering Dolphin to pick them up.

Ladka chambered a round from his weapon's high-capacity magazine, and with his finger on the trigger, put the gun in the pocket of his loose-fitting raincoat. He whispered, "Give me three minutes," and flashed the Lieutenant Commander a thumbs up. Then he strode into the Passenger Compartment...making his way along the undulating deck...toward where Albert Tremaine sat clinging to a table that was bolted to the floor.

Throughout the enclosed deck dozens of children were wailing as frantic mothers rocked and otherwise attempted to soothe them. Everyone was seasick, and even the burliest men were, for the most part, rendered incapable of helping their panicky wives. Some of the younger passengers held howling babies for mothers with more than one child to care for. And four valiant crewmen with first-aid kits tended to the injured. Most of the storm's casualties suffered minor cuts and bruises, but at least two children experienced broken bones that required splinting. Only a few older travelers had chanced the hazardous trip, and oddly, one of them seemed to be sleeping.

He was the eldest person on board...the extremist, Omar Inbula...and Karol Ladka sensed intuitively that he must be their man.

Who but a schemer, the General wondered, *would pretend to be asleep in the middle of a gale at sea?* And there was something else that disturbed Ladka. That sallow complexion on the pale cheeks and chin of the nodding fellow's otherwise ruddy features. Clearly, the old man had recently sheared-off a full beard...at a time of year when most hirsute-inclined men were *cultivating* such growth. Furthermore, he had cut himself at least twice while shaving; the man was plainly unaccustomed to the procedure.

Karol scanned Inbula's clothing for some sign...a sagging pocket...an unusual bulge...a telltale tucked pocket flap, or unbuttoned jacket...all were potential indicators of the presence of a weapon.

That could be anything, of course...a gun, a knife, or even a bomb...but the tipoff of its presence was how easily such a device might be accessed. In the case of the 'dozing' eighty-something man, whatever he was armed with was in the drooping right-hand pocket of his suit jacket. That side of the suitcoat hung at least two inches lower than the left...and unlike the left, its pocket flap was tucked inside, where it would not inhibit his reaching for the pocket's contents.

Convinced that he had established *who* his quarry was...and *where* he kept his weapon...all that remained was for Ladka to disarm the man. But *how*? It had to be done in such a way as to preclude his injuring any of the passengers…or, for that matter, killing his elderly target. That was vital. The General was certain that the old man was an Islamic operative. Surely he knew the details of Wilkinson's radicalization. For that reason, he had killed the activist from Yale, and probably Carter and Mary Banning as well. Whatever else the octogenarian knew about Peter Wilkinson's involvement in the Southwick incident, Karol Ladka needed to know it too. And one cannot interrogate a dead man.

Clearly the old fellow was right-handed…that was obvious. You don't carry a weapon where you must reach all the way across your body to access it. If Ladka could engage his quarry's right hand through some ruse, the General could then neutralize him effectively. Perhaps Albert Tremaine could play an effective role in the delicate maneuver. Karol had an idea.

With cautious steps, he ambled on the rolling deck toward the long bench where Tremaine was seated. As usual, the electronics expert was thumbing his smartphone. Tremaine did not recognize Ladka until the General was within an arm's length of him, and even then, he knew better than to register surprise. Karol made the first move. Stepping into the sight line between the young man and Omar Inbula, he gestured toward the electronic device that his informant was manipulating with obvious success. Speaking loud enough to be heard throughout the deck, he said, "I see you've been able to establish a wireless connection."

The informant understood. He played along. "Yes, Captain. Thank you."

"Perhaps you will permit me to send a dispatch," said Ladka.

"Of course," said Albert Tremaine…and he handed the phone to the man in the yellow slicker.

Karol thumbed a message on the Samsung's keypad and passed the smartphone back to Tremaine. "Thank you, son."

The inscription read:

target opposite you—blue suit—armed
throw phone to me as I approach him
I will disarm
prepare to provide back-up
we have 20 seconds

General Ladka placed a reassuring hand on the shoulder of a young mother to Tremaine's left and he continued circling the deck, issuing words of comfort to the worried travelers as he went. By the time he'd returned to where the old man in the blue serge suit sat, fifteen of the allotted twenty seconds had passed. From the far side of the enclosed passenger compartment Albert Tremaine abruptly called out, "Captain…your message," and the technician hurled the Galaxy smartphone on a line with Inbula's head.

Ladka danced to one side and reflexively the startled terrorist flung a protecting arm across his forehead. Ladka disregarded the flying cell phone, but instead dove directly for the revealing lump that he was confident was the weapon in the old man's suitcoat. Karol snatched a Russian-made pistol from Omar Inbula's pocket, and the cell phone smashed into the bridge of the Islamist's prominent nose, causing blood to gush from his nostrils.

As instructed, Albert Tremaine had launched his lithe body at the old man, and though blood obscured Inbula's vision, he reached blindly in his waistband. The cyber specialist assumed correctly that his adversary was reaching for a knife…and with one well-placed kick to his temple, Albert Tremaine brought the confrontation to an end.

The three Navy SEALS burst through the door from the catwalk and one of them placed Omar Inbula in wrist and ankle restraints while the others assisted the two children who had suffered fractured bones.

Already the pounding gale seemed to be subsiding, though the temperature had fallen well below freezing…and it seemed possible that Pedro Avila would be able to put the MH-65 on the *Barnum's* upper deck after all.

Chapter Fifty-two

AS OBDURATE as the pig-headed Omar Inbula was, his obstinacy was no match for that of the determined Karol Ladka. When you spend a good part of your life in the employ of America's Central Intelligence Agency, as Ladka had, you eventually learn ways to plumb the physical limits of your adversary...and more importantly, how to take advantage of them. Therefore, less than twenty minutes after the Dolphin chopper had lifted its human cargo from the deck of the *Barnum,* the once-tough, old insurrectionist had been reduced to blubber. In gangland parlance...*he'd sung like a canary.*

Even the hardened Navy SEALS were impressed by the General's innovative interrogation techniques. Particularly efficient, they agreed, was the suspending of the terrorist from the side hatch of the helicopter by a rope...at one hundred miles per hour! A few minutes dangled head-first that way, while being lowered ever closer to the choppy surface of The Sound, provided what the leader of the SEAL unit euphemistically termed *the perfect verbal laxative.*

Subsequently, Inbula had told Ladka everything, of course... everything about Peter Wilkinson...Professor Baghdadi...about the targeted VA Hospital...and above all, about the Phosgene stacked on the ventilation unit. The Lieutenant Commander nodded his admiration. "Quite the convincer, General. Where'd you come up with it?"

"Guy from The Bronx," said Ladka, slapping a strip of duct tape over the gasping Inbula's mouth and a longer one across the man's terrified eyes. "...name's Eric Hoffer. Hoffer always says, 'To find out what a guy's afraid of...watch how he tries to scare you.'" He motioned toward Tremaine. "When Albert here told me how our friend drowned the Wilkinson kid...I knew the best way to make him talk."

"You think it's too late, General?" one of the SEALS asked. "...to get rid of the Phosgene pellets before the bags decompose?"

"We'll soon find out," said Ladka. "Pedro's got us maxed at 175 knots. We'll be at the hospital in eighteen minutes."

Albert Tremaine was strapped into a jump seat in the rear of the Dolphin's dim lit fuselage. Characteristically, he was feeding data into the smartphone on his lap. He looked up from the display screen and made a megaphone of his hands. "According to NOAH Weather," he called, "...Southwick just got hit with an ice storm. Hail accumulations are reported Moderate to Heavy."

"Shit," Ladka cursed. He duck-walked to the cabin and cupping Pedro Avila's ear, he relayed the new information. The pilot nodded and pointed to an irregular, red blotch on his radar screen.

"I'm on it, Boss. It's a quick hitter," Avila hollered. "Secure the cabin, General...we're goin' upstairs!"

As Karol Ladka and the SEALS hastily prepared for the aircraft's ascent, Albert Tremaine dialed the single word 'PHOSGENE' on his Galaxy's keyboard.

He tapped 'GO' and immediately *'Chemical Compound with the Formula COCL2'* came up, followed by the black and white illustration of an ominous Skull & Crossbones.

Albert tapped on *COCL2*.

A number of defined specifications were listed starting with, *'Boiling Point* and *Melting Point.'*

But of more interest to the technically savvy Albert was the designation...*Neutralization Temperature.* It was listed as...*10 degrees Fahrenheit*...the exact reading that his smartphone now showed for the area surrounding Southwick, Massachusetts. At this level, Tremaine knew, calcified Phosgene was nothing more than a congealed, white ash...a harmless frozen powder that would become lethal only with a sudden jump in the surrounding temperature.

He dialed-up the Southwick weather forecast for the next six hours.

Unchanged...flashed on the handheld monitor.

Albert Tremaine pondered the thousands of local revelers who must be hoping for a resumption of the unusual holiday warm spell. *Be careful what you wish for*, he said silently...*especially if you expect to be inside the Southwick VA Hospital...at least for the next hour or so.*

* * * * *

JEAN GUSTAVSON could clearly smell the gunpowder that permeated the second floor hallway. It seemed the acrid stench had originated in the area of Meili Song's Examination Suite and was slowly wafting in Jean's direction.

With her back firmly pressed against the cold tiles of the corridor wall, she groped her way toward the Dermatology Clinic...the last Consulting Room on her left.

The nurse's only guide was the vague, red, Exit sign above the east stairwell, and as she approached it, a rose-colored reflection of the soft-glowing marker told her that the security gate in front of Meili's vestibule was in the 'Down' position.

Her eyes were beginning to tear, but rather than washing away the irritation, the resulting moisture served only to mix with the smoky residue and form a film that obscured her limited vision even further.

Everything seemed to be conspiring against Gustavson, and she stopped her snail's-pace forward progress. Resisting the temptation to call out to the office where her friend must be, she wiped her eyes on the harsh sleeve of her heavy jacket and slid slowly to her knees.

Jean hugged herself and rubbed her shoulders. God, it was cold!

Then she caught her first break.

The tall windows along the northern wall of the corridor began to light up with a jagged, reflected radiance…and Jean knew immediately that its source must be the approaching sand-spreader's flashing utility lights. The amber reflections were indistinct because the high panes of glass that lined one side of the hall were now covered with frozen rivulets that had, in turn, trapped thousands of small hailstones in their icy wakes. All along the beige-tiled walls of the walkway the irregular traces of mirrored light took on ill-defined forms like so many uneven pieces of a glacial mosaic.

As the rumble of the oncoming truck grew louder, and the brilliance from its emergency light inexorably increased… abruptly Gustavson saw something that made her gasp in alarm… and she bit painfully into a knuckle of one hand to keep from crying out. What she saw was the body of a uniformed man… and he lay across the hallway floor at a forty-five-degree angle to the shielding brass gate in front of him. He was prone and unmoving at the far end of the corridor, and at first the startled woman thought he must have been shot.

But with the intensifying illumination from the ice-covered windows, Jean Gustavson could now see that the man on the floor, far from being dead, was in fact training his pistol through a gap in the security grille. Obviously his weapon had been the source of the cordite odor. And clearly…for whatever reason… the gunman was intent on shooting Meili Song!

The man hadn't detected her presence, Jean knew, and that fact in itself gave her an advantage...if only a small one. But how could she use that to help her friend? The man had a gun... she did not. And even if he had *not* been armed, the fellow in the blue uniform would certainly be strong enough to subdue her in a struggle.

She wondered if she should try retracing her steps to the west stairwell. That might have worked moments ago when the hall was in total darkness...but not now. Now the sand spreader was embarked on a zig-zag route up and down the nearby hospital parking lot, and God knew how long its lights would be focused on the windows.

Then Gustavson thought of something. It would be risky... but it might be Meili Song's only chance.

On her hands and knees, she crawled backward to the side-by-side lavatories...entered the pitch-black Men's Room...and locked the door from within. Then, feeling her way to the nearest stall...she took her cell phone and dialed a favorite Shakespearian video excerpt on YouTube. It was actor Orson Welles plotting with another performer in a scene from *'Othello.'* Jean flushed the toilet, turned the sound on the cell phone up to full volume, and placed it on the floor. Then, in the darkness, she scurried out of the lavatory, and into the Women's Room next door.

The unexpected noise of the gushing water resonated with what seemed to the policeman like a roaring flood along the empty hallway. It was a clear indication of someone else's presence in the darkened corridor. Automatically, his head jerked in the direction of the noise, and his pistol rattled in the brass grate when he swiftly withdrew it.

As the splashing noise from the washroom diminished, the muffled din of two men conspiring could be dimly heard.

> *"Within three days let me hear...*
> *That Cassio's not alive."*

*"My friend is dead.
...at your request. But let her live."*

*"Damn her,...O damn her...
Furnish me...some swift means of death..."*

"I am your own forever."

    The uniformed man sprang to his feet and placed the pocket flashlight in his mouth. With both hands gripping the pistol at chest level in front of him, his teeth clamped on the light, he followed its beam like a worker in a coal mine, advancing step-by-careful step toward the echoing sound of the schemers. When the beam of the flashlight illuminated the Men's Room entrance, he called the single word, "Police..." and booted the door open with one, powerful kick.

    In the adjacent bathroom, Jean Gustavson realized that, for an instant, she seemed to have won her gamble. With the gunman occupied in search of two non-existent men, at least his attention had been diverted from Meili. Jean dashed from her hiding place and raced down the corridor to the stairwell she'd recently climbed. At the bottom of the second flight, she started to burst through the doorway...and collapsed in the arms of Building 200's emergency Security Guard.

    "The Doctor..." she gasped. "Doctor Song..." Gustavson pointed, exhausted, over her shoulder. "She needs help..."

    The guard shone his light in the nurse's frantic face. "Are you okay?"

    "Yes. Please hurry."

    He drew his pistol. "What's going on up there?"

    "Clinic 2-H," Jean panted. "Quick. He's got a gun."

Chapter Fifty-three

AS QUICKLY AS THE STORM in The Sound had kicked up…that's how fast it subsided. This, of course, was the best kind of news for the passengers and crew of the ferries *Barnum* and *Grand Republic*…and a source of considerable relief for Karol Ladka and the Special Forces team.

The bad news, however, was that when gassing up the big Dolphin helicopter, and determining weight and balance for his flight plan, Pedro Avila had no idea that the MH-65 would be transporting five additional adult males more than one hundred miles farther than he'd counted on. Making it successfully to Southwick with the additional weight that Omar Inbula, Albert Tremaine, and the three Navy SEALS represented would be problematic at best. A thousand pounds of unanticipated cargo is a lot in flying parlance when one is talking about an aircraft designed to transport half that load.

And the stiffening northern headwind associated with the weakened gale only added to the problem.

The pilot looked worriedly at his fore and aft fuel gauges… one read empty and the other was vacillating noticeably near the red line. Avila beckoned General Ladka with a quick bob of his head. Karol checked Inbula's handcuffs, leg irons, and the stout nylon strap that secured him five feet from the Dolphin's partially open side hatch...and Ladka made his way to the cockpit.

As the two men conversed in a quiet, but obviously intense exchange, Colonel Avila pointed to a gauge between the two fuel indicators on the helicopter's instrument panel. It told the pilot exactly how much fuel consumption he must anticipate under current flying conditions. By Avila's calculation, the way things now stood, the MH-65 would come up twenty miles short of Edgewood Links and the VA Hospital. There its tanks would be exhausted...unless the chopper were somehow lightened by approximately two hundred pounds.

"There's no time left to dawdle about this, Karol," said the General's old friend. "Either we lighten the ship, or we land in Granby."

"That's twenty-five miles this side of Southwick."

"Correct," said Avila. "Twenty-three miles, to be precise."

"You're the pilot-in-command," said Ladka. "You call the shot."

Colonel Avila looked over his shoulder at the shackled Iraqi terrorist who was struggling with the nylon restraint that held him lashed to the floor. "The raghead," he said. "How badly does he want to get to that open side-hatch?"

There was no need for idle conversation. Karol Ladka hadn't risen to the highest echelons of the CIA by being indecisive. "Gimme your survival knife," he said.

The pilot unsheathed the razor-sharp blade on his hip and placed it exposed on the seat next to him. "You going to kill him, General?"

Ladka picked up the knife. "What's our altitude?"

"Twelve hundred feet," said Avila.

"Then our friend's going to do the job himself," the General said...and he crawled back to where the terrorist was pulling at the nylon strap that secured him to the chopper's steel floor. With one, swift, unexpected swipe of the survival knife, Karol Ladka severed the thick strap that had held the sweating man in place. Instantly the Radical Omar Inbula jumped in two quick hops on manacled feet to the Dolphin's partially open starboard hatch. *Allahu Akbar*, he shrieked…and he squeezed through the opening in the sliding portal…his piercing scream fading as he tumbled through the night sky.

Immediately, the helicopter gained some thirty feet of altitude, and according to Pedro Avila's instruments, it picked up about ten knots of airspeed. "We're going to make our destination, General," the pilot called over his shoulder. "And our reluctant captive gets his wish to boot. He should be landing just north of Windsor Locks about now."

"It'd be a plus if he winds up on the bottom of the Connecticut River," murmured the SEALS' team leader. He peered toward the jet-black surface of the wide waterway through one of the MH-65's rear portholes. "Save a lot of explaining about the forty pounds of government-issue restraints he's wearing…know what I mean?"

"Just sex toys any S & M pervert can buy online for fifty bucks," said Ladka. "Don't worry about it." And he pulled the starboard hatch all the way closed.

"Speaking of toys…" Colonel Avila held his right hand back and to the side. "…could I have my knife back, General?"

* * * * *

THE EMERGENCY SECURITY GUARD instructed Jean Gustavson to sit on the bottom step of Building 200's west stairwell and stay there. "Don't use your light until I get back," he ordered. "Does anyone else know you're here?"

The nurse's voice was weak and faltering. "N…n…No."

With his flashlight in one hand, and his pistol in the other, the guard bolted up the stairs two-at-a-time, leaving Gustavson to sit, teeth chattering, and hugging her knees against the sudden early morning chill.

At the second floor landing of the staircase, the uniformed man stopped for breath and pressed his ear against the cold metal of the door that opened onto Corridor Two. He heard nothing. Switching off his light, he gingerly eased the door open. He was surprised to see the mosaic-like pattern of moving light that partially illuminated the hallway...it was the big salt spreader, he knew, following its precise back-and-forth pattern in the near parking lot.

The smell of cordite in the hall was unmistakable.

With his gun pointed at the ceiling, and his back to the wall opposite the high windows of the second floor hallway, the guard slithered along the cold tiles, eyes squinted in the hope of seeing the gunman Jean Gustavson had described. Two-H...Doctor Song's Dermatology Clinic...was at the far end of the corridor... *that must be where he is,* the Security Officer thought.

The odor of gunpowder was becoming ever-more distinct, and pungent.

He increased the pace of his forward progress...passing the partially recessed door of a Ladies' Room...bumping his left hip against a stainless steel water fountain...and feeling his way past another door. This one bore a sign that he could barely make out in the ultra-dim glow from the salt truck's lights. It said 'Men.'

As soon as he had cleared the Men's Room entrance, he heard the heavy door open behind him...and he saw the beam of a flashlight playing on the polished floor where he stood stark still.

"Hands high," said a gravelly but calm voice. "I'll take that." And he felt his raised pistol being wrenched from his grasp.

The emergency guard had no idea that the man who had emerged from the lavatory was himself a police officer...a Sergeant. He knew only that he had been accosted from behind... by a tall man with a deep voice...who now had taken possession of his weapon—an unforgivable circumstance for any peace officer.

The gravel-voiced policemen shone his light in the guard's eyes, effectively blinding him. "Who are you?" the Sergeant said. "I've never seen you."

"Emergency Security Detail," said the officer. "From Springfield."

"And why the weapon?"

"I was alerted to a gunman in 2-H."

"Get down. On the floor. Face down. If you move, I'll kill you with your own pistol."

"You'd never get away with that," said the man Gustavson had summoned.

"Wrong," the Sergeant announced in his hoarse voice. "I'll shoot you in the face…then put the gun in your hand. If you don't believe it…go ahead and try me."

"You win." The guard from Springfield conceded…and he began to kneel.

With that, the overhead lights throughout the hospital flashed back on. As did computer monitors in every room. The typical low hum of ventilation resumed. And warm air began to blow from ducts in the ceiling. But most importantly, the brass security gate that had held Meili Song captive in her own Examination Suite, now responded to a command prompt that she pressed on her computer keyboard…and the grille began to retract ever so slowly from the floor of Clinic 2-H.

Warily, the emergency security guard eyed his uniformed captor for the first time. "You're a cop," he said, disbelieving.

"Who the hell did you think I was?" said the Sergeant, "…Jesse James?"

"They told me there was an active gunman in 2-H. That's all I know."

"Well they told you right, Officer. And I was one of them," said the raspy-voiced policeman. "But somebody else fired first…and I don't take kindly to that shit."

He pointed to the newly accessible vestibule of Doctor Song's clinic and started to hand the security guard his gun. "Now back me up while I find out what the fuck's going on around here." Then the Sergeant yanked the pistol away briefly. "But don't get any cute ideas, Junior…I've got eyes in the back of my head."

A terrified Meili Song emerged from her suite at the east end of the second floor hallway. Immediately she spotted the two policemen and ran toward them.

"In there," she cried, pointing. "On the floor."

"What's on the floor?" the Sergeant demanded.

"A man," Meili sobbed. "He's dead. I killed him."

"Get her down to the ER," the tall policeman commanded. "Tell 'em she's in shock. I'll take care of things up here."

Chapter Fifty-four

THE HEADWIND TOOK a capricious turn to the west, and the VA Hospital's prominent, newly illuminated Building 200 came into view on the northern horizon. It became clear that the Dolphin would safely reach its destination, the seventh fairway of Edgewood Links, with fuel to spare. That would put Karol Ladka and his men less than a dozen yards from the HVAC unit where the neutralized Phosgene was stacked.

The remainder of the operation was going to be easy, thanks to the self-reliance and adaptability of the Navy SEALS. These warriors have been known to perform tactical miracles with nothing more than a ball of twine and five paper clips!

Thus, within minutes of setting down and clambering from the MH-65's broad hatch, they had fired-up a backhoe from the maintenance shack pointed out by Avila...dug a narrow, ten-foot-deep trench adjacent to the Heating Ventilating and Air Conditioning facility...and hauled the Phosgene from the roof into its deep, earthen grave. Where they quickly covered it with dirt.

They then dug a broader trough farther up the sloping fairway and bulldozed the carcasses of the twelve poisoned deer into it. Later they would be asked to prepare a single five-by-seven-foot grave, six feet deep. Subsequently, the open burial place would receive the corpse of poor, orphaned Freddie Young. It was generally concluded that in death he would have wished for the distinct honor of being buried beside his *Dongsaeng*...his four-footed *'Little Brothers,'* that had inhabited Edgewood Links.

Of course, there was the inevitable paper work to be completed...some things never change...but the murder of Peter Wilkinson on Long Island Sound was unreported...as was the suicide of his cohort, Omar Inbula.

There seemed little reason for Albert Tremaine, the one verifiable witness to both deaths, to conclude that he had not totally imagined both vicious scenarios.

Epilogue

Of the twenty-three key characters involved in 'The Southwick Incident,' ten were killed in a matter of three days. Six of those dead were terrorists who will, appropriately, be forever unsung—while four victims were innocent American patriots. They are: Carter and Elizabeth Banning, Major Amanda Bragg, and Freddie Young, the innocent PTSD patient who unfortunately wandered into harm's way.

Certain readers will decry the fact that the six dead Radical Terrorists of the story: Hugh Harmwell, Evrim Yildiz, Professor Mujab Baghdadi, *Imam* Ali Aziz, Omar Inbula, and the turncoat student Peter Wilkinson, might have been characterized somewhat harshly. Such complaints are inevitable in an increasingly permissive society, where the lines distinguishing sincere dogmatists from fanatic extremists have become increasingly blurred.

Among those who survived this tale's planned mass slaughter in the Massachusetts town on the Connecticut border, two Southwick medical personnel were traumatized most bitterly. They are Dermatologist, Meili Song, and veteran Charge Nurse, Jean Gustavson. As we have seen, only the most fortuitous quirk of nature spared them and many other staff members an agonizing death unheard of in ferocity since the cold-blooded gassings of World War I.

The exploits of General Karol Ladka and his team of Navy SEALS, though usually far-ranging worldwide, were concentrated during this project in a hundred-mile-square area east of New York City, and residents of the US Northeast Corridor will have no trouble recognizing the region involved… or the neighborhoods that surround the specific locales.

Clearly, they're all there, and actual names of places and institutions have been meticulously retained…from Long Island…to Istanbul (the only city on the planet situated on two continents)…to ancient Stonehenge…and modern-day New England.

Even American government facilities in chaotic Turkey are situated precisely where I've designated. That is to say, their locations in that far-flung country are accurately indicated.

As is ever the case, incurable romantics will want to know what became of the embryonic relationship that sprang up so quickly between Meili Song and General Ladka. Alas, the unfortunate news is that the General was too much the CIA operative for his occupation to dovetail with that of the humanitarian Doctor Song. Meili admired the older Karol for his resolve…was even impressed in an oblique way by his dour severity…but these were aspects of the General's personality that ultimately smacked too much of the morose to win her tender heart.

Obviously, the peaceful village of Southwick still functions in its historic upper middle class fashion. The inhabitants there won't forget what they've been through, but they'll seldom if ever discuss it. These are New Englanders, after all. Many of them trace their roots directly to the American Revolution…and stoic provincialism, like patriotism, is practically part of their DNA.

What *has* changed is the Security System at the Southwick VA Medical Center. Now, all incoming shipments of supplies… both perishable and non-perishable…are subjected to meticulous examination by a state-of-the-art gas chromatograph. The device identifies unmistakably the precise chemical composition of everything arriving at the hospital…from generators…to peanut butter.

Never again will the Southwick Medical Center's thousands of patients and staff be put at risk because some unknown substance has been maliciously injected into its closely controlled atmosphere...or so it is hoped.

Acknowledgments

This is one of those books that I'll always remember writing…and for some fairly diverse reasons.

I started putting *'The Southwick Incident'* together shortly after New Year's Day, 2016, a particularly good time to launch a novel, it seemed to me, when there's not much else weighing on an individual's mind…or demanding of one's time.

We were experiencing one of the warmest Christmas Seasons on record in the Northeast, and with that experience ongoing, I used it to overcome the inertia that frequently seems to get in the way when I'm most eager to start a tale percolating. Thus I began setting the stage for the story by calling upon one of the most historically common dinner table axioms there is: When all else fails…talk about the weather.

It's a device I borrowed from author Boris Pasternak, who used it to open his remarkable work, *'Doctor Zhivago.'*

Accordingly, more than was the case with any of my eleven other novels, this one got off to a robust, if rather un-Russian-like start weather-wise.

The upscale town of Southwick, Massachusetts seemed appropriate as the setting for most of the action because I wanted my Yale graduate antagonist to hail from a privileged background like those typified by families living in the historic town on the Connecticut border. Also, many of my friends (notably Lawrence DeLion and Jim Teese) are Yalies, and they were typically generous with inside Ivy League information…though certainly not of the sort my fictitious antagonist would have been privy to.

It was clear from the outset what the book's central theme was going to be. The newspapers had been (and still are) full of disturbing accounts of 'homegrown' American radicals, and their strange motives have always put me in mind of Shakespearian villains like *Iago*, or *Richard III*, or *Lady Macbeth*...antagonists whose fiendishness is described by Samuel Taylor Coleridge as deep enough to be *"...motiveless in its malignancy..."* In other words, their wickedness is so formidable that it's essentially incomprehensible!

I know! Talk about biting off more than you can chew!

In the first place, to do justice to such a convoluted theme, one should ideally be a psychiatrist, I'd been told...or at the very least, be somewhat familiar with psychological theory.

That, I concluded, left me out...and alas, out the window would go my story. Or so it seemed.

"But hold on," said I. "I've played *Iago* and *Richard* in college productions of 'Othello' and 'Richard III,' and at no time did I find the malevolence of my characters perplexing, or even difficult to understand." These Shakespearian villains were merely evil! And the fact is, like it or not, we have all met people who embody Coleridge's unexplained nastiness. In short, I refused to give up on my bad guy just because he typified the deepest, darkest sort of individual we find among us in today's world.

Essentially, therefore, I decided to base *'The Southwick Incident'* on the *What* of my antagonist's actions, and not the *Why*. Thus the story would become a *plot-driven thriller*, as opposed to a *psychological analysis* of deep-rooted iniquity...a much more manageable chunk of business for this writer to chew on.

Of course, no novelist creates a tale of any sort in a vacuum. There are always innumerable persons to thank for providing inspiration. For me, chief among these individuals are Professor Matthew McSorley...Dramatist John Oetgen...and Actor/ Director Jeffrey Sanzel. Together, these friends and advisors have *forgotten* more about dramatic interpretation than most theater impresarios ever *knew*!

Then, there is that vast cadre of supporters who lend more backing and encouragement than even *they* realize. For instance, my favorite Motivational Writer Cindi Sansone-Braff generously supplied the front cover blurb for this book…inimitable Publicist Debbie Lange Fifer (with me from day one) pushed the project across the finish line…Copy Editor Lynn Muller is simply the most attentive reader I know…and a cadre of Specialists at the Northport Veterans Administration Medical Center (like the magnificently named Doctor Solomon David) volunteered candor and insight. Many of these professionals appear by name…though fictitiously…in 'The Southwick Incident.'

In this novel-writing business, one can never be sufficiently grateful for one's first reader. Sometimes we authors make the near-fatal mistake of assuming that booklovers know our characters and locales as well as we do. It is the first reader who typically catches us in these fallacious notions…and frequently saves us from our misguided selves. My initial editor is the smartest person I have ever met—my wife Elizabeth. A voracious reader, she willingly puts aside the latest Lee Child, or Jodi Picoult, or Daniel Silva novel, and focuses her critical lens on my thousand-or-so words for that day. I don't deserve Elizabeth, but bless this amazing woman for her good-natured patience…and her insight.

To all of the enthusiasts who have been supportive enough during the past fifteen event-filled months to inquire frequently about this timely manuscript's progress…I can only say, "Your interest is the glue that, applied in layers along the way, ultimately holds the finished product together." Because no book is ever really completed until it's read…it just sits there. Thus, when you get right down to it, we authors are merely the conceivers and composers of our tales. Those of you who are now scanning these pages are the ones who have actually brought the story to fruition.

Thank you for partnering with me by contributing that necessary function…the vital role of Reader

And here's hoping you will have had as much fun poring over what I hope are the exciting chapters of *'The Southwick Incident'* as I did in jotting them down.

Jeb Ladouceur
JebLadouceur@aol.com
Presidents' Day, 2017